GYPSY BLOOD

JEFF GUNHUS

SEVEN GUNS PRESS

Printed in the United States of America

Edited by Mandy Schoen

Library of Congress Cataloging-in-Publication Data

Gunhus, Jeff

Gypsy Blood/ Jeff Gunhus

Visit Jeff Gunhus at:

www.JeffGunhus.com

www.facebook.com/jeffgunhusauthor

www.twitter.com/jeffgunhus

ALSO BY JEFF GUNHUS

ADULT FICTION

Night Chill

Night Terror

Killer Within

Killer Pursuit

The Torment of Rachel Ames: a novella

MIDDLE GRADE FICTION

Jack Templar Monster Hunter

Jack Templar and the Monster Hunter Academy

Jack Templar and the Lord of the Vampires

Jack Templar and the Lord of the Werewolves

Jack Templar and the Lord of the Demons

Jack Templar and the Last Battle

ACKNOWLEDGMENTS

Every book is a journey filled with excitement, frustration, love, joy, hate, doubt, and every other emotion you can imagine. Like most journeys, it's made more pleasant by the fellow travelers along the road and the characters you meet. By this time, novel number thirteen, my companions are a rogue's gallery of past war campaigns, the Avengers of book publishing, brought together to fight the incredible odds of beating my initial draft into something coherent and worthy of you fine people who plunk down your hard-earned cash to take a peek inside my very scary mind.

Mandy Schoen reads my stuff first. The developmental edit where she says kind things like, "Do we need this?" "Would she say that?" "What's wrong with you? You're supposed to be good at this writing stuff." OK, that last one isn't Mandy, just my inner demons and paranoia. She's much more tactful and skilled at finding the issues, pointing them out, and then sending me packing to go fix them. My books are always made better after she gets ahold of them. If you're a writer, and you want someone to make you look good, you can hire her too. www.Mandyschoenedits.com. However, I get dibs on her schedule. Just saying.

After Mandy comes Diana Cox who proofreads and is a fussy

fussbucket (in the best possible way) with all those darn grammar rules. You also can let Diana prove to you that you missed nearly every grammatical error imaginable in your manuscript. Just visit her at the best URL ever for proofreading, www.novelproofreading.com

For either Mandy or Diana, mention my name and they'll charge you an extra 20%. Their motto: any friend of Jeff's is bound to be a pain in the ass. But seriously, writer friends, these are good people who do good work. Check them out.

This is the first time I used Diren Yardimli to create one of my covers. I was cruising the Internet, looking for ideas to share with my usual designer, when I came across this premade cover. After some tweaks, it was perfect, fit the story (as you'll see) and I'd heard good things about Darin. The people saying those good things were correct and it's been a terrific experience.

Thank you to my friends who tolerate me capturing some of their mannerisms in my pages. If you think you recognize yourself, for legal purposes, it's not you. (Although it probably is.) Thank you to my writer friends for constant support.

My kids always support Dad and his crazy book writing thing. Some of my favorite pages were written with kids sitting on the couch next to me, reading a book of their own, suggesting periodically that I should write more like Rick Riordan or Neil Gaiman so I could sell more books. Good advice!

This book, like the others, is dedicated to my tireless and forgiving wife. I suggest everyone have their own Nicole. I've found it to be amazingly helpful.

The ending bit here is for my readers. You are a crazy bunch. I love your enthusiasm, your clever reviews, your lobbying for more books in my series and, most importantly, your trust. There are so many ways you can spend both your money and your time. I'm endlessly grateful you choose to invest some of each on my stories.

Cheers, best wishes, and hope you enjoy the hell out of Gypsy Blood.

Best,

Jeff Gunhus

For Nicole

Always

1

Corbin Stewart thought the conversation was going well. His only confusion was whether he was seducing the woman in front of him, or if he was the one being seduced. As he sipped the last of his wine and waved to the nearby waiter to signal for a refill, he decided he didn't care. It might have mattered more to him if he'd known the night was going to end with his hands covered in blood.

"Let me see what you've been working on," Margot said, reaching out for the notebook on the table. Corbin noticed, not for the first time, how long and slender her hands were, like a piano player. Or a pickpocket.

He put his hand gently on top of hers. Not as a flirtation, but as a defense to prevent her from taking the notebook.

"You must not know many writers," he said. "I can't show you a work in progress. You'd turn into salt."

She smiled. Full lips framed white teeth so perfect that the odd thought of whether they were real popped into his head. She let her hand linger under his for a few seconds before slowly pulling it back. He was disappointed she didn't leave it there, but she hadn't yanked it back in revulsion, so that was a plus.

"That's a big claim."

"What's that?"

"Are you implying the contents of that notebook are on par with the delicious depravity of Sodom and Gomorrah? That I'll turn to salt like Lot's wife purely from looking at it?"

"Maybe."

"Now I really want to read it."

Corbin pulled the notebook closer even though a thick rubber band had been wrapped around its width to protect it from unwanted eyes. He was happy she'd caught the Biblical reference. Not because he had any use for religion, but he loved the continued proof that the woman was intelligent and sharp-witted. Gorgeous and smart. The downside being that it also meant she was way out of his league. "Sorry," he said. "You'll have to wait for it to be published like everyone else."

The waiter arrived with two new glasses. Hers was still a third full, but she downed it in two gulps and handed the empty to the man serving them. As the waiter turned, he gave Corbin a wink as if to say, *Looking good, kid. Don't screw this up.* Corbin didn't think Margot saw the wink so he tried not to react to it. "Would you like some coffee next, perhaps?" the waiter asked. Corbin wondered if the old man thought he needed to slow down a little. It was probably a good idea, but a good idea never stopped him from making a bad choice.

"Merci, Monsieur. Je suis chaud." The man gave him an odd look and a less than charitable smile and then left.

Margot had her hand to her mouth, laughing at him.

"What?" he said. "Did I say it wrong?"

"How long have you been in Paris?"

"Nearly four months."

"Let's hope your command of English is better than your French."

"I said I was warm. What's wrong with that?"

"*J'ai chaud.* I am warm. You said, *Je suis chaud.* It means I am hot. As in, I'm horny," Corbin nearly spit the wine he'd just sipped. Margot grinned, clearly enjoying it. "He's probably in the back trying to decide exactly what you were hoping he would do about it."

Corbin glanced back at the restaurant from their sidewalk table but didn't see the waiter. "It's the effort that counts, right? Most Americans don't even try."

"I'll give you that. Not even the horny ones." The bells of Notre Dame pealed from across the river and she turned toward them. She closed her eyes and soaked in the sound, swaying gently in her seat as if the bells were a symphony playing just for her. She'd told him she was a local, so he should have wondered why the bells mesmerized her so. But he didn't wonder. He missed it completely.

Instead he used the opportunity to explore her face, wondering at the uncommon beauty that had unexpectedly walked into his life. Her olive skin was accentuated by the white men's dress shirt she wore, buttoned low enough to be sexy without revealing too much. The setting sun turned the sky behind her into soft pinks and oranges that made her black hair even more striking than when she'd first approached him and asked to share his table three hours earlier. He realized it was the first time he was really taking her in, because up to that point her eyes, the ones that seemed to alternate between green and brown depending on the light, had held all of his interest. He knew the wine had a lot to do with it, but he felt with some certainty that this was one of the most beautiful women he'd ever seen.

The bells stopped and she opened her eyes. He looked away quickly but she'd caught him.

"You were staring."

"Guilty."

She took another sip of wine. "That's all right. I don't mind."

Corbin felt a stirring in his groin and shifted in his chair.

She leaned across the table, suddenly turning earnest. "How long is it going to take?"

His mind wandered, trying to link the question to its meaning. Was she coming on to him? Was he slow-playing this too much? Was she giving him an opening to suggest they leave together? He felt a rush of heat and the muscles in his stomach tightened. She smiled again, guessing that he'd misinterpreted.

"The book," she said. "How long will it take to finish the book? You said––"

"I said you could read it when it came out," he said, the heat now on his neck and cheeks from embarrassment.

"How long will that be? You've been here four months, so you must have a good start."

Corbin reflexively put both hands on top of the notebook, gently snapping the rubber band against the leather cover. There was months of work in the notebook. The fruits of his labor at cafés all over Paris, living the life he'd imagined for himself during all those years when he was teaching *Introduction to English Literature* to revolving hordes of disinterested college freshmen, eighteen-year-old kids who only wanted to drink, screw and smoke pot. Seven days a week, morning until dusk, he'd been at work on his second novel. The one the publisher had already paid good money for a few years ago. The one he ought to be eighty thousand words into. At least.

"You haven't started, have you?" Margot said, her voice suddenly soft and tender. It was framed as a question, but it was a statement. She knew. Somehow she knew.

"Why would ... I don't know why you would ..."

She reached out again, but this time she put her hand over his. "It's all right. It doesn't matter to me, Corbin. Why should it?"

He shouldn't have had so much wine. His thoughts flitted around like the small birds pecking for crumbs around the café tables. Still, underneath the sloshing heaviness of his wine-addled brain, a voice warned him there was something wrong. He just didn't pay attention to it.

"Can I see?" she asked, pulling gently on the notebook.

He let go and immediately regretted it. He reached out to take it back, but it was too late.

"Don't," he said.

"It's all right." She pulled back the heavy rubber band and opened the notebook near its middle. There was a two-page spread of a pencil drawing of Notre Dame Cathedral. It was well-shadowed and detailed enough to show he hadn't done it by memory. "Very nice," she said.

Corbin took a swig of his wine. He knew he was no artist. *Nice* was being kind. His work rose to the level of a semi-talented high school art student. Maybe.

She turned the page and there was another drawing. St. Sulpice this time. The next page had two drawings of the the Pont Neuf Bridge, one in morning and the other at sunset.

Margot's eyes narrowed as she flipped page after page. Drawing after drawing. Not a single page of writing. No notes. No outline. Not a single line of prose.

He might as well have scribbled *All work and no play makes Jack a dull boy* on every page.

"Is this it?" she asked. Her tone was different, like a gear change in a car. "Is there work somewhere else? Tell me there is."

He took a deep breath, his rusty powers of observation, the trade-craft of any writer, finally kicking in. He settled back in his chair, the sexual tension draining out of him like a relief valve had been cranked open. He looked past her, at the happy tourists snapping selfies with the Seine River behind them. At the young lovers holding hands as if they were the only ones in the world. At the Paris skyline darkening as the sun descended.

"When were you going to tell me?" he asked.

She didn't seem surprised by the question. "You didn't respond to calls or emails. For months."

"So they sent you all the way from New York to find me? Seems a little desperate."

"They did pay you a considerable sum for your next book. And that was a while ago, from what I understand." She tossed the journal back on the table. "But don't flatter yourself. I'm based in London. This was just a side-trip."

"So, what you're saying is, I'm not getting laid tonight?"

Margot shook her head and held up his notebook. "You don't need my help. It looks to me like you're screwing yourself just fine."

"Yeah, but it'd be a lot more fun if we did it together."

He expected her to stand up and take her leave. She'd gotten what she'd come for, the answer to the question his publisher had most wanted to know. *How's the book coming?*

The question had started around six months after they'd paid him the money. Back then, they were just curious as to the topic of the book. Just the broad strokes so they knew he had something. He'd cobbled together some bullshit idea about a father-son road trip across 1960s' America, a final journey before the son left for Vietnam, where father and son learned about themselves and America all at the same time. They'd eaten that up and left him alone to work. Then his baby girl got sick. Six months after that, it was condolences. A nice flower arrangement at the funeral. A handwritten note from his editor. Apparently, the grieving time allowed for a father who'd received a large advance was about three months, because that was when the questions about his progress started again. After a while, the inquiries felt like his only constant. They were there through his bout with depression, his marriage counseling, his divorce, his move into a one-bedroom apartment.

Question: *How's the book coming?*

Answer: *Pretty shitty, actually. Kind of like my life.*

Two years had passed before his agent suggested they might actually ask for the money back. With nothing left for him in the States, he'd exiled himself to Paris figuring he'd not only cross something off his bucket list, but that he'd finally get to work. Little good that had done. Blocked was blocked, regardless of the scenery.

Now that the truth was out, he imagined he'd be soon left to his wine and his notebook filled with drawings as Margot went to report back to her bosses.

But to his surprise, she didn't leave. She smiled, then raised her hand to the waiter to signal for more wine. He said nothing, but just watched her with interest as she finished off her glass before the next one arrived.

As she sipped, she spilled some on her white shirt, four drops ballooning out on the fabric. Later that night, as he stared at the blood soaking through that same shirt, he'd remember the way she'd try to blot the wine away, just making the stain worse until she gave up. She wouldn't even try to wash away the blood. It was no use. There would be too much of it, drenching through the shirt until it soaked her skin.

Like the wine, touching it just made things worse.

2

Corbin paid the bill with a credit card, holding his breath that it would go through. The real problem with the publisher wanting their money returned was that there wasn't a penny of it left.

While his first book was a literary triumph, as heralded in the *New York Times Book Review* of all places, he'd quickly discovered that the literary part of the equation meant rave reviews from important people, but not necessarily massive sales volume. *Amethyst Dreams* did great business, better really than anything he could have imagined, but the economics of publishing was such that his pile of gold at the end of the rainbow looked more like rent money than house-in-the-Hamptons money.

After his agent, the tax man, his student loans and credit card debt, there had only been a little left over. He and Amy had thought they'd been so mature putting most of the balance into a college fund for Rose instead of buying a new house or a new car. All that fund, everything they had really, had gone to medical bills instead.

"You all right?" Margot asked, coming back from the ladies' room.

Corbin shook himself out of the past, a dangerous place with dark traps that could snare him for days if he wasn't careful. He turned his attention back to Margot. The wine spots on her shirt were paler now but surrounded by halos of wet fabric.

The waiter walked up and presented him the leather folio with his credit card and the receipt. Corbin searched the man's face for any sign that something was amiss. Seeing none, he opened the folder and was surprised to see his Visa next to a Platinum American Express card.

"What's this?"

Margot snatched the folio and handed him his card. "I figured you were broke," she said, scribbling her name on the receipt. "Expense report. It's not my money. You're cute, but not that cute."

Corbin followed her out, on the drunk side of tipsy, and more than a little giddy at the thought of what might lie ahead of him that night. He tried not to think about it. Once he thought about it too much he knew there was a damn good chance of him screwing things up. He realized he still had his napkin in his hand. He bound it up and tossed it toward a busboy's tray, but missed the shot by a foot.

"You didn't miss your calling in basketball, did you?" she said. "Where to?"

"Looked like you knew where you were going. I was following you."

"You're a blocked writer living in Paris. I'm thinking you know every bar in a five-mile radius."

He pretended to be offended. "Do you think so little of me? My bar knowledge extends to a ten-mile radius, at least. I know just where to go, especially if D.H. Harris Publishing Group is buying."

She brandished the American Express card. "Yes they are."

He offered her his arm and she took it. Even in his state, he breathed in her fragrance and felt his legs weaken. He felt like a teenager with a crush, and he welcomed it. He hadn't felt this alive in years. He steered her toward the river.

"Pretty impressive sleuthing skills finding me here," he said.

"I read a lot of detective novels. It was easier to find you than I thought it'd be."

"Okay, I'll bite."

"I followed you from your flat. You still get royalty checks sent to you by mail. It's quaint."

"I like to see the check. Hold it in my hands."

"The fruits of your manly labor and all that."

A chill passed through him and his mood darkened. He looked away, shoving his hands into his pockets.

"Wow, where'd you go?" Margot said.

He shook his head, a bad idea given the wine in his system. "Sorry, triggered a memory is all."

She squinted her eyes and wrinkled her nose at him. "The fruits of your manly labor triggered a memory?"

"I didn't want to bring it up, but ..."

"Tell me."

He took a deep breath. "When you mentioned fruit. There was this melon I had once in the Monte Carlo, so juicy, so succulent. I just went to that day and—"

"Shut up," she said, punching him in the arm. "Seriously. What is it?"

It was the word *manly* that did it. His father had held strong views about what it meant to be a man and had gone to great lengths to instill the same values in his two sons, beating it into them as necessary. His father was long gone, burning in the fires of hell while rats chewed his feet and birds picked at his eyes if there was any justice in the afterlife, but he'd left his mark. So much so that a single word could make Corbin think about the son of a bitch instead of the woman on his arm.

"It's nothing," he said.

She cocked her head to the side. "Writers. Always a moody bunch. No idea why I fall for them." But she was laughing as she said it. Corbin felt the dark shadow of his father's ghost fall away from him, and he gave himself to the half-drunk buzz that had been fueling his self-confidence. And to the phrase *fall for them*. He liked the sound of that.

They turned up Rue de Dauphin, putting their backs to the river and walking deeper into Saint-Germain-Du-Pres.

"Figures you like this area," Margot said. "Isn't this where all the artists hang out? Hemmingway? Picasso? Proust?"

"Hung out. They're all worm food now."

"That's a pleasant way of putting it."

"I'm a pleasant person."

She laughed easily at that, and he tried to think of something else funny to say just so he could hear the sound again. But the harder he tried to think of something, the further away any idea seemed. It reminded him of his writing.

"I'd thought you'd be more of a Harry's New York Bar. That's the famous one, right? Home of the Bloody Mary?"

"Over by the Louvre, so it's a hike. And the tourist crowd has long trampled any cool vibe. But if you want to see it, we could just—"

"No, wherever we're going is fine. Closer's better."

He came to a stop at the entrance to Alle du Dauphin, a side alley shortcut to Rue Mazine where the finely crafted cocktails of The Prescription Bar awaited them. But he hesitated, trying to decide if he'd heard disappointment in Margot's voice about Harry's Bar. It was a ten-minute cab ride at most, a small price to pay to give the lady exactly what she wanted. He looked up the street on the off chance a taxi driver with psychic ability was rushing to pick them up, but there was not. That's all it would have taken to avoid what was about to happen, a taxi that just happened to be on that street, just happened to have dropped someone off and been hungry for another fare.

But there was no taxi. And his Uber account was suspended because of his maxed-out credit cards. His buzz was wearing off, which made him think that hers might be too and she might soon come to her senses and realize there was nothing to gain from spending an evening with a destitute, blocked, one-hit wonder writer. Things were going so well and he wanted to keep the momentum going. Wandering around for a cab or asking her to call and pay for an Uber wasn't how he wanted to play it.

"This way," he said, steering her to the side street. "It's not far."

She balked at the sight of the narrow alley. "Are you sure? Maybe we should go around on the main street."

"I cut through all the time. It's fine. Trust me."

Unfortunately, she did. They went down the narrow alley. And, in some ways, they never came back.

3

It wasn't as if he'd taken her down some rat-infested, garbage-strewn back alley. He wasn't crazy. The Alle du Dauphin was fairly clean and wide enough for a delivery truck to park next to the slide-up metal doors for deliveries. Some of these had graffiti on them, but not much. It was well kept and usually well used. But that night, they were the only ones in the alley. Or at least Corbin thought until he saw the old man leaning against a wall, watching them approach like he'd been there for hours waiting for them to arrive.

Corbin thought later that maybe the old bastard had done just that.

The alley was darker than the street they'd just left. The sliver of sky above them framed by buildings on either side was an inky blue as dusk took firm hold. Still, the alley created its own shadows, and the few lights on the street did little to cut through them.

The man was just a dark shape at first, blending into the surroundings. It was only when he drew in on his cigarette and the red glow of its end fired in the dark that Corbin noticed him.

Corbin slowed a half-step, a subconscious reaction to the unknown that warned him of the danger of strangers, especially those in dark alleys hidden in shadow. Smoothly, he tugged on

Margot's arm, pulling her behind him and putting himself between her and whomever the person happened to be.

If nothing else, he thought the act might make him look chivalrous. Anything to impress.

But then the shape stepped away from the wall and into the weak, sputtering light of a streetlamp, and he came to a complete stop, pulling Margot to stop as well.

The man was ancient, which should have reduced Corbin's trepidation. One of the earliest skills a person learned was the ability to size up a physical threat. The calculus was a fundamental survival skill from elementary school onward. Even the modern man, the one who bought facial scrubs and beard oils and who meticulously counted calories, even he retained the ability to instantly size up an opponent and calculate his odds should there be a fight. By that measure, one look at the old man should have put Corbin at ease.

As he watched, the man shuffled toward them, hunched over and curled to the side from a twisted spine. He wore baggy pants cinched at the waist with a black rope. On top he had on a loose dress shirt, unbuttoned to mid-chest to show a white tuft of wild, curling hair, and a dirty jacket with patches at the elbows. The jacket had an Old World cut to it, with a high collar and tails, like it was something once worn to high society cocktail parties before spending a few decades being seasoned by daily wear on the streets of Paris.

But none of this made Corbin stop. It was the man's face that did that.

In his novel, Corbin had described one of his characters as having a face that told the story of a hard-lived life, the sadness and hardship of existence carved into skin like a roadmap to his damaged soul. A little over the top, his editor had thought, but Corbin had fought for it and kept it in. The old man's face was exactly what his line had meant to convey. Dry, leathery skin, made splotchy by decades of sun. Deep wrinkles that looked like cracks in a dry lake bed. A misshapen nose that bent in odd ways like something broken and allowed to heal on its own over and over. Large ears with drooping lobes, both of them pierced and hanging with hooped earrings. Eyes that seared through the space between them, carving through the air.

And he was staring only at Margot.

Corbin felt her go stiff next to him. She let out a short gasp.

"Do you know him?" he asked, not sure why he was whispering. The man was still a good thirty feet in front of them.

She shook her head. "No, you?"

A pang of guilt worked its way into the dread he felt in his gut. This was just some old man who'd seen better days. Probably a panhandler whose greatest threat to them was to ask to relieve them of their loose change.

"C'mon, we're almost there," he said.

But she was planted in place. "Let's go back," she said, a tremble in her voice. "I don't like––"

"Chey," the old man called out, his voice stronger than Corbin had imagined it would be. Deep and resonant with an accent he didn't recognize. "So keres, Chey?"

Corbin searched his limited command of French for the words but found nothing. The way the man said Chey made him think it was a name. "Does he think he knows you?"

She pulled his arm backward. "Come on. Let's go."

"Does he think you're someone else maybe?" he said.

"Don't go," the man said, still looking only at Margot. "I'm sorry, I didn't mean to surprise you here. Tell this *gaujo* to leave so we can talk."

The man's English was perfect, but still laced with an accent he couldn't place. Still, the inherent bias of human nature worked its magic and hearing English made Corbin relax. As if the shared language somehow made them part of the same tribe. "He's harmless," Corbin said, digging into his pocket. "He just wants some money."

Margot turned and looked behind them. Corbin knew exactly what she was looking at. The alley curved in a half-moon shape and they were at the apex of the arc. The busier streets at either end were cut off from sight. Good place for a mugging. But the man had to be eighty years old. Hell, he could have been a hundred. Then again, if he had a gun, it wouldn't matter how old he was.

The man turned to Corbin as he approached and smiled. It wasn't the most genuine smile he'd ever seen. In fact, it looked like the effort pained him, as if Corbin were a thing to be barely tolerated. The man licked his lips, and Corbin could have sworn his tongue was purple, although he reasoned it was just the shadows and odd light in the alley.

"C'mon, it's fine," he said, hearing the uncertainty in his own voice.

They continued down the alley and he dug through his pockets to find some change. He had some Euros and pulled them out, hoping that would be payment enough for a hassle-free encounter. And it didn't hurt that he'd look fearless in the process, striding through the dark alley like he owned the place. Margot would be impressed. The old man would get some cash. Everyone ended up a winner.

But the closer he got to the man, the more he wished he'd listened to Margot and turned tail when she'd asked. It was ridiculous because the man was so old, but Corbin felt like he was walking into a predator's cave. His body reacted instinctively. His skin prickled and turned to gooseflesh. He felt a thin sheen of cold sweat on his neck and forehead. Not only that, but he could have sworn the air temperature dropped ten degrees, like swimming into a thermocline in the ocean. A shiver passed through him. He hoped Margot hadn't noticed.

"Here you go, man," he said, trying to sound casual even though he heard a tremble in his own voice. He reached out a hand with the money. *Take it. Just take it and let us pass.*

The man looked down at Corbin's outstretched hand and then back up to his face. The black eyes bored into him, and Corbin thought he saw a flash of anger there. Maybe injured pride, he thought at first, but decided that was wrong. It was more like hate. And inexplicable rage.

Again, he felt the visceral sense of danger. Every part of him screamed to turn and run. But the desire not to look like an idiot in front of Margot was a powerful deterrent, and he foolishly stood his ground.

But then the man reached out his hand, palm open, as if for the money. Corbin hesitated. The hand was thick with callouses. The fingers slightly bent showing long nails made jagged as if the tips had been gnawed off instead of cut. Corbin slowly lowered his hand with the money, wondering if it would be rude to drop the coins from enough distance to not have to touch the man.

He didn't have a chance to find out.

The man grabbed Corbin's hand.

Instantly, like the flash of a camera, an image burst into his head. The man's face loomed inches from his own. Lips pulled back in a snarl. Purple tongue pressed against rotting teeth. His powerful hands were clutched around Corbin's throat. Nails gouging into his skin, ripping through flesh.

"You think me a beggar?" the man shouted, spittle peppering Corbin's face.

Corbin felt the pressure build in his head, as though he might burst in a fountain of blood and bits of brain. The man's clawlike fingers turned hot and wet as blood poured from the wounds opening in his neck.

"You will beg for my mercy, *gaujo*."

Corbin heard a desperate, gurgling sound, only distantly recognizing it came from him.

"You will beg," the man shouted.

Corbin kicked his feet and, with every bit of strength he had, jerked backward and ...

... staggered across the alley, gasping for breath. He reached to his neck, expecting to find blood gushing. But there was nothing. No wound. Not a scratch.

Something grabbed him from behind. He spun around, arm cocked back to punch whatever it was.

"Wait," Margot said. "It's me. Jesus, what's wrong?"

Corbin swallowed hard and tried to get his bearings. His legs shook uncontrollably and he worried he might topple over. That he might vomit right there on the street. He looked back to the old man, expecting to see him grinning like a madman or rushing toward him.

But he was neither. He just stood there, calm as could be, the barest sign of a grin on his face. He clenched Corbin's money in a fist and then slowly opened his hand, letting the coins fall to the pavement.

"Let's go," Corbin whispered.

But Margot clamped her hand onto his forearm and held him in place, nodding to the far end of the alley.

Three men stood there, shoulder to shoulder, black hoodies pulled up over their heads.

"I think it's too late," she said.

4

The men were dressed all in black. Shoes, pants, hoodies. But one look at their faces made his throat catch. The three men were identical. They had dark, empty holes for eyes. Anguished mouths turned down as if moaning in pain. Skin so white that it glowed in the shadows.

Then it clicked in his head that he wasn't looking at some kind of mutant beings, they were just men wearing masks. Greek tragedy masks to be precise. Standing perfectly still. Blocking their way.

"That can't be good," he said.

He spun around. The other end of the alley was still open. It occurred to him that if the freaks with the masks were working with the old man, then there might be more of them coming. They had to get out of there while they had a chance. He was about to hustle Margot out that direction when he saw the old man swing his arm in a grand gesture.

It took Corbin a second to see what he'd done, but once he figured it out, he had to blink again to make sure his eyes weren't fooling him in the low light.

The old fool had pulled out a knife that was so long that it looked like a short sword. He held it in his right hand as he faced the three men, slowly carving shapes in the air, looking proficient with the weapon. But if it was meant as a deterrent, it clearly didn't work. The three men pulled long knives of their own and marched down the alley, shoulder to shoulder. Corbin realized they weren't muggers looking for a quick score off a couple of tourists. They were there for the old man.

"Oh God," Margot said.

"Hey," Corbin called out to the man. "Get out of there. Come with us."

The man ignored him. He faced the approaching men, standing as tall as he could with his crooked back, squaring his shoulders to confront them.

Corbin pushed Margot toward the other open end of the alley. "Go."

"What about you?"

"I'll get the old coot and be right behind you. Go. Get help if you can."

She turned and ran, leaving Corbin to wonder if he was over-doing the whole impress-the-lady thing. As he glanced over his shoulder at the three knife-wielding, masked men, he knew he ought to be running away right along with her.

"Dammit to hell," he said to no one in particular. He sprinted to the old man, the others only yards away. "Come on," he said, grab-bing the man's arm. "Back to the main street. Let's go."

But the old man spun and lashed out at him with his knife. Corbin felt a sting on top of his left leg. A stripe of red appeared across his thigh where the man had slashed through his pants and his flesh. It wasn't deep, but it hurt like hell.

Corbin stumbled back, pushing himself away from the man. "Jesus, stay here then. Suit yourself."

He clutched his wound and sprinted after Margot, limping heavily on his injured leg. The blood spread and he worried that the cut was deeper than he'd thought. He'd done research for his first book about the ways a leg wound can cause a man to bleed out. He wondered if the son of a bitch had somehow managed to sever an artery or something. The thought of it pissed him off enough to glance back as he struggled down the alley.

The three had the man surrounded. None of them seemed eager to be on the other end of their target's knife. They feinted in and out, making the man turn in a circle to fend them off. As Corbin watched, one of the masked men dropped low and stabbed the man in the hamstring. He rocked back and grabbed his leg, and that was the opening they needed. All three of them fell on the man, knocking him to the ground. Their arms chopped up and down, knives puncturing him over and over.

Corbin stopped, not wanting to believe what he was seeing.

"Hey!" he cried out. "Leave him!"

Something instinctual took over, some sense of justice or fairness, or maybe just stupidity mixed with wine. Regardless of what it was, it made him run back toward the butchers.

He yelled as he ran, a guttural cry he'd never heard his body make before that moment.

He hit the nearest masked man with a lowered shoulder and lifted him off the ground with his momentum and sent him sprawling.

Corbin remained on his feet, standing in front of the old man's body on the pavement behind him. The other two men had stood up, knives in hand, facing down their new adversary.

Blood dripped from the knife blades, and the men's black clothes glistened in the low light, wet with blood.

The masked man he'd knocked over got back to his feet. The hoodie was thrown back and the mask was gone. The man had short, spiked white hair and a pale complexion almost as white as the mask. Even in the low light, his skin seemed nearly translucent with veins visible just under the surface. His eyes shone bright blue. An albino. As if all this wasn't enough, an angry red scar jagged across his face, starting at his chin, tearing up through his cheek, then turning toward a deformed flap of skin where his ear ought to have been.

Corbin jerked back when a siren squealed from the road behind him. It had an impact on the attackers too. The albino with the scar replaced his mask and pulled up his hoodie. A quick signal and the other two turned and jogged with him out of the alley. Corbin watched them go, noticing that they cut to the left suddenly, darting into a dark doorway and disappearing into the night.

A gurgling sound came from behind him.

He turned and dropped to his knees in front of the old man. He'd come to rest in a pool of light so Corbin had a good look at him. They'd stabbed him dozens of times. All over his body. Blood ran everywhere.

Corbin knew he ought to do something to stop the bleeding, but he didn't know where to start. He crouched over him, wishing the police would get there. Meanwhile, his internal voice was screaming at him.

Don't touch him. Don't touch the blood.

The man reached up a hand toward Corbin, his eyes pleading for help.

"Goddamn it," Corbin said.

He reached out and clamped both hands on the two gashes on the man's throat. The blood squirted through his fingers. He felt the pressure as the man's heart pumped the blood through the opening.

"Help!" he screamed. He couldn't remember the French word for it. "Someone help."

The man wheezed heavily, trying to breathe. Corbin shifted in place, keeping one hand on the man's throat, but turning to apply pressure on the puncture wounds across his chest.

"Help!"

The man convulsed, legs kicking.

Then someone was helping to hold the man in place.

Corbin expected a policeman. Instead, it was Margot. Face white and stricken. Blood covering her shirt. His question must have been written on his face because she immediately said, "They're coming."

Just as he turned back, the man's chest heaved and he let out a hacking cough. Corbin felt blood spray across his face. He tasted the saltiness in his mouth and spit it out. He blinked hard, blood stinging in his eyes.

An image flashed, just like before. The old man, leering at him with blood-covered teeth. Only this time he grabbed Corbin's face with clawed hands and pulled him in, nails digging into his scalp.

Hot stench filled the air as the old man's mouth gaped open. Thumbs dug into Corbin's jaw. He fought it, but the man was too strong. His mouth opened.

Then they were together, the putrid taste of the man's breath inside him. Corbin struggled, bucking and kicking, but he couldn't get away.

The old man's tongue pushed into his mouth, slick with blood and mucous. It squirmed into the back of his mouth like a thick worm, over his tongue, into his esophagus, down his throat. Deeper, deeper. He felt it in his chest, then his abdomen, wiggling around inside his guts.

Then strong hands pulled him back and the man was gone. A policeman held him. In fact, there were police everywhere. Flashes from cell phone cameras went off all around him. A crowd surged forward to get a look at the mutilated old man lying in the street.

Corbin bent over and retched into the street. Red wine and the appetizers from the café gushed out of him and sprayed over the pavement. He didn't care. He wanted that tongue out of him.

Oh Jesus. I drank his blood. It's in my eyes. In my mouth. I drank his blood.

Margot put an arm around him. He steadied enough to look up and watch two paramedics pull on gloves and face masks before going to work on the old man's wounds. Margot's shirt was drenched with blood. For some reason, the idea popped into his head that at least the wine stain would blend in now. So that was a silver lining.

Then he dropped to his knees and retched into the street again, over and over until his stomach muscles cramped.

A single thought screamed in his head as he puked.

IdrankhisbloodIdrankhisbloodIdrankhisblood.

5

Alexis watched from the rooftop at the busy scene below. He shouldn't have lingered but he had to make sure the task was done. He needed to see Gregor die with his own eyes.

With the mask pulled from his face, he breathed in the cool night air. His guards stood behind him, watching for any sign of danger. They were good men, men he trusted. He had no doubt they were both furious that he'd been hit by the American. If the decision was theirs, there would be two bodies in the alley instead of one.

Good thing the decision wasn't theirs to make. The murder of a decrepit old Romani beggar would barely warrant a mention in the papers. The theatricality of the masks might increase interest, but there would be no outrage. Some members of polite society might even secretly wish the same thing would happen to the rest of the beggars in the city. Not that they would ever say such a thing out loud, but they would think it. Alexis knew their kind. If it was just a homeless beggar, they would whisper that Les Fantômes de la Nuit had done a service to the community. If the police wouldn't clean the streets, then why not a vigilante group with strange masks? It was in his interest to keep them thinking that way.

But an American stabbed to death in Saint-Germain-Des-Pres

would have been a different matter. The media would have been all over it. And there was no telling who the American might be. If he was even a minor celebrity, the US twenty-four-hour news would have turned it into a crisis.

But the man had seen his face.

That was his only concern. And he knew his face wasn't something easily forgotten, a fact he remembered every time he caught his reflection in a mirror.

The paramedics down below applied compression to Gregor's wounds, but it wouldn't be enough. Alexis wished he'd decapitated the devil just to be sure, but there hadn't been time. And he didn't think it would matter given the massive pool of blood encircling the old man.

People stepped back from the body, and one of the paramedics attached defibrillator paddles to the man's chest. Even from his vantage point, Alexis could see the body jump as they shocked Gregor's heart. He wondered if the devil's black soul had already left the body. He looked up, as if he might catch a glimpse of the old man's wraith floating up into the night sky. Then again, Gregor wouldn't have been floating anywhere. If anything, the maw of the Underworld would rip open beneath him and winged minions would claw him back into the depths of hell where he belonged.

After shocking him three times, the paramedics below gave up the fight. Frantic activity gave way to slow, methodical procedure. A tarp was pulled over the body for decency. The police began to politely but firmly push the line of spectators back from the alley, clearing it out. Within a few minutes, the area was transformed from a medical emergency to crime scene. The only civilians left were the American who'd seen him and the woman who'd been with him.

The Romani woman.

He thought about that. Was it a coincidence? Or was she connected to Gregor? It was possible she was part of the cell he was in Paris to destroy. But what was her connection to the American? Maybe she was setting him up for something with Gregor before he and his Fantômes had done their work.

Or maybe she just happened to have Romani blood in her veins. That alone wasn't a crime, but it made him suspicious. If she was part of it, she would also have to pay.

He turned to his men behind him, M'akiwe and Njau. They still wore their masks and were of similar enough tall and wiry build that it was hard to tell them apart. Even their blue eyes were the same, a by-product of their albinism. It was integral to their order to sacrifice the individual to the power of the collective, something the masks helped facilitate. When he first got them as boys, they still spoke of their tribe, of their family lineage. By the time he was done with them, all they identified with was Les Fantômes de la Nuit, their new tribe, family and religion. And Alexis was their ruler, their father, even their god. He knew the men would carry out his instructions regardless of who he assigned a task to. They owed Alexis their lives, and he expected no less than full payment.

"Follow the American and the Romani woman," he said. "I want to know everything about them."

"He saw your face," the man to his left said. It was Njau, the voice was unmistakable, a deep and resonant African voice laced with the accent from his past British colonial rulers. "We ought to eliminate him."

Alexis nodded. "And we might have to, but not if it can be avoided. He's weak. He vomited like a child from seeing a little blood."

"He faced the three of us, unarmed. To protect a stranger," M'akiwe said. "This is a man who can cause problems for us."

And knocked me to the ground, Alexis thought. *Don't forget that.* "Perhaps. Watch him and report back. Once the adrenaline wears off he'll do what Americans do."

"What's that?"

"Lose interest."

"And if he doesn't?" M'akiwe asked. "If he proves to be an issue?"

"Then we will eliminate him. But only after I give the order. Is that understood?"

The men nodded. Alexis knew the question had been unnecessary. All of his men followed his orders without fail.

"And the woman?" Njau asked. "Is she one of them?"

"I don't know," Alexis said. "If she is, I wouldn't have expected her to run."

The men stood silently as he considered the woman. Even with her fine clothes and American accent, they all knew she was Romani. A lifetime of hunting had honed their ability to find them wherever they tried to hide. But their fight wasn't with all of them.

"Follow her. Be discreet. Use more men if you need to. If she is one of them, she can lead us to the others."

The men turned and left him alone on the roof. He walked back to the edge, peering over to the scene below. The American sat on the ground, back to a wall with his head cradled in his hands as two police officers questioned him. The woman stood a few yards away, talking with another pair of policemen. Even covered with blood, she stood tall and seemed composed. Of the two, he had a feeling she might be the one to cause him more problems.

But that was to be expected. The Romani had been causing his kind problems for centuries. But Alexis intended to bring an end to that. Forever.

6

"I told you everything I know," Corbin said. "It's exactly what I told the guys before you. And the young guy before that. And the first cops at the scene got the same story, even if they didn't speak English. So I think we're done here."

He stood up, the metal chair he'd been in for the last two hours scraping loudly against the concrete floor. Enough time had passed for the sharp edges of the night's horror to wear down, replaced with a little embarrassment for his reaction to the old man's blood getting on him. Certainly there were medical concerns. He'd made a stop at an emergency room, under police escort, to have his leg stitched and his blood drawn. They'd given him some Cipro as a preventative measure and told him to report any symptoms. Corbin hadn't mentioned the vision of the old man sticking his tongue down his throat. He had the sense it wouldn't have added to his credibility in the interview process.

The Commissariat de Police du 6e Arrondissement where he'd been questioned was housed in a historic building on Rue Bonaparte, two stories of natural stone façade with tall windows and arched doorway entrances. But the interior of the building looked like any other police station. A waiting room outside the intake area. Old, metal desks covered with paperwork no one wanted to do. There were mostly uniformed cops on the first floor. The detectives who'd escorted him and Margot to the station had taken them upstairs. The ambiance up there wasn't any better.

At least they'd let him clean himself off in the men's room and provided a police windbreaker to put on after he stripped off the blood-covered clothes. He'd found Listerine in the men's room too. He gargled with it for almost two minutes even though he was pretty sure that any disease the old man might have carried in his blood wasn't going to be stopped by over-the-counter mouthwash hours after the fact. Still, after he spit it out, he'd taken another swig and gargled again.

"Monsieur Stewart," the most recent detective to ask for his statement said. His English was excellent with a soft accent that reminded Corbin of how an actor might play a French detective in a movie. Not overboard, but just enough accent to remind the audience of his nationality. "If you'll just indulge me for a few more minutes, then I think we will be done here."

Corbin remained standing. "What was your name again?"

"Detective Maurice Besson. I've now been assigned to this case."

"I thought it was the other guy. The young one. Lasso or something."

"Allesandro," he said. "He was originally assigned. But that changed."

The way he said it made Corbin think that Detective Besson wasn't going to elaborate. And it made him think that he was the kind of man that could swing into an investigation and take it over if he chose to. Corbin took another look at the man now that he sensed he was finally talking with someone with real authority.

Besson was older than himself by at least a decade, likely in his mid-forties. While the other detectives so far had appeared in wrinkled suits and run-of-the-mill dress shirts, the man with him now wore a tailored blazer with perfectly pressed wool pants. His shirt was a fine knit that showed a little texture as it moved under the light. Gold cuff links adorned his wrists. Besson was handsome in a rugged

way, the kind of man with an oversized nose, heavy brow and a
perpetual five o'clock shadow that comes across manly instead of like
a Neanderthal. His hair was carefully groomed, cut low to his scalp
and edged in a way that spoke to the man's attention to detail. His
sides were grey and added a level of sophistication.

Corbin just hoped that the detective wasn't interviewing Margot
as well. Even with the terror of the evening, he found himself
thinking about her. He didn't need her comparing this good-looking,
well-spoken guy to his own performance puking in the streets of
Paris. Weak stomachs weren't really a turn-on for most women.

"I'd like to review your statement once again."

"Why you?" Corbin asked.

"Excuse me?"

"I'm guessing from the looks of you that you're not the B team
they bring in on low-level cases."

"No, I am not the ... B team, as you said it."

"Then why are you here? What changed?"

Besson smiled and Corbin had the uneasy sense that the man had
already judged him to be an idiot. Just another American to be tolerated. He indicated the chair at the table. "Please, will you sit? Only a
few minutes, I promise."

"Where is Margot? Has she been released?"

The detective feigned surprise. "Released? No one is being
detained. I apologize if that was the impression——"

"You know what I meant."

Besson lost the surprised look and regarded him with narrowed
eyes. Corbin wondered if the detective was recalculating his impression of him as well. "Ms. Vinci has answered my questions. I believe
she is waiting outside in the corridor for you."

Corbin glanced at the door leading to the hallway and nearly
went to it. After what they'd been through together, he felt protective
of her. And a little guilty. She had, after all, not wanted to go down
the alley to begin with. And she'd been the first to suggest turning
around when they'd first seen the old man. Part of him wondered

whether she was just waiting outside to let him know how badly he'd screwed up.

"Just a few questions."

Corbin pulled out the chair, dropped into it and waved for Besson to begin. The detective opened a file and placed it flat on the table as he sat across from Corbin.

"I have the initial report you gave and the longer report you gave to Detective Allesandro, so we don't need to go over that."

Corbin's curiosity clicked up a notch. "So what do you want to go over?"

"The man you saw, the albino——"

"I never said he was an albino."

Besson flicked through the pages in the file. "Yes, I see that. But I think from your description it's apparent that he was."

"Maybe. I don't know. Does it matter?"

The detective smiled. "Not really. But you got a good look at him. Your description is very detailed. Creative even. You're a writer, yes?"

Corbin didn't like the insinuation. "I saw him. Pale skin, blue eyes, nasty scar from here to here." He drew the outline of the shape from his chin, across his cheek and over to his ear. "And his ear was all mangled, like whatever had cut him lopped the ear off too. Why would I make up such a thing?"

Besson shrugged. "Creative types," he said, as if that explained everything.

"I told you exactly what I saw. And I don't appreciate your tone. I tried to help the man. Against three deranged lunatics wearing creepy-ass masks. Maybe a thank you is in order."

"Is that what you want? A thank you?"

"I'd prefer a case of wine, but a thank you wouldn't be bad either."

Besson rocked back in his chair. "How long have you known Ms. Vinci?"

"Who?"

The detective scowled. "Please, Monsieur Stewart. I promised only a few minutes, but these games will make things take longer."

"Do you mean Margot?" Corbin realized he'd never gotten her last name.

"Yes, the woman you were with."

"I met her this afternoon for the first time."

Besson opened a new page to the file. "She says the two of you met today for drinks."

"That's right."

"The decision to go down Alle du Dauphin? That was your decision or hers?"

"Does it matter?"

"Perhaps not."

"Then why ... you think she set it up?"

"I didn't say that. I'm simply trying to——"

"It was my idea to go that way," Corbin snapped. "I've done it hundreds of times before."

"Hundreds? How long have you lived in Paris, Mr. Stewart?"

"All right, maybe a dozen times."

Besson scribbled a note. "Creative types."

"I don't like this conversation," Corbin said. "I want to place a call to the US Consulate."

Besson pulled a photo from his file and slid it across the table. It was a grainy picture of the old man in the alley, with good posture and better clothes, but it was unmistakably him. In the photo, the man was sitting in a park, tossing what looked like bits of bread to pigeons. "Gregor Purem. A person of interest in an investigation I've been working for a very long time."

Corbin flipped the photo over and was surprised to see a date from last year written on the back. He wondered how that man had aged so much in a year. At the same time, he felt an inexplicable relief that the old man was a wanted criminal. The vicious butcher of an old man for no reason was a breakdown in society and basic humanity. An execution of a criminal by a rival crime gang was still a terrible thing, but somehow more acceptable.

It was the same reason people in the suburbs got bored easily with reports of gang violence. It had little to do with them. They weren't in a gang so they weren't subject to the danger it represented. But when an innocent passerby was struck by a stray bullet, the news trucks were on the scene, candlelight vigils were held and society took notice. Ostensibly because it was a tragedy. But the real difference was that random violence made them feel unsafe. That the same could happen to them. Human nature ensured the first question was, how does this impact me? The gory death from that night was sure to make some headlines, but once it was clear it was an execution, people would move on quickly.

He pushed the photo back to Besson. "Looks like you found him if you have this picture. Why was he still on the streets?"

"The picture was uncovered during the arrest and interrogation of one of Gregor's associates. There is a gypsy group. Call themselves the Tacho R'asa. The True Tribe. Other Romani don't really appreciate the name, as you can imagine. The implication is that the R'asa are somehow more pure than the others."

Corbin shrugged. "I still don't see what this has to do with me."

Besson withdrew a second photo from the folder, hesitated, and then slowly slid it across the table. "The person I interviewed had a series of pictures. This one I found particularly interesting."

With a deep sigh to show how done with the conversation he was, Corbin grabbed the photo. It took only a second before adrenaline flash-flooded his system, hitting him so hard that he jerked back as if the photo had conducted an electrical charge.

He leaned closer, squinting as if that might change the truth of what was clearly in the photo. But there was no denying it.

Gregor remained on the park bench, only now he wasn't alone. There was a woman with him.

A woman whose last name he'd learned only minutes before. Margot Vinci.

"Oh shit," Corbin whispered.

"Oui, Monsieur," Besson said. "Oh shit."

7

"What the hell is going on here?" Corbin asked. His mind rifled through the day. The moment Margot had walked up to his table. The easy way she'd engaged him in conversation.

"You see," Besson said, pointing a finger at him. "That's exactly the same question I have for you. What the hell is going on here? Once we figure that out, you're free to go."

"Free to go? I thought you said I wasn't being detained."

Besson shrugged. "I am also creative."

"I want to call the American consulate. That's my right, isn't it?"

Besson shook his head. "You've been watching too many movies. Americans always want to call the consulate. What do you think is going to happen? That they're going to send in the Marines to pull you out of here? No, I don't think they will."

Corbin swallowed hard and found that his mouth was so dry the act nearly gagged him. "A lawyer? Am I entitled to a lawyer then?"

"Do you need a lawyer? Have you committed a crime, Mr. Stewart?"

"No ... I didn't say ... Jesus Christ, I was a witness. I came here to help you out. You said that I just need to come down—"

"I said? I said nothing to you. We just met. I personally didn't give you any indication as to the purpose of your being brought here."

Corbin rubbed his eyes, pressing the bridge of his nose to push back the headache that was forming. "I'll take that water now."

Besson fixed his eyes on him for several long seconds, then straightened. "Of course. Right over there."

Corbin saw the small water cooler in the corner of the room. He stood and walked over, his legs feeling weak. The leg that had been sliced open throbbed with each movement, and he had to grab onto the cooler to steady himself once he reached it. He pulled a paper cup from the side and filled it, noticing that his hand shook as he did.

He needed to think this through. Somehow Margot was connected to the old man in the alley. He tried to remember exactly her response when they'd first seen him. The few minutes leading up to the attack was a blur, drowned out by the image of the men in the masks and the bloodbath that followed.

But there was something. When they first walked in the alley, the old man had called out to Margot. He said something twice.

"He called her a name," Corbin said, turning.

"What's that?"

"The old man. When he first saw her, he called her a name."

This got the detective's interest. "What name?"

"It was hard to hear. He had an accent. Shay? Schway? Something like that?"

"Chey?" Besson asked.

Corbin nodded. "Yeah, could be. He said something else in a language I didn't understand."

Besson pointed to the folder on the desk. "You said he spoke English."

"He did. After that he did."

"And what was Ms. Vinci's response?"

"What does it mean? Chey?"

"How did she respond?"

Corbin tried to remember. But when he thought back all he saw was the old man with blood gushing from his wounds. The feel of the blood spraying on his own face. The man's tongue worming down his throat. And before that. The moment when he'd grabbed Corbin's wrist and transformed into––

"Monsieur," Besson said. "I asked you a question."

"She ... she ... didn't want anything to do with him," Corbin said, remembering. "She wanted to leave the alley. Go back the other direction."

"But she was the one who wanted to use that shortcut."

"No, I told you, I wanted to use it. She wanted to go to Harry's Bar. I said that in the report." Besson looked away as if he'd been caught at something. "Look, let's get something straight here. I was sitting at a café, writing my novel." He winced at the words. He hadn't been writing shit. "A beautiful woman sits next to me and chats me up. I chat right back at her. Who wouldn't?"

Besson held up his left hand and pointed to his wedding ring. "Me."

Corbin's fingers went to his own wedding band on reflex, twisting it in a circle. He didn't feel the need to explain himself to the smug detective, so he moved on. "It turns out it wasn't a chance meeting. She works for my publisher and was sent to check up on me."

"Are you someone that needs checking up on?"

"Apparently. We have words about her lying to me, but we get past that and decide to go for drinks. That's the only time I've seen or met her. If she has some connection with the man who was killed or the men with the masks on, then it has nothing to do with me." Corbin crushed the paper cup in his hand and tossed it at the trash can in the corner. To his surprise, it landed perfectly.

"Nice shot," Besson said, giving him a curious look. "Two points."

"More like three, motherfucker. I've had enough of this. That old man got his blood all over me, so I'm going to go back to my place, take a hot shower and scrub a few layers of skin off myself. If you have more questions, I suggest you ask Margot."

Corbin walked to the door, feeling impressed with his little speech and the tough way he delivered it. Besson stopped him with one word.

"Daughter," he said.

Corbin turned. "What?"

"Chey. In Romani. It means daughter."

He felt cold wash through him again, drenching even the hot pain radiating out from his bandaged leg. Could it be? She'd seen her father and wanted to run from him? But her reaction afterward was off. She'd been shaken up, but it was the reaction of a bystander witnessing a savage crime, not a daughter watching a parent bleed to death.

"You think she was his actual daughter? Or could it have been like, you know, a term of endearment or something?"

"I don't know. The R'asa have their own ways. Their own nuances in language. It's hard to say."

"Why don't you ask her. You said she was right outside waiting for me." Besson's expression gave him away immediately. Corbin felt a surge of anger. "That was another lie, wasn't it?"

Besson nodded. "Margot Vinci, whereabouts unknown. I went to question her and she was gone."

"Gone? Gone where?"

"That was my other question for you."

Corbin didn't like the way the detective was eyeing him. "How would I know where—"

Besson held up his hand to stop him. "Funny thing is that I believe you. I don't think you know what all this really is. I hope that remains true." He walked over to Corbin and handed him his card. "If things start happening to you, odd things, I want you to call me. I might be able to help."

He took the card. It was plain with only the name Gerard Besson and a single phone number. There was no official seal. No title. Just the name and number.

"If things start happening to me? What kind of things?"

Besson opened the door for him. "The doctors told you to watch for symptoms, yes?"

"Yeah."

"Some things you will want to call the doctor for. Others, you'll want to call me."

Corbin felt a headache start right behind his eyes. He blinked hard and hoped it wasn't the sign of something bigger on the way. "What are you talking about? What kind of symptoms would I call you about instead of a doctor?"

"What did your Supreme Court Justice Potter Stewart say about pornography?"

"I know it when I see it."

Besson smiled. "Any relation? Never mind, doesn't matter. Good night, Mr. Stewart. Thank you for your cooperation."

Corbin let himself be ushered into the hallway. It was late and the building was darker than when he'd arrived. Someone had turned out the main lights so only every third light was on. The door closed behind him and he was alone on the floor. Noise came from the stairwell at the far end of the hallway. He guessed that the lower level with the uniformed police was still a busy place at night, but the detectives probably worked more reasonable hours. Or perhaps they were still at the city's crime scenes, looking at blood-splayed walls and desecrated bodies.

He didn't like the way things had ended. *You'll know it when you see it?* That felt to Corbin that the detective had a good idea that something might happen to him. He didn't see the value of being kept in the dark.

Corbin turned and reopened the door. "Hey, I want to know ..."

The room was empty. Besson was gone.

8

C orbin needed a drink. He didn't much care what it was, as long as it was wet and stiff. He limped his way up the road, knowing no respectable street in this part of Paris would allow too far a distance between drinking establishments. Sure enough, a narrow, hole-in-the-wall bar presented itself after a half block. He grasped the doorframe as he walked in, grunting from the pain in his leg.

His head felt like he'd already downed a couple. He hadn't felt good as he left the station, and he seemed to be getting worse with every step. The world around him seemed to move on its own volition, tipping precariously from side-to-side as if he were on a boat. And he felt cold. Cold enough that shivers coursed through him. Except for his damn leg. That was on fire with heat and pain. But none of it compared to the headache that had started as a dull ache and now felt like someone had used the claw end of a hammer to split his skull in two.

The headache had kicked up a notch right after he'd gone down-stairs in the police station and asked around for Detective Besson. Person after person assured him, nicely at first, and then with rising frustration and anger, that no one by the name of Gerard Besson worked at that station. When Corbin showed the desk sergeant

Besson's business card, the man laughed at him and said something in French that he didn't quite understand. The word *stupide* translated well enough though.

Confused, pissed off and tired of feeling like he was the last one in on a joke being played at his expense, he'd left the police station with the intention of heading home to take a shower and sleep it off. But the more he walked, the more his leg hurt, and the more he needed a drink.

"Que puis-je vous?" the bartender said, looking him up and down as if not liking what the cat had just dragged into his establishment.

Corbin tried to muster the French words for his order, but they wouldn't come. "I'll take a whiskey. Neat."

"Of course," the bartender said, easily switching to English.

Corbin's jaw ached as he watched the man pour the drink. He licked his lips, waiting. The whiskey glass made a solid *thunk* on the wood bar as it was set in front of him. He grabbed at the glass and lifted it quickly to his mouth, dribbling some from his lips as he put it back like a shot.

"Reload," he said. The bartender may or may not have been familiar with the term, but there wasn't any doubt he was familiar with a person who needed a drink. He refilled and then walked to the other end of the bar even though there were no other customers at that end.

Corbin finished the second drink in two swallows and then caught his reflection in the mirror. He looked even worse than he felt, something he didn't think possible. His hair was uncombed, sticking out in odd directions after he'd washed the blood from it in the men's room at the police station. He still wore the light windbreaker the Paris police had been kind enough to let him keep. It was two sizes too big so he looked like a kid wearing his dad's clothes. But his eyes were the worst part. Bloodshot and wild, he looked like he'd just been in a fight, or was about to get into one. No wonder the bartender had drifted away from him.

What if the old man gave me something?

Some things you will want to call the doctor for. Others, you'll want to call me.

He fished out his wallet to throw some euros down but remembered his little cash problem. Carefully, he pulled out the one credit card he thought still had a chance of working and waved it at the bartender. He considered one more round. If the credit card was going to get declined, a little more booze would make the embarrassment more palatable. But something told him that the bartender might refuse him, so he decided to just pay up. He twisted the glass nervously in his hand as the bartender ran the card.

He grew nervous. It felt like it was taking longer than it should. Corbin eyed the exit and wondered how far he'd get on his bum leg before someone tackled him. The idea struck him as funnier than it should have and he stifled an odd giggle.

God, his leg hurt. The doc that had stitched him up said it wasn't that deep, but what did he know? It felt like it was down to the bone.

He wiped a hand across his brow and it came back wet with cold sweat.

"Monsieur?"

The bartender nodded to the leather pad holding his card and the receipt for him to sign. Corbin picked up the pen, fumbled it, then focused hard and gripped it long enough to make a slanted mark on the receipt.

"Are you all right?" the bartender asked.

Corbin lifted a feeble hand at him and tried to give him a thumbs-up, only his thumb seemed impossibly heavy now. He held his fist out and gave a little jab in the air. "I'm fine. Tough night is all."

He turned around, trying to remember where the goddamn door was. The room wasn't helping out, spinning around him on some unseen axis, making it impossible to focus.

But then he saw the first one.

Up against the far wall, pretending to talk with a girl.

A man in a tragedy mask. Black holes for eyes. Gaping mouth turned downward.

The man turned and looked right at Corbin, his empty eyes burning into him.

Then the woman with him turned, her face covered by the same mask.

"No. It's not me you want," Corbin mumbled. He lurched toward the front of the bar where he felt the door had to be located. But the second he put weight on his leg, it buckled, fresh bolts of pain tearing through him. He grabbed a chair. It barely kept him from falling over.

A couple at the table nearest him spun around to look. Their faces covered with masks.

Corbin's mind turned over on itself. He blinked hard, sure that the masks weren't real. Couldn't be real.

He twisted his body back toward the bar. The bartender stood there, tragedy mask covering his face, staring at him.

Get out of here, Corbin. Get out of here right now.

But he couldn't. Everything hurt now. And he was cold. So cold.

Get out. Last chance. Get. Out.

But there were too many of them. Every person in the bar turned to look at him. All wearing lifeless masks.

He took one step forward, fell, and sprawled out on the floor, face up to the ceiling. His chest heaved in short panting breaths, but he couldn't get enough air. The pain in his leg flared, and for a few seconds the world turned bright white as the pain washed out everything else.

When the wave of pain passed, he saw that a circle of people had gathered around him. Embarrassment hit him first. He'd fallen in the middle of the room. So many people staring at him.

But when he looked up and his eyes focused on what was in front of him, he couldn't breathe.

Faces. Dozens of them. Covered with tragedy masks.

Staring down at him.

With dead, empty eyes.

The thin cord that held his sanity in place snapped and he was cut loose, pirouetting into a storm of madness that was all noise and tragedy masks and gypsies and black blood. He raised his arms over his face and did the only think left to do.

He screamed. And screamed. And screamed.

9

Alexis watched from the street, glancing through the window as the bar patrons scrambled to help the American who had fallen to the floor in a drunken heap. He spotted the bartender on the phone, probably calling the police or the paramedics. Either way, Alexis suspected Corbin Stewart was on his way to a hospital.

He would have preferred if the American had just gone home from the police station. His people had already been there; a walk-up apartment on the Ile Saint-Louis, the island in the Seine directly behind Notre Dame. The American lived there alone and it would have been simple to have a little chat with him there. Just a clearing of the air to make sure he wasn't involved with Gregor and the woman. And perhaps a little payback for knocking him to the ground. Alexis wasn't the type to let something like that go unanswered.

A siren wailed behind him and he took a step farther back into the shadows. It was an impressive response time for an ambulance, but the police station was just down the street so he figured they would be en route too. He imagined the American had given them a description of him, so he had to be careful.

The ambulance driver popped two wheels on the curb and came

to a stop. Several seconds passed before the doors opened, and when they did, the paramedic who got out was texting on his phone, clearly in no hurry to get inside. A passed-out drunk wasn't enough to get the adrenaline pumping.

Alexis pulled his hood lower over his face as the driver joined the first medic and together they went into the bar. Pedestrians slowed and craned their necks to look in. Since the terrorist attacks in Paris, the general population was on edge, thinking every siren meant a gunman or a bomb. But once they picked up on the way the paramedics moved lazily about their work, and how most of the customers in the bar were back to their drinks, some even eating, they continued on their way.

He glanced around the area, looking especially in the shadowy spots where he would hide, making sure no one was watching him. Gregor's men were the main concern, but he found that the face he was looking for in the crowd was the woman's, Margot Vinci. He still found it hard to believe that his men had let her slip through their fingers so easily once she'd left the police station. Njau and M'akiwe were out scouring the streets for her now, trying to make up for their failure. With them occupied, he'd decided to follow the American himself.

While the paramedics got the man to his feet and then into a chair, Alexis thought through all the mistakes he'd made that night and how they could have been so easily prevented. One additional man at the other end of the alley would have guaranteed them enough time with Gregor. Maybe even time to have a little fun with him. To make him feel some of the pain he'd inflicted on others over the course of his miserable life.

But while that could have prevented everything else, it wasn't the only mistake. Once the American had seen his face, Alexis should have killed him, simple as that. Concerns about increasing the profile of the case be damned. The more he thought about the way the man had fought back, trying to defend an old man he'd never met before, the more he chided himself for not removing him from the equation.

A few years earlier, he would not have hesitated. Maybe he was losing a step?

Corbin Stewart may have looked soft, but there had to be some steel in his backbone for him to have done what he did. As the only cooperating witness for the police, he had to die. Not yet, but soon.

And the same for the woman.

He couldn't be certain whether her slipping out of the police station showed skill or blind luck, but he wasn't a big believer in luck. She'd run from the police, the people who she ought to have sought for protection. The old adage echoed in his head: the innocent don't run. There was some truth to the saying, but then again, how many innocents had he seen in his life that had run only to be chopped down by evil men? A thousand? Two? More than could fit into the nightmares he had every night. Nightmares where the corpses rose back from the dead, bodies black and bloated, decayed flesh hanging from their bones as they clambered after him, demanding that he bring them justice.

No, the fact that the woman ran didn't make her guilty, but it raised enough suspicion that she needed to be found and eliminated. Even if he was wrong about her, a single innocent life wasn't enough to bother his conscience. He'd done far worse in pursuit of the R'asa. He'd rather be careful. Besides, there was a good chance she was one of them and deserved the death coming to her.

The American was on his feet in the restaurant now, a paramedic on each arm as they walked him out. Alexis turned to the side, using the cut of his hood to hide his face in shadow. Since childhood, he'd been an expert at keeping his face from being seen, a skill that had often meant the difference between life and death when the hunting parties tore through his village looking for albino children. He'd been good at it. He'd known too many others who had not. They populated his dreams too.

The people in the bar weren't about to let a drunk tourist ruin their evening. A few of them clapped as the American walked by, raising their glasses of wine to him in a salute. The man didn't seem to know they existed. His eyes were glassy, staring at the ground in front of him. Even from his position, Alexis could see that the man's face was covered with sweat, his hair wet as if he'd just finished a long run. This was more than being drunk. He was ill.

That was even better. It meant they'd admit him to the hospital. He wondered if the woman would try to visit him. Try to warn him of the danger he was in. He supposed it was worth the chance. He'd keep the American alive long enough to use him as bait for the Tacho R'asa.

Alexis was so deep in his thoughts and plans that he didn't see the reflection in the window until it was too late.

He heard the sound of a gun being cocked first, and then he saw the faint image on the glass, wavy and distorted, but clear enough. Police. Three of them.

One of them barked an order for him to raise his hands.

He didn't comply. He was too busy calculating his odds against the men. He'd hidden the knife he'd used on Gregor, so he wasn't armed. But there were only three of them, and fighting his way out was possible. That's if there hadn't been a gun. Guns always complicated things.

What had he been thinking to be on the streets without a guard of any kind?

He raised his hands and slowly turned in place. The officers stepped back as his face came into the light. Two of the men had guns out. The third grabbed a Taser from his belt and pointed it at him.

Alexis closed his eyes, searching for the sequence of actions that would enable him to fight his way through them. But each scenario ended with three dead bodies. And only two of them were police.

He followed the next set of instructions shouted at him and lay down on the ground, twisting his hands behind his back. As they cuffed him, he cursed his own stupidity. Of course the American had given them his description. The police had likely come to the scene based on the call from the bartender. And there he'd stood, his own face reflecting on the window, an easy target. He would have punished one of his men with an amputation of a finger or toe for such foolishness. Alexis acknowledged that he was getting reckless, skipping steps, not taking essential precautions. But he felt the end of his chase for the Tacho R'asa approaching. And at the end, great risks had to be taken lest the quarry get away.

As they pulled him to his feet, he watched them load the American into the ambulance. He and the woman, Margot, were the only ones who could testify that he'd killed the old man. He just needed to make certain neither of them lived long enough to do so.

10

The rats gnawed on Corbin's feet. He felt their teeth rip through the soft flesh, tearing off strips of callused skin, pulling out his toenails with vicious twists of their heads. Then they reached his bones, breaking them open to get at the tasty marrow inside. The pain took away his ability to scream. His mouth stretched wide in a soundless cry, every muscle of his body flexed so hard that his back arched like a seizure victim.

But the rats still came. Up to his ankle, then his lower leg, feasting on his juicy, blood-filled calf muscle. Chewing and chewing and chewing.

He tried to draw in a breath but he couldn't. The pain froze everything in place. His lungs refused to work. His eyes wouldn't move. There was nothing in the world except the agony of being eaten alive.

And the sound.

The high-pitched squeaks from the feeding frenzy. Punctuated by short screams when the rats bit one another in their eagerness. Getting louder as they worked their way up his body. Devouring him, inch by inch. Blood, marrow, bone. When they were done, there would be nothing left of him. Nothing but traces of his DNA in the piles of rat shit produced hours after the feast was over.

Somehow, he grabbed a corner on the edge of his pain and pulled it back just enough to gasp in some precious air. But his body didn't want it for breath. It wanted it for a release. It wanted it to put a warning out into the world that enough pain existed to drive a man insane. Gathering up all of his strength, he screamed and screamed and ...

... and screamed, as he sat up in his hospital bed.

A nurse ran into the room, flipping on a switch, flooding the world with bright light.

"What is it?" the nurse asked, her accent heavy. More like *What eiz eet?*

Corbin tried to catch his breath. His heart pounded in his chest as he looked around the room for the rats. There were none. None that he saw anyway.

He pulled his covers aside. His legs were there, of course. Nothing had chewed them. It was a dream. That was all.

Sweat covered his body, drenched like he'd broken a fever. He was embarrassed to see it was more than that. He'd urinated in the bed. He felt shame like he was a little boy again, wetting the bed during a sleepover at a friend's house. The nurse noticed it but appeared unfazed, a response that gave him an odd sense of relief.

She took his wrist, placing cold fingers on his skin, and watched the clock on the wall.

"Where am I?" Corbin asked.

She gave him an annoyed look, then refocused on the clock. The message was clear: *Don't bother me. I'm busy.*

He took stock. The hospital room looked like any number of rooms he'd been in during his life. His father's after his first aneurysm, the small one before the one that turned his lights off for good. His mother's as she lay dying of what the doctors told her was congestive heart failure and what she assured them was a broken heart after a drunk driver killed her youngest son. His wife's when she gave birth to their daughter. His daughter's five years later where she'd battled cancer and lost. They all looked the same to him. Only it was the first time he was the one in the bed.

He was surprised to have a room to himself. His impression of European hospitals and socialized medicine was that there was chronic overcrowding and that it was hard to get treatment. He considered he might still find the last part to be true.

The room was small but orderly. He traced the IV coming from his arm to the saline bag on the stand next to him. Wires led from his chest to a bank of monitors keeping track of his vitals. The crazy spikes of his heartbeat were drifting off the screen, replaced by a more regular pattern as he calmed down.

"Can't you just use the machine for that?" he asked the nurse, obviously still counting his pulse compared to the clock on the wall.

"Machines can be wrong," she said quietly. "I'm never wrong."

Corbin immediately liked the nurse. "Then you can tell me what I'm doing here."

Before she could answer, a young man in a white doctor's coat walked into the room. He had deep brown skin and closely cropped black hair. His walk and demeanor exuded the confidence of a young doctor not yet beaten down by years of practice. "You don't remember?" he said.

"Blood pressure 180 over 76. Pulse 68," the nurse reported, speaking English still.

"Yes," the doctor said, pointing to the machine. "I can see that."

The nurse let out a not-so-subtle grunt that made Corbin smile. She walked from the room. "I'll return with fresh sheets."

The young doc sniffed the air, obviously picking up the smell of urine but nice enough not to mention it. He lifted an iPad from his side. "I'm Dr. Gupta," he said. "Says here you're from Maryland. I grew up in Jersey."

"You're American?"

"Yeah, my grades in medical school were pretty bad, so I had to come here." He waited a beat. "That was a joke."

Corbin wasn't in the mood. "What happened? Why am I here?"

"I understand from the the police you were involved in a mugging last night."

"Yeah ... I mean no ... how did you know I was from Maryland?"

Dr. Gupta looked up from his iPad. Corbin didn't much appreciate the way the young doctor made him feel like he was some animal to be examined. Like a hamster in a cage.

"You told the intake nurse. And we found your license in your wallet. What's the last thing you remember from last night, Mr. Stewart?"

Rats eating my goddamn legs, was what he wanted to say. Instead, he closed his eyes and tried to recall. Suddenly, an image burst into his head: a restaurant full of people turning toward him, tragedy masks covering their faces, empty sockets staring at him.

"The restaurant," he said, leaving his eyes shut. "There was something wrong with the people in the restaurant."

"Something wrong? How do you mean?"

Corbin caught something in the doctor's voice. He was judging him. He knew if he opened his eyes, the man would have a smirk on his lips.

"Nothing," he said, opening his eyes. "It was just that ... just ... what's wrong with your face?"

Corbin watched in horror as the young man's mouth drooped down at the corners, like he was having a stroke. Then the skin under the doctor's eyes sagged, wide half-moons rippling down his cheek like melting wax.

His eyebrows slid out in opposite directions, pooling up at the edges of his brow before slipping down the sides of his face.

"What the hell's wrong with you?"

The doctor took a step closer to the bed as his eyes filled with blood.

"What are you talking about, Mr. Stewart?"

The doctor's left eye burst first. Corbin heard it go, just a soft, wet sound as it collapsed inward.

Then the right one bulged out, like something was inside the man's head trying to get out.

Pop

The eye squirted out, liquefied in the socket, pouring down his cheeks in black tears.

"Get away," Corbin said, pushing back against the bed, kicking his legs, trying to disappear into the mattress. "Stay away from me."

The doctor opened his mouth as if to scream and teeth poured out in a torrent of dark blood. A stench filled the air, the same as the old man in the alley, a heavy putrescence of rotting, infected flesh.

A thick purple tongue lolled inside the mouth, forcing out the few remaining teeth through the mushy, soft gums.

Corbin clawed at the bed, but he couldn't move any farther back. The man's face froze in place, the eyes now black holes, the mouth stretched into an open wail.

A tragedy mask made of flesh and bone.

"No ... no ... no ..." he cried, holding his hands in front of his face.

Something touched him and he fought back, flailing his arms, kicking his legs even though they were still under the sheets.

"Mr. Stewart, relax. Just relax. Nurse!"

He had to get out of there. He had to run. He had to ...

Something yanked his hands down from his face. He didn't want to see those eyes again. He couldn't see them again and not go insane.

But the face was right there, right in front of him. Unavoidable. Unmistakable. And ... unremarkable.

Just the doctor.

No dark holes for eyes. No melted skin. No gush of blood and teeth.

Nothing but an exasperated look of a man watching someone dance on the brink of sanity.

There was movement to his right as the nurse and a big orderly burst into the room. The nurse had a syringe in her hand. The orderly had straps, the kind they used to tie crazy people to their hospital beds.

Crazy people like me.

"Wait, wait a second," he said, holding up his hands. "I'm all right. Sorry. I'm all right."

The nurse glanced at the doctor, and Corbin had the impression she would have stuck him with the syringe with the barest nod of his head. Probably a sedative. Maybe not a terrible idea to get his malfunctioning brain to shut the hell up. But the thought of the rats coming back if he went back to sleep made him shudder. "I'm all right. Really. Look, see? I'm calm. Everyone's calm."

Dr. Gupta pushed a hand through his hair, pulling himself together. "Are you sure? Because I didn't see that coming. At all."

"Just a little disoriented. I'm good now." He took a deep breath and felt himself calming down. He pointed to the machine next to his bed showing his heartbeat slowing. "See?"

The doctor indicated that the nurse and orderly could both stand down. The orderly looked especially disappointed. He seemed to be the kind of guy that enjoyed tying people up. The nurse left, but as the orderly began to follow her, the doctor said, "Jean, you can stay."

Corbin realized the doc thought he might freak out again and he wanted some muscle in the room if he did. He didn't blame him.

"Been through a lot last night," Corbin explained. "Could I get some water?"

Dr. Gupta's skepticism was thinly veiled and he didn't seem eager to be alone with him again. After a long pause, he turned to the orderly. "Would you mind?" The man grunted, but he left the room in search of water, his restraints thrown over his shoulder. "Your blood-work came back fine."

At the mention of blood, Corbin remembered the taste of it in his mouth. "Are you sure?"

Dr. Gupta eyed him oddly. "We just did a basic panel. Some tests take longer, but we should have them later today. Are you expecting something to be there?" He poked the iPad screen. "You gave no indication of prior history when you were admitted."

"I don't even remember coming here last night. I might have told you I was President of the United States for all I know."

Dr. Gupta's easy demeanor was gone. "Mr. Stewart, if you have a disease you're managing, I need to know about it."

"No, nothing like that."

"Then what?"

Corbin weighed what to tell the young doctor. The doctor he'd seen right after the attack had taken his blood and given him an antibiotic. He didn't want to drag this out any longer than he needed. Then again, if he did pick up something from the old man, then maybe Dr. Gupta could hook him up on a quicker treatment plan.

"I witnessed a murder last night."

"Yes, I know. There were police with you when you came in."

"He was a homeless guy. I assume he was homeless, anyway. He was old, wore dirty clothes. And after he was ... after they ..." He felt the hot blood splashing against his hands and arms. Then the spray in his mouth. "After they attacked him and ran off, I tried to help him."

"And you were in contact with his blood."

"Yes. On my skin. Some got into my mouth."

"Hmmm."

"Hmmm? What's that mean?"

Dr. Gupta looked far too serious. He liked it better when the doc was trying to crack jokes. "As I'm sure you know, there are several blood-borne illnesses that are somewhat common for men who live on the street. Malaria, syphilis and brucellosis are possible. But hepatitis B, hepatitis C and HIV are obviously of greater concern." He poked at the iPad and then appeared to find something. "Shows here you were treated in emergency. They took blood for analysis and prescribed Cipro."

"That's in there?" Corbin asked, surprised.

Dr. Gupta smiled. "This isn't the US. Electronic records here. Huge step forward. Once you're in the system, all docs can see your history."

"That's got to be hell on pill addicts."

"They still find a way around it. Increased the trade in fake IDs. But do you want to talk about electronic records or whether you caught a nasty disease last night while you were playing Good Samaritan?"

"They say no good deed goes unpunished."

The orderly walked in with a bottle of water and handed it to Corbin. He glanced at Dr. Gupta as if hoping for a sign Corbin was being bad and needed to be tied up after all. But the doc gave a nod to the door, and the big man left sulking.

"You understand there's a risk, especially with the mouth. But the real problem would be any cuts you had. Blood on blood contact. A puncture wound."

Corbin pointed to his leg. "My leg got sliced open with a knife." He realized that the leg hadn't been bothering him. That was one thing he did remember from last night, the fire in his leg. Barely being able to walk on it.

Dr. Gupta poked at his iPad again, his expression going from curiosity to annoyance. He soon gave up searching and put the iPad down. He reached for the blanket covering Corbin. "Do you mind?"

"Go ahead."

The doc pulled the blanket down. Corbin felt a little ridiculous in his hospital gown, but he stifled his modesty. A loose gauze pad was wrapped around his upper leg. "Let's take a look at it." He pulled back the tape and carefully unwrapped the leg. Corbin wondered at how there was no pain. He lay back and raised his knee off the bed so it was easier to unwind the gauze. Still no pain. He wondered if they'd given him a shot or something.

Finally, he felt the cool air on his skin as the doc removed the final layer.

"Is this right?" Dr. Gupta asked.

"What?" Corbin asked.

"Look for yourself."

Corbin lifted himself up, resting on his elbow so he could look down at his leg.

There was no wound. There wasn't even a mark.

11

Electronic records didn't make the discharge process any easier than in the States. Corbin worked through the levels of bureaucracy to get himself checked out over the objections of Dr. Gupta who argued that he ought to wait until the full bloodwork panel came back. But there was zero chance he was going to sit and wait in the hospital. It would have driven him crazy. Especially staring at his miraculously healed leg.

He'd made excuses for the leg with Dr. Gupta. Maybe he hadn't been injured after all. Maybe he'd pulled a muscle in his leg and with all the blood from the man, he'd just assumed it was cut. Maybe the paramedics who said they stitched him up on scene had just pressed the wrong button on their tablet. Maybe it was just all a misunderstanding.

Or maybe it was all just so goddamn weird that he didn't want to talk about it.

Dr. Gupta had relented, mostly because he had other patients on the floor and had to make his rounds. He promised to call Corbin once the bloodwork came in and then left after a perfunctory handshake. Finally, the original nurse came in and handed him a tablet to sign with a stylus, the last piece of the puzzle to get him out the door.

She gave a short sniff as she looked over the hospital scrubs he was wearing out into the world instead of his dirty clothes. She obviously didn't approve.

After he signed the tablet, the nurse handed him a small envelope.

"What's this?"

The nurse shrugged. "A boy gave it to me. Said it was for you."

He tore open the envelope and pulled out a small card, the type one might find attached to a flower arrangement. On it was scrawled a simple message that got his heart racing.

NOTRE DAME. *3pm.*
Don't let them follow you.

HE FLIPPED THE CARD OVER, looking for a name, but it was blank.

"Where is the boy?" he asked the nurse.

"I didn't like the look of him so I sent him away."

Corbin looked over her shoulder and into the hall. "Are we done here?"

"Yes, of course."

Corbin snatched up his bag of dirty clothes, gave her a quick nod and a smile so as not to add to the rude American stereotype, then jogged out the door. He ignored the looks as people watched him run through the hall in his ill-fitting doctor scrubs that were cinched at the waist to keep from falling. He scoured the halls for any sight of a boy.

Seeing none, he grabbed the elbow of an orderly. "Did you see a boy walk through? Un petit garcon?" The orderly shook his head. Corbin headed to the exit. It seemed reasonable that the boy would have gone the same way. He wanted to know who'd given him the card. He wanted to believe it was Margot, but he was self-aware enough to know he just wanted to see her again. But why not just sign the card? Why the mystery?

He squinted as he left the hospital, the midday sun blazing. It was a Saturday and Mother Nature had graced the city with an unseasonably warm day so there were people everywhere. He scanned the sidewalk, looking for anyone who might stand out. There were young boys in the crowd, but they all seemed to be part of a family or walking in groups. He turned left and right, growing more exasperated.

"Are you looking for me?" came a voice behind him.

Corbin turned as Besson walked toward him. He was in a different suit, a tan linen that perfectly fit the season and the warmer than usual weather. A muted crimson tie lay against a white shirt. He looked well rested and in good spirits. Corbin felt like a truck had run over him and felt inexplicably annoyed that Besson looked so good. As the detective, or whatever he was, walked up to him, Corbin slid the card from Margot into his bag of clothes.

"No, wasn't looking for you at all," he said, glancing around to make sure there were plenty of witnesses. Despite Besson's smile, Corbin didn't trust the guy. "But there are some police officers back at the station who are looking for you. Turns out none of them know who you are."

Besson waved the comment away. "I'm in a special division. The people who needed to know I was there knew I was there." He smirked, responding to the doubt on Corbin's face. "What? You think I'm just some guy off the street? Why else would they give me access to you unless they knew who I was? I had your folder, remember?"

Corbin felt his face warm as his elaborate conspiracy theory crumbled in front of him. "I came back in the room. You'd just ... disappeared."

Besson laughed. "Because I'm magic, didn't I tell you? I walked through the wall, levitated over the street and flew away." He laughed at his own joke, clearly pleased with himself. Corbin grew more irritated by the second. Finally, Besson wiped a tear from his eye. "Remember that tall mirror on the far wall of the room? It's a door into the observation room. In case things get out of control during an interrogation."

"You mean if a prisoner gets violent?"

"Or if the man asking the questions does," he said, dropping all humor in his voice. "Sometimes you want answers so badly that you'll do anything to get them." He locked on to Corbin's eyes for a long beat. Corbin had the same unsettling feeling he had when faced with a big dog guarding his territory. He wasn't sure if Besson was about to wag his tail or bite his face off. Fortunately, he wagged his tail. "But if this helps, you can see my ID." He pulled a leather bi-fold wallet from his pocket and flipped it open, showing a badge on one side and an identification card on the other. He tossed it to Corbin.

Corbin made a show of examining it, even though he had zero clue what the ID ought to look like.

"I bought your book, you know," Besson said. "Well, I downloaded it for free on Amazon. I'm only through the beginning, but it's not bad."

Corbin tried to resist liking Besson because of the compliment, but it was hard. Like most writers, he was a sucker for a new fan. He relaxed, suddenly aware that he'd been clenching his teeth the entire time. "Thanks, hope you enjoy the rest. Leave a review if you like it. If you don't, keep it to your damn self." It was a line he used at book signings and it always got him an easy laugh. Besson complied with a faint chuckle.

"I'll do that." Then his tone changed. "I wish I was here just to talk about your book," he said. "They caught the man with the scar."

The words sent an electric sensation through Corbin. He pictured the man's face, snarling in the harsh alley light. "That was fast," he said.

"It was your description that did it."

"Happy to help."

"I'm glad you said that, because I need you to identify him in a row of suspects."

"A row of ... you mean a lineup?"

"Yes, exactly. A lineup. I'll take you there."

Corbin's stomach turned. All he wanted was to go home, take a hot shower and sleep for a week. "Really? You don't have him on other evidence? The old man's blood or something."

Besson's lips turned down into a disappointed frown. "A man was killed. I don't mean to inconvenience you, but——"

Corbin cut him off. "No, you're right. I'm sorry. It's been a rough twenty-four hours." Actually, twenty-four hours ago, he was having a late lunch and would soon be getting drunk with a beautiful woman while sitting in a café. That part didn't suck. Identifying a homicidal maniac in a lineup so the police could put him away for life? That wasn't nearly as fun.

"How much time do we have? Can I go to my apartment and change clothes?"

"I think that would be preferable," Besson said, looking over his outfit. "I'll take you. My car is right here."

Corbin had the feeling that refusing the ride wasn't an option, so he didn't even bother. And he had no real reason to ditch Besson other than he wanted to be by himself to think through everything that was happening to him. He checked his watch. It was only eleven. He just needed to get this done with before three to meet Margot. If she was the one who'd sent him the note, that was.

"You're walking better," Besson said, glancing back as they walked to his car.

Corbin added a small limp into his step. He wasn't sure why, but something told him that he didn't want Besson to know about his miraculous recovery. For all of the good guy, I read your book talk, at a visceral level he sensed Besson was a dangerous man, coiled up for violence, ready to strike when needed. He didn't want to give him any reason to take more of an interest in him than he already had. "Painkillers," he said lamely, wincing with faked pain as he rubbed the leg.

Besson slowed a step, but then continued to the car. In that split second, Corbin saw something in the man's eyes he didn't like. It wasn't just the look of disbelief that unnerved him. Besson's eyes telegraphed that some new information had been processed and a conclusion had been reached. With it came a change in the man's physicality. Besson tightened up his shoulders. His hands curled into fists and then opened up, like a gunfighter in an old Western getting ready for a shootout.

Besson was dangerous, all right. And Corbin made a mental note not to forget it.

12

Corbin's apartment was a mess. The fact that it was small didn't help, giving him less square feet per pound of detritus spread across the floor and furniture. He was on the second floor of a seventeenth-century building, accessed by a narrow staircase that spiraled one rotation as it went up. On his drunker nights, that spiral had saved him from falling all the way down the stairs. An added benefit to be sure.

The building was on Ile Saint-Louis, one of two islands in the Seine River. The other island, connected directly to the river by the Pont de Neuf, was the original settlement for Paris, properly named Ile de la Cite, or Island of the City. Once a viciously guarded battlement to ward off invaders, it is now home to the Cathedral du Notre Dame and vendors hawking goods to the hordes of tourists that descend on the area each day.

Ile Saint-Louis was nothing more than a rock pile for most of Paris's history. Then the wealthy merchant-class paid to fill in the area in the seventeenth century, creating a new island for summer homes, their own little getaway right in the physical and emotional heart of the city. The beautiful homes are all still there, four- and five-story stone facades facing out to the passing river. Only now most of them have been carved up into high-end multi-family units and short-term rentals for tourists.

Corbin liked the place because it felt like walking back in time. Everything he needed was on the little island. A few restaurants, cafés, a bakery, a cheese shop and a liquor store. He also loved hearing the bells of Notre Dame in the near distance, a reminder that there were still people in the world that believed in God and in the idea that good things could come of that belief. On some of his darker nights, the ones where the hole in his life gaped so large that it threatened to pull him down, to convince him that breathing and circulating blood through his body was overrated and worth bringing to an end, on those nights the sound of the bells had been the only thing that brought him back from the edge.

They were ringing in the distance as he finished his shower and pulled on fresh clothes. He'd scrubbed every inch of his skin until it glowed red, his stomach turning as the water on the shower floor turned a rust color when he first started to rinse off. The old man's blood had been caked into his pores, stuck under his nails, stained into his scalp. Some of it was his own blood too. He knew that was true even if there was no evidence of any wound on his leg. He pressed where he remembered his cut to be, stretching his skin in different directions, thinking it might be like a paper cut, invisible until pulled apart or until blood beaded up on the surface.

But there was nothing there.

It was so odd that he started to question his own memory. He inspected his other leg, just on the off chance he'd confused himself. It was a ridiculous idea, but he was getting desperate.

Wounds didn't just heal overnight by themselves. He knew that. But the evidence was undeniable. He even considered the possibility that he'd been in the hospital for a week in a coma, giving it time to heal. And the doctors didn't want to tell him because ... because why? It made no sense.

But what part of any of it made sense?

"That was the station on the phone," Besson called out from the small living room. "They're waiting for us."

"Be there in a minute."

Corbin pulled on socks and his favorite pair of hiking boots. *To climb out of the pile of shit I'm in*, he thought to himself as he laced them up.

If this was one of the books he liked to read, a Jack Reacher book by Lee Child maybe, he'd have a gun squirreled away somewhere in the room. He'd slip it into a shoulder holster or even tuck it under his belt, ready for action. But he didn't have a gun, not that he knew how to use one anyway. He did, however, have a tiny pocket Taser. A gift to himself after the terrorist attack in Paris the first week he was in town. He'd carried it around for a few days and then felt stupid having it. What good was a personal mini-Taser going to do against a pipe-bomb or an AK-47? Still, it would have been awfully useful to have facing down the three amigos wearing the tragedy masks the night before.

He went into the bathroom and closed the door. Holding the Taser in his right hand, he flushed the toilet with his left to make some noise and tried the tiny device. It spit and crackled, still fully charged. He hoped the door and running water had been enough to block the sound from reaching Besson. He didn't want the detective to know he had it.

Maybe it was an irrational thought, but he didn't consider anything happening to him recently to be particularly rational. If he was sick or losing his mind, a weapon wasn't going to help him. But the next time someone's face melted or turned into a mask, it made him feel better knowing he could jab the Taser into them. Not only that, but on a more practical level, he didn't completely trust Besson either. A weapon seemed like a reasonable precaution.

Corbin slipped the Taser into his pocket and opened the door. Besson stood on the other side.

"Everything all right?" he said, lips turned up in a fake smile that made Corbin shiver.

"My stomach's upside down a little," he lied. "I'll be fine."

"Guilty conscience."

"Excuse me?"

"My grandmother told me that an upset stomach comes from a guilty conscience."

Corbin had a hard time imagining Besson having a guilty conscience over anything. Hell, he found it hard to imagine the man having a grandmother.

"Yeah, well, sometimes it's just the idea of identifying a crazed lunatic for the cops. One who still has friends on the loose. Are we doing this or not?"

Besson stood to the side and let him pass. He noticed that the detective stuck his head in the bathroom for a second to look around, even though he'd looked through the entire apartment when they'd first arrived. Satisfied there was no one else there, he followed Corbin to the door. "Maybe I should tell you more about the man you're identifying today. Out of fairness."

"Do I really want to know?"

Besson considered for a moment. "No, probably not. But I'm going to tell you anyway."

They walked in silence to the car, a BMW 6 series, which seemed like a nicer car than a detective could afford. The detectives he'd met in the States while researching his novel drove mid-range SUVs and sedans. But most of them were family guys, stringing paychecks together for orthodontics, travel soccer fees and new appliances to keep their wives happy. Besson didn't seem like the family-type, despite his little shtick with his wedding ring during their interview.

"You know a little French, yes?" the detective asked as they buckled in.

"A little."

"Les Fantômes de la Nuit. You can translate?"

Corbin could, but he didn't really want to. He didn't think he was going to like where the conversation was going. "The Ghosts of the Night."

Besson nodded. "Exactly. Very good. That's what they call themselves, the men you saw with the masks. They are a very dangerous group."

"No shit," Corbin said. "I hadn't figured."

The detective didn't acknowledge the remark. He checked his rearview mirror and changed lanes. Corbin noticed the man didn't use his turn signal.

"They wear the masks to symbolize the tragedy of the immigrant's plight in Europe."

"They're political?"

Besson pursed his lips as if weighing the word. "Some think so."

"You?"

The car came to a stop at a red light. Besson turned to him. "Are you a religious man, Mr. Stewart?"

Corbin was thrown off-guard by the change of direction. "No, not really."

"I've never understood men without religion. How do you survive? How do you not drown in the sorrows of life?"

The sorrows of life? Corbin felt the slow burn of anger heating up in his chest. He assumed the man knew about his wife. His daughter. That he was using them to get a rise out of him.

"I manage," was all he could say.

The light changed to green. The car in front of them didn't move, so Besson laid on his horn until the car rolled forward. "Without religion, do you still believe in the concept of evil?"

"You can't watch the news and not believe in evil. It's almost harder to believe in the concept of good."

Besson nodded. "True, but there is duality in the world. Male and female. Light and dark. One cannot exist without the other. Don't you agree?"

"I didn't take you for a philosopher," Corbin said.

"See enough death and a man must become a philosopher. Otherwise, madness." It was a quote from Corbin's book. The bastard had done his research.

Corbin shifted uncomfortably in his seat. "You obviously want to tell me something. Why don't you just come out and say it."

Besson pulled into a handicapped parking spot in front of a police station and turned off the car. "You're doing a brave thing today, but you should know how brave."

"Okay."

"The man you identified may be the leader of Les Fantômes. He may be a foot soldier. There's no way to know. But what I can tell you is that if you go in there and ID him, you're going to make enemies that are more powerful than you can imagine. Ones that base their existence on fear and intimidation. And on ensuring a reputation that if you cross them you will die a terrible death."

"Like the old man," Corbin whispered.

"Like Gregor. Who was no saint."

"What did he do?"

"I can't tell you that."

"It would help——"

"I can't tell you."

"But——"

Besson put his hand firmly on Corbin's shoulder as if to put an end to the conversation. It worked. Corbin fell silent.

"I'm not saying you shouldn't identify this man," the detective said. "If you do, it will be some good in the world. Some bravery even. And if you do, we will try to protect you."

"You'll try?"

"Both good and evil come at a price. When someone comes to collect what's due, I want you to have made your decision with your eyes wide open." He opened the door. "Are we getting out?"

Corbin put a hand on his door, but hesitated. He wished Besson would tell him what the old man had done. It shouldn't have mattered. What could he possibly have done to deserve being brutally hacked to pieces in that alley? Then again, if the old man had been a murderer, would he feel differently about helping then? What if he had killed little kids? Or sold them into the sex trade? Would Corbin have even come to the station at all? Maybe. But it would have been to shake the albino man's hand and apologize for getting in his way.

Something felt off about Besson though. And it had been off from the first time they'd met. He'd never expect anyone in law enforcement to do anything to dissuade a witness. Funny how the man doing something decent in warning him was setting off alarm bells.

"Let's go," Corbin said, opening his door and getting out. He felt good about his decision for about three steps from the car to the station. It took only that long for rational thought to cut through the testosterone. He followed Besson into the station wondering just what in the hell he thought he was doing.

13

Any sense that Besson was some kind of imposter went out the door once they were in this new police station. He was greeted with warm handshakes and rapid conversation in French that Corbin couldn't follow. Not that he needed to. Men busting each other's balls had an international cadence that he recognized immediately. Besson was known here, and he was respected. There was a little fear in the way the other men deferred to him.

Corbin was offered a water, which he declined, and then led deep into the police station. Past rows of desks with bored men and women working on computer screens and shuffling papers. Through a double set of doors into a more secure area with a guard posted on duty. And finally into a small, dark room with a row of metal chairs facing a glass wall. On the other side of the wall, which Corbin assumed to be a one-way mirror, was an empty room painted stark white with glaring fluorescent lights bolted to the ceiling. Three men were in the dark room with him. Besson and two detectives whose names Corbin was told, although he forgot them seconds later. His stomach churned and he was glad he hadn't eaten anything recently as he thought he might have thrown it up in the corner of the room.

"Let's begin," Besson said. Whatever his actual job title was, it seemed to rank him above the other two men as they jumped when he spoke.

On the other side of the glass wall a door opened and five men shuffled into the room. They were all of basically the same height and build, all dressed in black as Corbin had reported the assailant to be last night. They all had spiky blonde hair and pale white skin. They even had scars on their faces which surprised him. How had they found so many men with scars to stand in the line? But on closer inspection, the answer was obvious. Four of the men's scars were makeup. Their strangely pale faces had to be too. The makeup job was pretty good actually, but under the intense light of the room, it was obvious. It made picking out his guy only slightly harder than if he'd been the only one in the room with a scar.

Not that it would have been hard for Corbin to identify the guy under any circumstances.

The killer walked in fourth, his head down, staring at the legs of the man in front of him. All the suspects presented a profile to the mirrored glass and then turned to face the viewing room. The second he looked up, the killer's eyes found Corbin's. Not close to him. Not in the correct general area, but right at him.

Corbin's throat constricted and it suddenly felt hot in the room. Like there wasn't enough air.

Besson put a hand on his shoulder and he jumped. "Take your time. Think it over," he said. Corbin knew he wasn't talking about deciding which of the men in front of him killed the old man in that alley. It was a decision of how involved he was willing to be in the French justice system's prosecution of a lunatic killer. One with friends on the outside.

Corbin's pride rebuked him for his cowardice. He knew what the honorable thing to do was. Any little kid could have made the call based on what was fair and right. He saw a crime. The man in front of him committed the crime. It was his duty to help bring him to justice.

But every kid also knew the mean truth of the playground.

Nobody likes a tattletale.

"I'm not sure," he said, hating the words as they tumbled from his mouth. "It was dark. Hard to say."

The other two detectives in the room didn't bother to guard their body language. Surely they'd experienced eyewitnesses buckle in the room before, but that didn't mean they had to like it. One sat heavily in a chair. The other took two steps back and leaned against the wall, letting out a low groan.

Corbin walked to his right, wringing his hands together. He closed his eyes, taking deep breaths. He stopped when he was at the far end of the room. When he looked up at the glass wall, the killer was still staring right at him. All the other men in the line looked straight ahead, but not him. Somehow he knew where Corbin was in the room.

"How can he see me?"

"He can't," one of the detectives said, although his tone made it clear he'd obviously noted the way the man had tracked Corbin's movements across the room.

Corbin walked the other direction. The man followed his movement, cold eyes boring into him. His scar an angry red against his pale skin that seemed to squirm over his skin as he turned his head.

"He can see me," Corbin said, unable to unlock his eyes from the man. "It's obvious."

As if on cue, the man's eyes wandered the other direction, as if tracking Corbin walking the other way. "See? Just coincidence," Besson said.

Corbin didn't buy that for a second. The man had seen him. Or sensed him. Something. Worse than that, he could *feel* that the guy knew he was there. It was that nagging extra sense baked into the primordial human mind that caused people to turn around once someone began to spy on them. It was unexplainable, but every person on the planet had experienced it to some degree. At that moment, Corbin didn't just think the killer knew he was on the other side of the mirrored glass. He knew it. And that was enough to put him over the edge.

"I ... I don't think ..."

"Take your time," Besson said.

Guilt seeped through his body like a poison. This was the coward's way out, there was no other way to put it. He was scared of the man in the room. He was scared of the men still out on the streets. And that fear made him feel small and weak. His pride tried to take a stand, arguing that he had to do what was right. He had to do his part. It was part of the bargain to live in a civilized world. But the fear was more powerful, knocking down the argument in one simple question. *What the hell makes you think you live in a civilized world?*

"No ... none of these guys ... not for sure..."

The detective leaning against the wall behind him murmured something in French. Corbin didn't need to know the translation to get the sense it wasn't a phrase the man's mother would approve of. The detective sitting in the chair looked up to Besson for guidance. Besson was the only person who didn't seem surprised.

"Do you want some more time to––"

"No," Corbin said, firmly now. He'd already crossed the river. His guilt already washed away by the torrent of relief he felt. "I'm sorry to waste your time. We're done here."

He walked to the door, but the detective against the wall stepped forward and got in his way. Corbin turned to Besson and waited.

"Thank you for your time, Mr. Stewart. I'll walk you out."

The detective stepped aside but continued to glare at Corbin as he walked past, even making a sucking noise with his mouth to signal his disgust.

Corbin felt it too as he walked out of the room, but he just wanted to be done with all of this. If that meant leaving a bit of his pride and manhood on the floor, he'd recover. He'd been through a lot worse and survived. If his current life could be considered survival, that was.

"This way," Besson said, turning down the hall.

Corbin walked behind him on weak legs, feeling like every eye in the place was on him. Like they all knew he'd chickened out and let a murderer go free. "I knew which one it was," he said to Besson's back as he followed, surprising himself with the admission.

"I know," he said without turning. "It's all right. I might have done the same."

Corbin thought that was bullshit, but he appreciated the attempt to let him off the hook. He'd been a coward and he knew it. Worse, now that it was over, the only thing he could think about was whether the man would still come after him once he was back on the street. He was, after all, the only witness. Even Margot had run before actually seeing the act. "What will happen to him? They'll let him out now?"

The hall widened and they were able to walk next to one another. Still, Besson didn't look at him when he talked. Corbin wondered if it was so he wouldn't see the scorn in the man's eyes. "I'll take another crack at questioning him. But I don't expect it'll get anywhere."

"I'm sorry, but I ..." He didn't know how to finish the sentence. *I'm sorry, but I'm a fucking coward? I'm sorry but I almost pissed myself when he looked at me? I'm sorry but I'm barely making it through life right now without all this shit thrown on me?* But he didn't want to say any of that, not out loud. So he said nothing.

"If it makes you feel better," Besson said. "You helped us quite a bit."

"This ought to be good. How do you figure?"

"Without you we wouldn't have had a description of the man. The uniformed cop wouldn't have picked him up. We now have photos of this ghost. His fingerprints. Samples of his DNA. He so much as jaywalks in my city, I'll string him up by the balls."

Corbin hated to admit it, but that did make him feel better. He hadn't gone all the way, but he'd done some good. And hadn't created sworn enemies out of a bunch of street vigilantes in the process. Not a terrible outcome.

He was about to thank Besson when the big man froze midstride, causing Corbin to slam into his shoulder. The man was so tense that it was like hitting a brick wall. Corbin followed his line of sight to see what he was staring at.

In the waiting room beyond the main reception desk sat an old woman and three young men. All of them had the dark complexion he remembered from the old man. The men had black hair and intense, burning eyes. They dressed in corded pants tied with thick belts and large buckles. All of them wore button-down shirts with vests, these affixed with horn buttons. One of the men wore a wide-brimmed hat and a scarf tied around his neck.

But it was the woman who drew Corbin's attention. She wore a voluminous dress, old-fashioned as if with layers of petticoats beneath it. The blouse was full-sleeved, puffed up at the elbows, and cut low to reveal a large, if wrinkled, bosom. A pleated apron was tied around her waist, finely stitched with a riot of patterns. She wore high-heeled black boots that were scuffed and dusty from wear. A scarf wrapped her head, although stray strands of grey hair stuck out from under the cover and hung dangling to her shoulders. Her face wore the markings of a long, hard life. The lines in her skin spoke of pain and hardship, but her eyes, heavy with black eyeliner, held a fire in them that spoke more of anger than sadness. And that anger flared when she spotted Besson.

Besson whispered, *"Ki shan I Romani, Adoi san' I chov'hani."* Then he looked at Corbin. "An old saying. It means, *Where gypsies go, There the witches are, we know.* That's Gregor's widow. And I think she's here to see you."

14

The old woman stood with the help of one of the young men. He was careful with her, his gentleness actually touching to see. His two companions made up for it with severe scowls directed at both him and Besson.

"Madame Purem," Besson said, bowing in an oddly formal style. "Toutes mes condoléances."

"English," she said, her voice a raspy whisper. "For this one." She pointed at Corbin. "I came for him. Not you. Not yet for you."

Corbin swallowed hard, amazed at how effectively such a frail old woman could lay out a threat so effortlessly in the middle of a police station.

"My name is Corbin Stewart. I was there when your husband died."

She turned her face up to his, squinting as if she might be able to see inside of him if she caught the light just right. "I am Mariyana Purem. You helped him. This I heard. You fought."

And then I let his killer go like a damned coward.

"I'm sorry I couldn't do more."

The old woman smiled, her mouth a collection of gold and silver. Her eyes glistened with tears of sadness that he didn't expect to see.

Anger maybe. He expected that. He preferred that. The sadness threatened to break his heart.

She put a shaking hand to her mouth, kissed it and then turned her palm toward him.

"Blessings," she rasped. "Blessings to you."

Now tears burned his eyes, obscuring his vision. All the guilt came roaring back from wherever it had gone, proving that it hadn't strayed far. With the guilt came an even more powerful emotion. Shame. So strong, so poignant that it felt like a physical weight pressing him down. He thought for a second he might come clean with her, blurt out what he'd done in the other room. But he didn't have a chance. And, it turned out, he didn't need to.

Mariyana shuffled forward, close enough now that Corbin smelled on her an exotic mélange of spices and incense. Of wildflowers and wood smoke. Of wet soil and new rain. The smell was mild at first, just a whisper, but then it filled the air. She reached out an unsteady hand, the one that had imparted a blessing only seconds earlier, and touched his bare arm.

There was a photographic flash, so brilliant that he reeled backward. He might have stumbled but for the woman's hand on his arm, now gripping him like a vise. Another flash and the world around him turned into a negative, all blacks, whites and greys. And it wasn't the right room. He was back in the viewing room, behind the glass. The killer staring at him. Only this time the albino was the only man standing there. The other four were on the ground, their throats slit open, pools of blood spreading across the floor.

But the dead weren't the four men in the lineup. They were all Gregor. All the old man, dying on the ground.

The killer smiled and pointed at Corbin. Then he screamed, a terrible sound filled with fury and pain and insanity. He ran full speed at the glass wall, smashing through it in an explosion of glass, the shards flying through the air, tearing into Corbin's skin. The screaming now louder, in the room, in his head.

Flash

Flash

And he was back.

In the police reception room.

Mariyana standing before him. Her hand now hovering over his arm, not touching him but somehow feeling like she was burning his skin. He pulled away from her, cradling his forearm against his chest.

One look into her eyes and he knew the unthinkable had somehow happened. She'd been in his head.

She knew what he'd done.

Corbin stared at the ground, but he felt the woman's eyes bore into him. Slowly he looked up, his head turned to one side.

The sting of her hand slapping his face was quick and powerful. Stronger than he would have expected from someone so old. His cheek lit up with heat, but it was almost a welcome relief. He deserved the slap.

The blow twisted him so that he was looking at her. Without warning, she spit into his face. He felt the spray on his cheek and around his eye. It reminded him of the way her husband's blood had covered him.

"Coward," she rasped, so softly Corbin was sure only he could hear. "You don't deserve what he gave you."

With that, she turned and went to the door. The young man helping her struggled to keep up and she shrugged off his attempt to take her arm.

Besson pushed his way toward her, but the two other men blocked his way. One of them reached into his coat. A gun? In a police station? Were these guys crazy?

Maybe they were, because Besson stepped back, his hands to his sides. The men waited a few more beats, giving the woman time to leave. Then they followed behind her, leaving Corbin and Besson in the reception area alone.

"What the hell just happened?" Corbin asked.

Besson shook his head, looking authentically sorry. "You avoided making an enemy of Les Fantômes today," he said. "But you managed to make an enemy, nonetheless."

"Her? It can't be that bad, right?" Even as he said it, he knew he didn't believe it. He glanced at his arm where she'd grabbed him. The area was bright red and shined as if it'd been scorched in a fire. He looked closer and saw that all of the hair where she'd touched him had been singed away. Even as he watched, the redness faded, like it was a thin layer of liquid evaporating in sunlight. He raised his arm closer until it was right at the end of his nose. Unbelievably, the hairs in the bare area poked up from his skin, rising like a time lapse video of grass growing out of soil. It twisted and curled until the hair matched the rest of his arms.

"Holy shit," he said. "Did you see that?"

But Besson still stared out the door where the men had just left, looking like a dog desperate to chase a rabbit that just hopped into a bush. Corbin grabbed the man's arm, his anxiety causing him to grab him rougher than needed.

"It's time you tell me what the hell is really going on here," he said.

Besson gave a weak smile, then clapped Corbin on the shoulder. "Nice to see you again, Mr. Stewart. Our business is concluded. Good day."

The detective turned, but Corbin pulled on the man's arm and spun him around.

"Good day? After what just happened? You need to tell me what's going on."

A flare of anger passed over the detective's face. He looked down at Corbin's hand and waited until he let go. Once he did, Besson smoothed out his suit sleeve. "I have work to do."

Then the son of a bitch turned heel and walked back into the station, leaving him standing there with a million questions going through his head.

"Hey, you can't just leave. Tell me what's going on here." He walked after the detective, but two armed officers stepped forward to block his way past the reception area. Corbin shouted past them. "Goddamn it. What the hell is going on?"

15

Besson walked away from the American, ignoring his protests. It took a couple of uniformed cops to block the man's way before he finally fell silent. He felt bad for the man; he didn't seem like a bad guy. Under different circumstances, he might have been someone he could have a drink with. Unfortunately, the man was likely going to be dead within a day. Explaining to him what was going on wasn't going to change that. Besson had learned long ago not to form bonds with people. All it did was make things more complicated later.

He walked back through the station, nodding at the men he knew, stopping a few times along the way to rib one of the detectives. Accepting their good-natured jokes about the fancy way he dressed, knowing there was jealousy behind the comments. And more than a little suspicion wondering how he paid designer prices. Not that any of them would ever say anything to him. Not if they knew what was good for them. Besson knew exactly what his reputation was in the police force. A reputation he'd carefully cultivated. He rewarded his friends and he brutally destroyed his enemies. Every time. Without exception.

His father had taught him that lesson well. As an immigrant from Algeria, he'd come to France with all of his belongings in the world in a single backpack, including a set of tools and a knack for fixing cars gained from working for the French military as a mechanic. But he'd also brought with him the air of leadership that other men found instantly compelling. Besson had seen it in his father only later in life, but men who knew him in those early years spoke of how even powerful men were attracted to Haida Besson, all of them falling into his orbit without being asked, simply from the pull of his charisma. There was something about his presence alone, the men said, something that felt powerful and irresistible. Added to that was a kindness that ingratiated people to him, along with a violent ruthlessness that turned his name into a synonym for terrible fear.

But Haida Besson's greatest character trait was that he was satisfied with only a small piece of the world. He didn't have the same hunger that usually reared its head with those who acquire some power and the loyalty of men. Haida's dream was simple. To wed and raise a family, and to do so without having to ever bow his head. His aspirations were sated by the control of only a small area of Clichy, a Parisian suburb, in which he turned himself into a respectable businessman. While keeping his other interests in play, of course.

By the time his sons were old enough to help with the family business, he had three auto repair shops. His side enterprise that ran behind closed doors provided even greater financial rewards. But Haida didn't chase money. His criminal activity only ensured that the small world around his family was protected, both by his men and by his reputation. It was in this side business where Haida taught his two sons the importance of an iron fist.

A rebellion in the ranks wasn't put down with a bullet in the back of the ringleader's head. It was abducting the man and then removing body parts, one at a time. A man walking the streets without ears, without a nose, without fingers and without a cock was a constant reminder about the cost of betrayal. Besson remembered the lesson well as he and his brother were made to cut the pieces from a man who'd wronged their father. For the year after, he heard the man's screams in his sleep. But after a while, the screams disappeared as such things became routine. Just another part of his teenage years.

Life in France was good for the Besson family. But then the Old World came and found the man who had tried to leave it behind. First to ask for his help. Then, when his father refused, to demand it in the only way a man like Haida could understand.

Besson remembered the night his father had sat him and his brother down in one of the repair shops, long after the mechanics had left. The air was filled with the smell of grease and oil, a smell he still associated with his father. Up until that night, he couldn't remember ever seeing his father scared. Not of any man. Not of any circumstance. But that night, Haida Besson's hands shook and his eyes filled with tears as he told his sons of his life in Algeria, the terrible past he'd fled and thought buried in the mass graves of his homeland. He told them of how he'd been part of a gang run by a small-time warlord. Not because he sought it out, but because it was the only way to survive life on the streets.

One of the money-making ventures his boss engaged in was trafficking sex slaves and albinos, the latter traded for the purported medicinal purposes of their flesh and bone. Both activities filled his father with shame, tears running down his cheeks as he admitted his sins to his sons. But it was the albino trade that had sown the seeds that grew into thorny vines reaching all the way from Algeria into their new country and into their new lives. As he told them this, a man entered the room from the shadows. A strange, mutilated man with pale skin, unlike any the boys had seen before. And that's when everything changed. All of them had a new master from that day forward.

Besson jerked back when something touched his shoulder, the memory of his father dissolving in an instant. It was a junior detective who just wanted to say hello. The young man was surprised at the reaction and immediately apologized for disturbing him. But Besson covered quickly with a laugh and play-fighting slow-motion punches at the man. It worked, for the most part. The detective laughed nervously and found a reason to move on quickly to leave Besson to his business.

And he did have business. Business that was waiting for him in

the back of the station, in a private room set up for special interroga-
tions. A room without cameras or a window in the door. Special care
had been taken to make it soundproof as well. In a city rocked by
terrorist attacks, there wasn't the same hesitancy to interrogate
suspects without a lawyer present as there was in the United States.
And sometimes people left the interrogation room with unexplained
injuries. On more than one occasion, they'd left the room on a
stretcher bound for the hospital.

A uniformed cop, one of Besson's, stood outside the room. He
wasn't guarding the room to prevent the prisoner from coming out,
the lock on the door was adequate for that job. The cop was there to
ensure no one disturbed Besson while he had his chat with the perp
inside.

Besson shook the man's hand and inquired about his kids, calling
them by name. The cop beamed, either proud of his kids or that
Besson knew him well enough to remember. Likely a bit of both.
Then Besson opened the door and stepped in the room.

Even though there was a table and two chairs, Alexis sat on the
floor in the far corner away from the door. He didn't bother getting
up. He just stared at his hands, rubbing them together.

Besson closed the door behind him and took a deep breath.
When he turned to face the room, the albino with the brutal scar was
staring right at him.

"I expect better service from you, Besson," Alexis said. "Now get
me the hell out of here."

16

Corbin was pissed. Overall, he was a pretty mellow guy, so it took a lot to punch his buttons. But considering his last twenty-four hours, his buttons had not only been punched, but nearly obliterated from the pounding they'd taken.

He left the police station with his head on a swivel, looking up and down the street for any sign of the old woman and her entourage. After Besson's warning, he imagined they were lying in wait for him somewhere, ready to attack him on the street. Or maybe shove him into a car to whisk him off to an abandoned warehouse to pull out his fingernails. At this point, nothing would have surprised him.

But there was no sign of them on the street. There was a suspicious-looking white van parked nearby that, in his ramped-up mind, had to be full of men in masks ready to jump out and grab him. The driver's door opened and he stopped in place, ready to make a run for it back into the police station. He had to laugh at himself when an old man wearing painter's clothes climbed out eating a sandwich.

Corbin checked his watch. Two thirty. At least he was going to make his appointment at three at Notre Dame to meet Margot.

Perhaps she would have some answers for him. Clearly she knew more about what was going on than he did.

Notre Dame was less than a mile away. He had the time to walk. And although striding down the sidewalk just reminded him about his leg, he needed some exercise to clear his head. Nothing much about what was happening made any sense, but most of it could be explained away as the product of his overactive imagination. The visions could just be offshoots of panic attacks. Or remnants of some fever dream he had from the night before. And then there was always the possibility he was just losing his mind.

But his leg was a tangible thing. Unexplainable in any way other than if he accepted that he'd never been cut. That the pain and the blood had all been in his head. How else could it have healed so completely?

There was something in the blood, you idiot.

Something that's changing you.

The voice was surprisingly clear in his head, as calm as a school teacher citing a fact from a textbook. As a writer, hearing voices in his head was part of the occupation. The dialogue he wrote echoed in his head with that character's tone and accent. Narration sounded a certain way depending on the point of view from which he wrote. But this voice was different. It was a voice he didn't recognize. And it made his skin crawl.

Corbin glanced over his shoulder, looking for any obvious sign that he was being tracked. Margot's note had warned him not to be followed, but he wasn't sure what to do with that. He supposed jumping in and out of taxis like they did in the movies, or ducking into a café and using the kitchen back entrance might help, but he felt foolish even thinking about it. If there were professionals following him, he doubted his feeble attempts would do much to stop them. He decided instead to stay with the crowds but take a circuitous route. If someone was following him, maybe they would get complacent and he'd be able to spot them. What he would do if he did see someone was unclear, but he resolved to cross that partic-ular bridge when he came to it.

He pulled out his cell phone and dialed as he walked. He'd saved the doctor's name in his contacts. Dr. Gupta had told Corbin that he'd call once the blood tests came in, but he didn't care to wait. He wanted to know whether he'd contracted something that might explain some of the craziness.

The call went to the doctor's voice mail, an overly cheery greeting first in French and then in English. Corbin left a short message asking the doctor to call him back as soon as he had any information. When he hung up he felt even worse than before. The not knowing ate at him. He considered he was more worried about the results than he was admitting. Perhaps that stress explained his odd behavior after leaving the police station last night. Even his mistaken belief his leg had been sliced open.

That last one didn't fit in because it'd happened before he'd come in contact with the blood. In fact, the hallucination he'd experienced when the old man had first touched him couldn't be explained away either. And the pain of the knife slicing through the meat of his leg was as real as anything he'd experienced. Still, there were only two options. That he'd somehow made a mistake. Or the cut in his leg had somehow just managed to heal overnight, leaving no mark at all on his skin.

He remembered the old woman's voice rasping in his ear. *You don't deserve what he gave you.*

What he did deserve were some answers. As the hulking walls of Notre Dame loomed up ahead of him, he felt more confident that some of those answers might come from Margot.

He made his way toward the massive cathedral doors. Even with his mind running in so many directions, he couldn't help but slow down to give his eyes time to rove over the ornate carvings in the portal around him. He preferred the left-hand doorway, but the right was less crowded so he chose that entrance. The Portail Sainte-Anne soared above and around him, showing the Virgin's parents, the Annunciation and the Nativity of Christ. The intricate detail in the work always astounded him, and he felt the eyes of the sculptures follow him as he passed inside.

No matter how many times he visited, he never grew tired of the sudden immensity of the sanctuary. The goal of medieval architects was to not only honor God with their creation, but to humble Man. It was impossible to stand beneath the soaring ceiling and colossal pillars and not feel they had succeeded in both. Even with the bustle of tourists from all around the world taking photos and listening to guided tours, the space held an undeniable solemnity. Corbin wasn't religious. His father had been a God-loving deacon in their Methodist church for three hours on Sunday mornings and an abusive, sanctimonious piece of shit every other waking hour of the week, so Corbin had never seen the appeal. Still, if Notre Dame had been his church every Sunday as a kid, he'd be wearing a cross and carrying a rosary.

He worked his way slowly through the crowd gathered near the entrance where the guided tours were organized. The noises from the assembled people drifted up into the enormous space above, getting lost among the vaulted ceilings. Even without a religious bone in his body, Corbin usually felt peacefulness emanating in the place that always reached inside of him and calmed his mind. But he didn't feel it that day. He was too anxious to find Margot and get some answers.

Like all cathedrals, Notre Dame is laid out in a long axis, the nave, intersected at a right angle by the transept. From above, it gave the building the shape of a cross. Corbin went to the aisle, just on the other side of the row of columns that lined the nave. It was darker there, providing some cover while he searched the vast cathedral. He thought he saw her more than once, but looking closer found it to be a false alarm. A quick look at his watch showed it was five past three. He began to worry that he'd missed her somehow. That his hiding in the shadows made her think he hadn't come.

He was about to march out into the open and park himself right on the altar if necessary, when his phone rang.

The ringtone he'd selected was an alarm klaxon for a submarine diving. The *ah-ooo-gah, ah-ooo-gah,* blared from his phone, seeming to echo through the hallowed space. As he fumbled his phone, people around him turned to stare. A tour guide wagged a disapproving finger in his direction as Corbin clicked the button to mute the ring.

He recognized the phone number and answered it, an act that turned the tour guide's frown into an outright scowl. Corbin turned away and tried to walk to an empty corner. His heart pounded as his finger hovered over the button to answer the call. Even though he'd been waiting for it, now that it was here, dread filled him. He considered putting it off. Just letting the call go to voice mail so he could listen to the news without having to react to it. But then he imagined the message would only ask him to return the phone call, just delaying the inevitable. He decided to rip off the Band-Aid.

"Hello, Doc," he said, using the softest voice he could, but still drawing a few looks. "What'd you find out?"

He tried to sound conversational, cavalier even, but he felt like he was breathing through a straw. It didn't help that he'd wandered over near a bank of prayer candles, the air heavy with the smells of paraffin wax and burning wicks.

"Mr. Stewart ... Glad ... caught you." The connection crackled. Seemed like thousands of tons of solid rock wasn't conducive to great cell coverage. Corbin tried moving around as if it would make any difference.

"Dr. Gupta. We've got a bad connection."

"... didn't know whether ... knew or not already ... bizarre ... and not good news."

Within all the static and garbled sounds, those three words sounded like a shout.

Not good news.

Then the phone cut out. "Shit," he said, and immediately drew a damning look from an old lady near him. He mumbled a quick apology and rushed outside. His brain churned through the kind of bad news he was about to get. A disease. It had to be some kind of disease. He redialed the phone once he was through the door.

"I'm here. Can you hear me now?" he said.

"I'm sorry. I know this comes as a shock," the doctor said. "If you want to call the police and talk to them, I have a number I can give you."

"Wait, what?" Corbin clung to the phone, squeezing it hard as if he might force answers to come out of it. "Why would I call the police?" He took a breath to steady himself. "What did I test positive for?"

"Nothing. Your bloodwork is perfectly clear. For now, anyway. Your triglycerides were a little high, but that could be diet. Maybe dehydration."

"But you said ... I don't get it," he said, certain something was still wrong. "You said you had bad news."

"Some diseases are easier to test when we have a sample from the host. Like when someone is bit by a dog, we can treat the victim for rabies, but we really want to be able to test the dog."

"You tested the old man," Corbin said, finally catching up. "What did he have?"

"I don't know. I wanted to get a sample to test, but I called the Institut Medico Legal where they would conduct the post mortem to have them send over a sample. And that's when they told me the disturbing news. The old man's body is gone."

"What do you mean gone? Like picked up by family?"

"No," the doctor whispered, as if saying the next words was some kind of indiscretion. "Someone broke in last night. They stole the body."

Corbin slowly turned around. Even before he did, he felt someone's presence.

"Thanks, Doc. Keep me posted if you get any news." He ended the call, slid the phone into his coat pocket and faced Margot. "I think it's time you tell me what the hell is going on."

17

C orbin walked with Margot around the outside of the cathedral, past the flying buttresses that so elegantly supported the structure's massive walls. She wore a head scarf and large sunglasses, nearly a caricature of a woman trying to hide her identity. Still, she glanced furtively around. It made Corbin do the same, looking at each person they passed with suspicion.

"Let's hear it," he said when they'd reached the backside of the cathedral away from the crowds. "I think you owe me an explanation."

"I don't owe you anything," she said, still walking. "I didn't need to come here."

Corbin was caught off guard by her tone. He'd assumed she'd reached out to him because she was scared and needed help. He wasn't picking that up from her at all. "Wait, are you angry with me?"

"I told you we should have gotten out of there, but you didn't listen to me. I told you."

Corbin stopped walking. "You didn't tell me that old man was your father. Maybe you don't mention it at first for whatever reason. But afterward? Why wouldn't you say anything?"

That stopped her. Rattled, she turned and stared him down. "Is that what that idiot detective Besson told you? That he was my father? That's ridiculous."

"He called you Chey. I heard him. That's daughter in Romani."

"Really? Is that what it means?" Her tone was angrier now. "Chey can mean daughter. Or just girl. Anything else you want to accuse me of?"

Corbin felt his own anger rise up. He was tired of being played for the fool. "He showed me a photo of the two of you. On a park bench together here in Paris a year ago." He stepped closer, jabbing a finger in the air as he spoke. "You want to know what I think? I think you knew he was going to be in that alley. I think you were setting me up for something. Until the freaks showed up and ruined it all."

"That's what you think?"

"I think it's possible. And you've given me no reason to believe otherwise." He hadn't realized until then how bottled up he'd kept his emotions. He worried that if he really started to let them fly he might not be able to get them back under control before he ended up in a sobbing mess on the ground.

"This was a mistake," she said, glancing around as if looking for an exit in a crowded room. "I came to warn you but sounds like you've got it all figured out. Good luck, jackass. You're going to need it."

She stalked off toward the Pont de l'Archeveche, the bridge off of the Ile de la Cite that led to the West Bank. He stood there, feeling the sting of being called jackass and slowly realizing that perhaps he actually was being one. She hadn't gotten far before he ran to catch up to her.

"Wait," he said. She ignored him and kept marching. "Just wait a second." Still no response. Corbin stopped, the pressure in him mounting, pushing against the seals. All things considered, he'd kept himself together pretty well. But now he felt himself teetering on an edge. He clutched his hands into fists and fought down the urge to unload a torrent of expletives that would make the gargoyles lining the cathedrals walls cringe. He reined himself in, but just barely. Margot was several steps from him when he shouted, "Goddamn it. What the hell is wrong with you? Why won't you help me?"

She spun around. "I came here, didn't I? Instead of running like I should of. I didn't know you were an asshole at the time; otherwise, I would have been on a train hours ago."

Corbin saw the truth in that. He took advantage of her looking at him to hold up his hands as if to say *you got me.* "You're right. I'm sorry. I'm just ... it's just ..." He lowered his voice so that she had to lean closer to hear him. "Some of his blood got into my mouth. I think ... I think it's ... I think something's happening to me."

She pulled her arms up across her chest, as if bracing from a sudden cold wind. Only the sun was out and there was hardly a breeze in the air. Her face slowly transformed from an angry scowl to the face he remembered from the coffee shop when they first met. Kind, inquisitive, beautiful. But now burdened with an unexpected emotion.

Sadness.

She walked back to him, her arms still crossed like she was comforting herself. "The cut on your leg?"

A chill passed down his spine. How could she have known? "I don't know if it was ever cut really ... it might have ..." But the lies he'd been telling himself caught in his throat. He'd been cut. Deep and nasty. A wound that ought to have taken weeks to heal. And the next day it'd been gone. "It healed. All the way."

"Not even a mark?"

He shook his head. There were a hundred follow-up questions rifling through his head, but he didn't ask a single one. He just waited, terrified of what she was going to say next.

"We need to do something right away," she said.

"What's that?"

She smiled. The anger was gone, but the fear was still there. "We need to find a bar and get a drink."

"I don't need a drink. I just need to know what's going on."

"I'll tell you what I know," she said. "But trust me, you're going to want a drink."

Once again, she turned and walked away, leaving him standing there like an idiot.

No, not an idiot, he reminded himself. A jackass.

He quickly decided the only reasonable thing to do was follow her, grab his drink and listen to what she had to say. He quickly caught up and fell into step as they rounded the back edge of the manicured grounds behind Notre Dame and turned left on the Quai de l'Archevêché, heading up to Pont Saint-Louis.

"See that spot over there," she said as if they were just out for a stroll through town. "The point of land that juts out into the river?"

He knew the spot but looked anyway. It was a nondescript, irregularly shaped point of land. There stood a low, concrete slab, only four or five feet high. Too low to be a building, although that's exactly what it was. Living on the other side of the river and with nothing but time on his hands while avoiding his novel, he'd explored every nook and cranny of the area. The concrete structure was the Mémorial des Martyrs de la Déportation, a monument to the two hundred thousand Jews deported by the Vinchy government during World War II to concentration camps to the north. A small door led down to a solemn memorial underground, purposefully designed to give a sense of confinement. It was a powerful memorial but unfortunately rarely visited.

"I've been in it before," he said. "What's that got to do with anything?"

"The Roma were rounded up by the Nazis too." She kept walking after only a quick glance at the memorial. "Did you know that?"

"Roma and gypsies are the same thing, right?"

She flinched at the word. "To the Roma, gypsy is an insult. A slur. It brings back every prejudice, every slander, every point in history when our rights have been violated."

He picked up the words, *our rights.* "You're Roma." He looked at her dark complexion differently now. The raven hair and wild eyes.

He thought of every stereotype in the movies and books. The seductive gypsy woman reading palms and staring into a crystal ball, scamming people out of their money. Margot had the seductive thing going on. So far, no crystal ball. But things had gotten so weird that he wouldn't be surprised if that popped out next.

"Yes."

"That old man. Gregor. He wasn't your father. He was your grandfather, wasn't he?"

It was hard to read her expression with the sunglasses covering her eyes, but he saw her tense up at the suggestion. "That's a longer story. You may not want a drink, but I do. There's a bar I know only a minute or two walk from here."

She fell silent and it was clear he wasn't going to get anything else out of her about Gregor until they were sitting down. "I remember in history class that the gyps ... the Roma were hated by the Nazis and sent to camps in the Holocaust."

"Hated by the Nazis? We were hated by more than that. For centuries, the Roma have been a people without a home. Wandering through Europe but welcomed nowhere. Scapegoated for anything bad in society. A disease outbreak? Blame the Roma caravan. A rash of burglaries or disappearances? The Roma must have done it. We became synonymous with the boogeyman. Eventually the stories hardened into hatred."

"So when the Nazis showed up race-baiting hatred for the Jews, adding the Roma into the mix was an easy sell," Corbin said. "But it wasn't like the Jewish Holocaust, was it? I mean, not that bad."

"Of the million Roma thought to be living in Europe before the war," she said quietly, "the Nazis killed two hundred fifty thousand. One out of every four."

"Oh shit."

"Yes, it was a terrible—"

"No, I mean *oh shit*," he said, pointing to the other side of the bridge. There were three men walking toward them. The men from the police station that had been with Mariyana, Gregor's wife. The one who'd stared down Besson leading the way. "I think we'll go the other way."

She didn't fight him. They turned and hustled back the other direction on the bridge. A quick glance over his shoulder confirmed his fear. The men broke into a jog, shoving the people to the side.

He grabbed Margot by the arm and they ran.

18

Besson watched Alexis walk down the street, hands in his pockets, strolling as if he hadn't a care in the world. He wondered whether any of the people on the crowded sidewalks were assassins carefully lying in wait for the perfect moment to strike and kill the albino. If they were, none of them seemed to pay any attention to the man with the grey hoodie pulled up, his eyes covered with large aviator sunglasses. Besson snorted and spat on the ground, his nose wrinkled with distaste. It wasn't just that he found the man repugnant. Besson hated the smell of his own fear.

The talk hadn't gone well. The man's insults still rang in his head.

"You're worthless," Alexis had said. "But then your entire family has always been dogs. No, worse than dogs. Dogs at least have a sense of loyalty. And obedience. All your kind can do is piss all over themselves when they get scared."

Besson had taken the abuse with a straight face, but he seethed inside. They were on his ground. Alexis had no men or weapons here. This was his world where no one knew who Alexis was. Not really anyway. How easy would it have been to end things right there? To grab the man's head in his hands and smash it against the cinder block wall until it cracked open. Until the evil thoughts just poured out with the blood and bits of brain onto the floor. There would be a short investigation to be sure. And it would show that the detainee attacked a detective in good standing and that detective had taken steps to protect himself. The medical record would state trauma to the head, but the photos of the scene would never make their way into any official record. The post-mortem would be simplified to a point where someone reading it would think that perhaps the deceased had hit his head from a slip and fall from a little spilled water. All Besson had to do was decide and it would be done and over in a matter of seconds.

Only it wouldn't have been done and over.

Not by a long shot. Once the Fantômes de la Nuit knew what he'd done, the retribution would have been fast and brutal. They wouldn't have attacked him, not at first, anyway. If he were the only one in danger it might have been worth it. No, he knew how they retaliated. His immediate family would have been killed first. His mother and father were already gone, but his brother was alive. He and his wife would have been killed outright. Their two children would have been spared, but not for long. The Fantômes would have sent them to Besson in small pieces. Fingers first. One at a time. Then a nose or an ear. Toes. Anything they could take and still keep the kids alive and suffering. All to make him pay for his betrayal. But his own wife and daughter was how they'd really take their revenge. The future that would await them would be long and horrific. He knew how the Fantômes worked, which was why he'd bitten his lip until it bled to keep from lashing out at Alexis.

"There's something you need to know," Besson said. "Mariyana was here."

"Where?"

"At the station. Minutes ago."

Alexis jerked his head toward Besson. "You killed her, of course."

"No."

The man climbed to his feet. Besson took measure of the man's speed. If it ever came down to a fight between the two of them, he hoped he had a gun in his hand. He had Alexis by thirty pounds of muscle, but that didn't fool him. Born and raised in Clichy-sous-Bois, one of the roughest neighborhoods in all of Paris, he'd been getting in to fights since he was five. The small, wiry guys were the ones who caused the most trouble. Alexis was well trained, but it was his fanaticism that made Besson fear him in a fight. Most men could be counted on to fear death. Or even fear pain.

He didn't think Alexis feared anything.

The albino circled behind Besson. The detective forced himself not to turn to follow his movement. He wanted to show he didn't fear being attacked. Not here, anyway. This room was his turf. The trouble was that most of the rest of the world was Alexis's.

"You let her go?"

"She was in the middle of the station. With three men."

"Any of my men would have attacked immediately. Even if it meant their own deaths."

"I'm not one of your men," Besson said. He stepped back slightly with his right foot, balancing his weight, just in case an attack came. But none did. Surprisingly, Alexis only nodded as if accepting the truth of the statement and then turned to face the wall. Besson could no longer see the anger twisting the man's face, but the muscles in the man's neck twitched and corded under his alabaster skin.

"You constantly remind me that you are not one of mine," he said, his voice flat and lifeless. He didn't speak for several seconds. "My father was a farmer in Algeria. Did you know this?" Besson didn't reply. "The soil was bad so he grew just enough to keep us from starving. Some seasons, enough to sell a little in the market. One year he bought three chickens. Egg layers. He was so proud of those chickens. It was like he'd bought us a mansion. But one of the chickens wouldn't lay eggs. We waited and waited, but she never laid a single one. Do you know what we did with that chicken?"

"Ate it, I suppose."

"You suppose? Of course, that makes sense. A hungry family. Food is scarce. But my father was so angry with the chicken. So disappointed that it failed to do what was expected of it, that his reason left him. He took a stick and beat the chicken with it. Over and over and over. Turned it into a pile of blood-drenched feathers and bones and organs. Then he kicked it to the dogs and let them eat it." Alexis turned and pointed a finger at Besson. "That's what happens to an animal that stops serving its intended purpose. Whether a chicken or a mongrel dog like you, it's the same."

"Your men weren't here to protect you. I was," Besson said. "Nor were they anywhere to be found when the uniformed police picked you up like a common pickpocket off the street. I'm here. And I'm what kept you from being picked out of a lineup and held without bail. That might be worth remembering the next time you threaten me."

Alexis glowered on the other side of the room.

"You should leave now, dog. I want be be a free man within the hour."

Besson rapped on the door and the guard outside slid the lock aside. As it opened, he turned back. "You should know that Gregor's body was taken from the morgue."

Alexis didn't turn. He spoke to the wall in front of him. "What do you mean, taken? Where was he moved to?"

"I don't know. No one knows."

"Impossible." Alexis's voice was almost indiscernible, barely a whisper. "My men were watching."

"The body was stolen in the middle of the night. It's gone. Your men will tell you the same. If they're still alive, that is." He was about to leave, but couldn't help himself. "I guess it would have been nice to have a dog watching the place after all." He wanted that to be the last word, to let Alexis soak in his rage, but he wasn't allowed the satisfaction.

"Besson," Alexis said so softly that he was barely audible. "Find them. The girl and the American. Find them for me."

He didn't say *or else*, but he didn't have to. Besson understood. The comment he'd made about the dog had felt good when he said it, but as he left to expedite Alexis's release, he knew it'd been foolish.

Still, as he closed the door behind him and heard the table and chairs being thrown around the room, he couldn't help but smile.

Alexis was a dangerous man. Perhaps as dangerous as Gregor, only in a vastly different way. Besson hated that his life was intertwined with the animal. He fantasized about the day he could kill the man. If he ever had the chance, he'd do it slow. Maybe feed him alive to wild pigs, making sure he was fully aware as they ripped the skin and flesh from his bones. Besson smiled as he imagined the man's screams.

Perhaps one day he could make it come true.

Until then, he had two people to find and an entire city to search.

19

Corbin tried to use the tourist crowds as cover, but he knew they were too exposed. The R'asa men had put aside all pretense and were sprinting toward them, shoving people out of the way. Margot pointed to the cathedral.

"Inside. We can lose them in there."

Running into a confined area didn't feel like the best option to him, but Margot let go of his hand and ran toward the doors.

"Wait," he called out. But it was no use. She wasn't turning around. He stood in place, not wanting to follow her inside, but not wanting to lose her either. He spotted the three men in pursuit and saw two of them follow her and the other head his direction. It was clear who the more important target was, and he wondered why. "Goddammit," he said, taking off after her.

He caught up just as she reached the entrance. They slowed down, matching the flow of traffic. Once inside, Corbin's eyes took a few seconds to adjust to the dark interior.

"This way," she said, pulling on his arm.

They struck out to the left side aisle which was darker than the nave, and less crowded. He pulled her behind one of the columns and pressed up against it. Out of the corner of his eye, he saw the three men enter, scanning the area as their eyes adjusted.

"Do you have a master plan?" he whispered, yanking off his jacket to at least present a slightly different look to their pursuers.

"We lose them in here, then sneak past them using a side door."

"What side door?"

"There's got to be emergency exits, right?"

Corbin looked around them. "Not seeing one, are you?"

She did the same scan, but then pressed harder against the stone pillar. "Oh shit. Back, back."

Corbin saw one of the men walk into the aisle, eyes peering into every dark corner. He reached into his pocket, searching for the mini-Taser he'd taken from his apartment. He wrapped his fingers around it, but the thing felt tiny in his hand. Not exactly the confidence boost he wanted, but it was better than nothing.

He and Margot tried to slide around the pillar to stay out of view but ran into a cluster of people on a tour gathered around a painting. They found themselves next to the guide with twenty tourists staring at them. Corbin crouched down and pulled Margot with him. The tour group gave them cover, but it wouldn't last long. The tourists were laughing and pointing at them, taking their pictures like they were part of an act.

"This is a private tour," the guide said.

Through the tourist's legs, he saw that the man was closing in on them, attracted by the commotion.

"We've got to move," Corbin said.

Margot didn't need to be told twice. She snuck past the guide, still working around the edge of the pillar. Corbin followed her, but then a man shouted behind them. His other two companions responded and moved toward them, shoving tourists aside.

"Run," he cried.

But Margot did the opposite. She skidded to a stop. Corbin looked past her and saw why. On either side of the exit, backlit so that their faces were hard to see with their hoodies pulled up, were two new men. On seeing him and Margot, they both slowly reached up and pulled tragedy masks down over their faces.

20

M argot grabbed his arm and pointed to a small door on their right. They ran through people milling around, hit the door at full speed, and ended up outside Notre Dame in a small area surrounded by a high metal fence. On the other side of the locked gate was a line that extended down the sidewalk along the cathedral. Corbin recognized where they were, the entrance to the stairwell that climbed up the bell tower.

A large woman wearing an official-looking jacket sat in a chair reading a paperback. She glanced up at them and muttered. "Not open. Ten minutes for repairs." She shooed them away with a hand and went back to her book.

"Can you open the gate?" Margot said. "Ouvre la porte, s'il vous plait?"

The woman lowered her book again, her face looking at the two of them with the kind of true disdain mastered by the French. She didn't lower herself to answer with words and instead shooed them away again, this time with a loud smacking of her lips.

A commotion erupted behind them. Men's voices and a woman yelling. Whether it was the R'asa or the Fantômes who'd reach them first, it was impossible to tell. Either way, they didn't have much time.

"Up there," Corbin said, pointing to the stone staircase.

"This goes up the tower," she said. "We'll be trapped."

He'd made the trek to the top of Notre Dame before and had been rewarded with one of the best views in the world for his effort. As he tried to remember his last time there, he racked his brain for any advantage. There was one possibility. A long shot, but something worth trying.

"There's a gift shop up here. Not quite to the top. Stop there," he called out. "Trust me."

He wasn't sure she'd heard him or if she'd simply reached her own conclusion that up was the only way out, but she launched herself up the stairs. He followed behind, the woman guard and a dozen or so tourists yelling at them for cutting line.

The angry shouts faded quickly as he ran up the spiral stairs. His legs burned and he was out of breath in the first thirty seconds of his climb up. He wondered whether Margot had heard him about stopping at the gift shop, but when he finally reached that level near the top, she stood there waiting for him.

The gift shop was housed in a room with a soaring roof and beautiful arched windows. If his memory served him right, it had been an apartment for important church workers through history. Too long of a climb for dignitaries, but a beautiful space. In the back left corner was the thing he remembered. An intricately carved spiral staircase that led to a small open door fifteen feet off the floor.

"Up there," he said, gasping for breath. "Hide and I'll draw them away."

"That's your plan?"

"Once they pass, head back down."

"What about you?"

He pulled out his Taser. "I have this." She started to object, but he didn't give her a chance. He turned and ran up the stone stairs that led to the top of the tower, hoping she wasn't following behind him. He pounded the stairs as hard as he could and made as much noise as possible. He even called out as if Margot was ahead of him on the stairwell, "Hurry! They're right behind us."

He burst out into the room on the top of the north tower, gasping for air and holding a side stitch. Drinking and sitting on his ass for the last four months hadn't prepared him for an afternoon of running for his life from murderous psychopaths.

Shouts from the stairwell gave him an extra shot of adrenaline and got his legs moving again. He remembered the tour started in the north tower, crossed over the length of the cathedral, and then ended with a walk down the south tower.

He ran to the small door that led out to the walkway between the two towers. The last time he'd been there he'd waited ten minutes to make his way across because of the quash of people soaking in the views and taking photos. He was thankful that the tour had been on a break because it was empty except for the two A-frame ladders and the construction tools in the walkway. He saw the reason the crowd was being held back down at the base. A section of the thick netting material that prevented tourists from throwing things off the top of the cathedral had been removed and was balled up on the floor. Probably due to a tear or something. A new roll leaned up against the railing, but there were no workers to be seen. Likely on a long lunch while a hundred-plus people waited below in line.

Corbin ran across the walkway, dodging the ladders. But just as he passed them, a man appeared at the far end of the walkway in the doorway that led to the south tower.

Corbin hoped it was one of the workers, but that hope didn't last long. The man stepped out from the doorway and onto the walkway, brandishing a knife that glinted in the afternoon sun. The R'asa.

He heard movement behind him. He spun around to look at the opposite end of the walkway where he'd come from. There he saw a man in a black hoodie and tragedy mask. A Fantome.

The day just kept sucking more.

Corbin ran back to the ladders in the middle of the walkway. He leaned out over the railing where the netting had been removed, looking for a way down. A stone gargoyle with a face curled into a mischievous grin stared at him, daring him to climb over the edge. Quasimodo the hunchback may have been able to climb down from the tower, but there was no way he would make it more than a few feet without falling to his death.

The Fantome filled the doorway where he'd just stood, tragedy mask pulled down into place. Corbin wasn't sure which person was more disconcerting, the mask or the grinning face of the R'asa slowly walking toward him from the opposite side, twirling a knife in his hand.

But then two emotions welled up in him, displacing the sharp fear that churned in his gut. First was a sense of familiarity toward the R'asa coming toward him, almost so strong that he felt protective of the man. As if he were his brother. The second emotion was a scathing, bitter hatred for the Fantome.

The next thing he knew, he was sprinting toward the Fantome, crying out like a half-mad warrior. The R'asa matched his cry and ran behind him, nearly catching up to him.

The Fantome pulled a knife and crouched low, ready to absorb a blow. Corbin pulled the Taser from his pocket, feinted high and then slid on the ground, knocking the man's legs from under him and jamming the Taser into the soft flesh of his thigh. The Fantome cried out as his body spasmed and he dropped his knife. The R'asa fell on the man, stabbing him over and over.

By the time Corbin got to his feet, the deed was done. The Fantome lay sprawled on the stone floor, blood filling the lines of ancient grout.

Just as fast as the emotions had come to him, they left. All that remained behind was nausea and disgust that he'd played a part in a man's murder. But the feelings before hadn't been his, perhaps not even his actions had been. Somehow, they had come from some *other* lurking inside him. But it didn't do anything to lessen the shame he felt.

The R'asa pointed the knife at him. "Where is the girl?"

Corbin shook his head, wondering if the man intended to kill him where he stood. He looked out over the edge of the railing, out over the Parisian skyline, even spotting the Eiffel Tower in the distance. If he was about to meet his maker, at least he'd go out while enjoying the view. The R'asa seemed obliged to give him a better look. He grabbed Corbin by the throat and heaved him back, up over the railing.

"Where?"

The R'asa pushed harder, his fingers digging into Corbin's neck. Then a string of expletives erupted as the man pushed Corbin aside and leaned over the railing himself. Something down below grabbed his attention. He quickly dialed his phone, shouting into it and pointing down into the square. Corbin stood just in time to see Margot for a second before she climbed into a taxi, shut the door, and drove off.

Margot had escaped. He felt a surge of triumph, followed quickly by cold dread as the R'asa man nodded for him to start walking toward the south tower where a second R'asa had appeared, this one holding a gun. He just hoped the man didn't intend to use it right away.

21

Corbin fought to control his breathing, but he was struggling. A cloth bag over his head forced him to rebreathe the same air, now heavy with carbon dioxide. Light-headed, choking. He was drowning in the darkness.

He was in a small space. The trunk of a car, he thought. Or a box. He couldn't move more than an inch in any direction, and his body was painfully folded over on itself, his knees up to his chest while his arms were pinned behind his back.

Waves of claustrophobia crashed over him, mixed in with equal measures of fear and panic. Riding high on these waves was the certainty of what was about to happen.

They were going to kill him.

He kicked his legs but they barely moved. He yelled but it just rang his own ears and made him feel even more light-headed. It was pointless. They had him now. And why else would they go through the effort of kidnapping him unless they wanted him dead?

With the thought came an unsettling flash of self-awareness. And with that, as usual, came more than a hint of self-loathing. Hadn't he been thinking for a while now that he wanted it all to be over? Wasn't that what the quiet voice in his head told him at night? The whisper that drifted out from every empty bottle of booze, the voice that told him he was better off dead? No more pressure. No expectation. No more pain of remembering.

For months, he'd thought maybe he was just too much of a damn coward to go through with it. Just one more deficiency to add to the list.

But as he lay there in the dark, he knew it was more than that. He didn't want to die. He wanted to escape. He wanted to live.

The vehicle hit a bump in the road and his body slammed upward into the roof of the trunk. There was something sharp there, a metal edge or a bur of some kind. It sliced a gash in his head. Hot blood gushed over his forehead and into his eyes. He squeezed them tight, they weren't doing him any good open anyway, but still felt the sting of the salt in them. He yelled and thrashed his body, but it was useless.

Reason reasserted itself and he grew very still. Energy expended now was just wasted. He needed to wait for an opportunity, and he needed as much energy as possible when it came. They could have already killed him if they wanted, stuffed him inside the box he was in now as a corpse. But they hadn't done that. Why?

The answers flittered through his mind as images instead of words. He saw himself being tortured, a man plunging a power drill into his leg. He saw men holding shovels opening a metal box with his dead, asphyxiated body inside. He saw himself strapped to a chair, arms tied down with thick leather bindings, one of his captors screaming questions at him about Margot.

None of those were good options. But it was clear that, barring them letting him just suffocate in the box on the way to dump his body somewhere, they were going to let him out at some point. That was going to be his chance. And he needed to be ready for it.

With intense focus, he was finally able to slow down his breathing. His muscles screamed at him as they began to cramp up, but he did his best to ignore them. He recalled stories from men who'd survived captivity for long periods by sending their minds somewhere else, leaving their tortured bodies behind. One man had said he played chess in his head. Another went to baseball games, watching the Cubs play an entire season. Pitch by pitch. Play by play. It wasn't memory, he'd only ever been to a few games in real life, but every game played out in his mind's eye in perfect detail.

Corbin knew exactly the memory to take him away.

Rose was four. He had her to himself because Heather was working. He knew he ought to be working too, that he ought to park her in front of the TV with one of her videos and sit at the kitchen table to work on his novel. He was three-quarters of the way through and had momentum. Whereas the story had spun away from him for a while, impossibly he'd recently gathered up the loose strings of the story back into his hands like reins on a runaway horse. He felt the power of the book pulling on him, threatening to yank the reins again and gallop off in unintended directions, but for that moment, he had control. And he ought to have worked on it. But Rose was four. And she was his sunshine.

"Daddy, can we go outside? It's boo-tiful." Her blue eyes crinkled at the corners, a new thing she'd started to do when she was trying to be irresistible. She didn't need to try too hard at that.

"Is it boo-tiful outside?" he said, actually curious. School wasn't in session so he was still in his pajamas and hadn't even looked.

"Sun's out. Roses need sunlight to grow."

She got that one from her mom, but it was still cute coming out of her mouth. "Is that so?"

"Is that so what?" she asked.

"Is that so silly?" he replied, tickling her side. But she dodged aside, not wanting to lose the battle.

"C'mon, Daddy. Will you play with me?"

He looked at his laptop sitting on the table next to his cup of coffee. His novel crouched inside, demanding to be dealt with, plot lines curving toward the climax, characters waiting for the verdict on their redemption or damnation. But one look at Rose and he knew it would all have to wait.

They got ready quickly, bundled up against the brisk fall weather, then had the best day of their lives. They played in leaves and chased squirrels through the yard. They went to an apple orchard and picked two whole bags. Then they ate a picnic down by the river. Had a tea party with two of her Barbie dolls and her one-eyed stuffed rabbit named Lucky. When Heather came home from work, Rose ran to her and told her all about the best day ever with her dad. The day that would nearly drive him insane when Rose was taken from him less than a year later.

Because it was a day that never happened. It was just the day he should have had instead of working on his novel while Rose watched TV, colored and periodically asked her dad if he wanted to go outside.

He'd redone his answer to that question so many times in his mind, lived the day with his daughter so many times, that it felt more real than what had really happened. A thousand words in his novel. Exchanged for a day with his daughter. He'd give every word he'd ever written to have that day back in more than just his imagination.

It would have been a boo-tiful day.

By the time the van slowed and then came to a stop, the blood from the cut in his forehead no longer bothered his eyes. His tears had washed them clear.

22

Strong hands pulled him from the box. His joints flared in pain as he stood, but it subsided almost immediately. His hands were still zip-tied behind his back so there was no chance of him making a stand here. Besides, the hood was still pulled down over his face. He didn't mind putting up a fight, but doing it blind and with his hands tied seemed like a bad idea.

"What do you want with me?" Corbin asked.

"Shut up. Walk."

Hands shoved him forward. He stumbled but caught himself. Without the use of his eyes, his other senses worked overtime trying to figure out where he was and what was happening. They were inside, maybe a garage. He smelled car oil and rubber. But that didn't last long. He was made to walk into a smaller space, a hallway maybe, the sounds of their walking bouncing off the walls around them. The ground was flat at first, but then dropped into a sharp decline, coinciding with the change of the smell in the air to wet soil and rock.

"Where are we going?"

His answer was a smack to the back of his head.

They kept walking down, the decline going on for twenty or thirty yards before ending in a short, flat landing and then doubling back on itself. Back and forth they went, ever downward. The air grew cool and musty. It smelled organic, like a damp forest, rich with soil and living things, even though Corbin could tell they were going deeper underground. The car ride hadn't been that long so they had to still be in the city. He worried that they were going into the sewers, not a bad place to dispose of a body. And it was easier to make someone walk to the spot where they were to be dumped as opposed to carrying the dead weight. He felt his pulse quicken again at the thought.

"Stop here."

He did as he was told because what was his other option? Run any random direction with a hood tied over his head and his hands bound behind his back? That would accomplish nothing.

He strained for any sound that might give him a sense of his surroundings. The air was damp and stale. Water dripped somewhere nearby. Two men murmured in low voices behind him and to his right. He tried to hear what they were saying but it was too soft and filled with strange intonations that made him think they were speaking in a language he didn't know.

Their conversation stopped as new footsteps came from in front of him. Corbin straightened, feeling that something was about to happen. One of those somethings could very well be that he was about to die. If that was the case, he intended to do it standing tall.

A voice rumbled, a woman's voice, but deep and coarse like a chain-smoker. He didn't understand what the words meant, but he didn't like the sound of it. There was an anger in the voice that he recognized. And that wasn't good.

Someone grabbed him from behind, pulling his bound hands away from his back so that his shoulders twisted in their sockets. The person kept lifting, trying to use the pressure hold to force him to his knees. Only he refused to go down. He'd rather the man rip his arms from his shoulders first.

The voice barked another command and the pressure stopped. Then he heard a sound that chilled him. The unmistakable scrape of a knife being pulled from a sheath. Next, cold metal pressed against his forearm, thankfully just the flat side of the blade. Then with a swift movement, the blade cut through the bindings and his hands were free.

Corbin ripped off his hood, ready to take his one chance to fight back. But once he could see, he stopped, frozen in place.

He was in a cave, lit by two lanterns held by his captors. The light cast shadows around the space as the lanterns moved and swung, giving Corbin a brief sense of vertigo. But that wasn't why he froze.

Mariyana, Gregor's wife, stood in front of him. Whereas the last time he'd seen her she'd been wracked with a mix of grief and anger, now she appeared calm. Almost serene as she looked him over. Her clothes were different now, but in much the same style. More ornate now. Heavy gold necklaces hung from her neck, matching the hooped earrings that dangled from behind the blue scarf on her head. She reached out toward his forehead and he flinched.

"You have dried blood on your face."

The statement didn't register at first. There were strange feelings welling up in him on seeing her. Respect. Gratitude. Even a sense of love. He didn't understand why she elicited those emotions in him, but they pushed past his fear and filled him up.

"Is there a cut?" she asked.

Corbin put a hand to his forehead and felt the flakes of blood there. "Sliced it open when the car hit a bump." He felt higher on his forehead, searching for the tender cut, but came up empty. There was no cut. It was just like his leg. The skin had healed over.

Corbin slowly lowered his hand, staring at Mariyana. The old woman looked down below his waist and laughed. He felt a rush of embarrassment as he realized she was staring at his erection bulging in his pants. Part of him was shocked at his arousal, but another, stronger part, wanted to use it. Wanted to throw this woman down and take her right there on the ground. He'd been between those legs a thousand times, but he wanted nothing more than to be there again.

She reached out and rubbed the front of his pants. "*Bi kashtesko merel i yag,*" she said. The men around them laughed. She smiled at him. "It means, without wood, the fire would die."

He gave a weak smile, confused both by his body's reaction and because he'd somehow understood what she'd said in her foreign tongue. The words were as clear as if he'd spoken the strange language since birth. He decided not to mention that fact to her.

The old woman lost her smile and turned to the men. "You are missing Mikal," she said.

"He was taken. He fought bravely."

"We will honor his death," Mariyana said.

Corbin listened, unsure now if they had switched back to English or not. He had the strangest feeling that they were speaking a foreign language, but that he was somehow able to understand it. But he pushed the question aside. It was trivial. Didn't matter. All he cared about was the movement of the woman in front of him, the way her dress shifted to show the outline of her body. He might have taken her right there in front of the guards, except for the old woman's throaty laugh as she looked him over. "Don't be ashamed. That's not you wanting me," she said. "That's my husband. The old fool still can't get enough of me." She reached down and rubbed his groin a second time. "Still, this old woman likes to see a young man's body react that way to her. Perhaps we'll have time later to see what my husband's desire can do inside your body." She smiled, then turned and walked down the tunnel. "Come, my love. We have much we can discuss."

23

Alexis entered the building from the back. As always, he'd been careful not to be followed. He knew Gregor's men would be out for revenge so he took extra precautions, doubling back several times on his journey and watching carefully who followed. It was possible that a three-man crew could have fooled his methods, but his adversary preferred blunt force to finesse, so he thought he was safe. His own men would watch the streets for a block in either direction once he was inside, so if anyone had followed him, he would know soon enough.

He was pleased that one of the Romani had been captured. He wanted Mariyana, it was crucial to complete the circle, but she'd disappeared. He hoped his new prisoner would shed some light on her whereabouts.

The apartment building had been abandoned for years, used by drug dealers and the homeless before Les Fantômes took it over. The detritus from those forsaken people still littered the rooms. Empty bottles of alcohol, baggies and balloons, hypodermic needles, porn magazines, moldy couches. The stench of human waste still filled the air, in some rooms worse than others, but pervasive enough that it felt like it was everywhere. The previous residents hadn't wanted to leave, but when Alexis eviscerated one of them, wrapped the man's intestines around his neck and skewered him on a pole in the rear courtyard for all to see, they'd gotten the message and moved on.

He wondered how long it would take the Romani to get the same message.

Alexis walked down into the cellar, the wooden stairs creaking in protest under his weight. While the building above was late-twentieth-century construction, the cellar was made of heavy, irregularly cut stones set in mortar. Like many of the buildings in the area, the foundation was a century or two older than the building that rested on it. As Alexis walked down the stairs, he had the sensation of walking back in time. He liked the feeling and was a little disappointed to see that the interrogation room was lit with electric lights suspended from the ceiling instead of something more atmospheric like open flames. It was more practical, but he preferred the old ways. It was why he pulled the long knife from his side instead of a gun or power tool.

The Romani was stripped naked, his arms bound over his head and hoisted up with a rope until his feet barely touched the floor. His head hung down, long, oily, black hair covering his face.

M'akiwe and Njau were there, waiting on either side of the Romani. Njau pulled the man's head back when Alexis walked into the room, grabbing a handful of hair and yanking it until the man's body arched.

The Romani's face was a landscape of pain. Nothing but bruised and swollen skin, mottled with purples and reds. His lips had shredded against his teeth, but many of those now littered the floor beneath him. One of his eyes bulged from his skull, filled with blood and staring blankly to the right, no longer moving with the other eye. The rest of the man's muscular body was bruised and scraped, but not as bad as his face. His fingers, toes and genitals were all still connected to his body, and there were no body parts on the floor, so the questioning had just started. Alexis knew that M'akiwe especially liked cutting off a testicle or two early on.

"Who is he?" he asked.

"He calls himself Mikal," Njau answered. "He was one of the men at the cathedral. We lost the targets, but we were able to take him."

Alexis felt his anger again at the failure, but this wasn't new information. It would do little good to waste emotion on it. Alexis reached for the man's face and squeezed it with one hand so that the prisoner's lips puckered out. He searched the face all over, carefully. Waiting.

After a few long seconds, he looked over to Njau. "You brought me here for this?"

"Wait," Njau said, his voice confident. "We were working right before you arrived. That is why you don't see it."

Alexis pushed the man's head back by placing the palm of his hand against the center of his forehead. Seconds passed. He was about to turn back to Njau when it happened.

It was the bulging eye first. The blood emptied from it like something inside his skull was sucking it back with a straw. Then it slowly pulled back into the socket. The man blinked hard and the eye once again moved in tandem with its partner. By this time the swelling had gone down, the purple bruises fading, slowly turning into the smooth dark complexion. The man's lips shrank down, the ragged bits of skin congealing until they were whole once again. Even the man's teeth grew back into place. In only a few minutes, the Romani that hung from the rope looked as if he hadn't been touched.

Alexis was delighted.

"Hello, Mikal," he said. "Do you know who I am?"

Mikal fixed his eyes on him. The hate that burned there told Alexis the answer to his question.

"Good," he said, patting the man's face softly. "Then you know that you will tell me where the others are hiding."

"*Ka xlia ma pe tute*," he said.

Alexis sniffed the air. "No, I think your bowels have released themselves already."

"I'll die before I tell you anything."

Alexis shook his head slowly. "No, you won't die. But you'll wish you could."

With a swipe of his knife, he cut away the Romani's testicles, and the man screamed. Alexis held them up to the man's face and waited for him to control his pain enough to focus on him. It took nearly a minute, but finally Mikal stared at him, still whimpering.

"Look at this, Mikal. I have you by the balls. I suggest you start talking, because if you don't, each time they grow back, I'm going to cut them off again. Do you understand me?"

Mikal nodded.

"Good, now tell me. Where are the others? Where is Mariyana? Where is Gregor's body?"

Mikal looked up as if to say something, but instead he spat into Alexis's face. M'akiwe rushed forward, a club wrapped with barbed wire in his hand.

"No!" Alexis called out. M'akiwe obeyed. Alexis wiped the spittle from his face, walked to M'akiwe and took the club from him. "This one's mine."

24

Corbin followed slowly, the distance between him and Mariyana growing. The separation helped resolve the problem in his pants as the throbbing need ebbed away. His hulking guard followed behind but didn't rush him. As he walked, Corbin rubbed the spot on his forehead where he knew he'd cut himself earlier, then felt his leg where he'd been sliced open the night before. At some intuitive level, he understood a truth that he didn't want to accept. It was Gregor's blood that was healing him.

But that wasn't all it was doing.

That's not you wanting me. That's my husband.

He couldn't believe the power of the lust he felt for the old woman. It was like he was a teenager again, the biological need to screw short-circuiting every other thought in his head. But it wasn't only the sexual desire that amazed him, but the powerful emotions he'd felt on seeing her. Those weren't his. Those were a man seeing his wife after a long absence. He remembered feeling that way about his own wife, years ago, in what seemed a different lifetime. But he remembered.

It's not just his blood that's in me, he realized. Somehow he's inside of me.

He was so lost thinking through the implications of that idea that he nearly missed the first skull.

It was lodged into the apex of a stone archway, tilted so that its vacant eyes stared down, offering a sullen challenge to any who passed beneath. The jaw hung open, giving the impression that it was screaming a warning. Corbin felt like it was a warning worth heeding and slowed his pace. The man behind him, perhaps lost in his own thoughts, didn't notice and bumped into him, giving rise to a string of cuss words.

"Move," the man said.

Corbin did as he was told, all too aware that the living man behind him was more dangerous than the dead one suspended over him. But as he passed through the arch, he wondered if that was true or not.

The tunnel maintained its width on the other side of the arch, enough for three men to walk side-by-side. But instead of solid rock, the walls were made up of an uneven surface that extended from the floor nearly to the ceiling ten to twelve feet above. A narrow band of black shadow appeared where the rough surface stopped, leaving a gap between it and the ceiling. The man carrying the flashlight behind him had the light trained on the ground, but soon the beam danced up one of the walls. Corbin sucked in a breath as he realized what he was looking at.

The wall was made of bones. Human bones. Thousands of them. Stacked one on the other, fitting together like pieces of a puzzle. They were dark grey, dried out and cracked with age. Corbin stopped to stare. This time the man behind him didn't cuss him out. Instead, he angled the flashlight so that it danced across the wall of bones. Then he held the flashlight over his head and illuminated the gap between the top of the bone pile and the ceiling. Corbin stepped back and got on his toes to try to see what was back there. All he saw was the top of the bone pile as it went farther and farther back into a deep vault, deeper than what he could see from his vantage.

"These are the catacombs," he said to the man behind him. Corbin had read about the city of bones under Paris before, but he'd never been to them before. He'd come to Paris to escape death, not surround himself with it. "You brought me to a tourist attraction."

The man laughed. "You won't find no tourists in this part of the catacombs. Come on. Mariyana waits. She don't like waiting much."

Corbin saw the candle was now twenty yards ahead of them, floating in the middle of the dark corridor. His escort shined the light from side to side in the tunnel, vault after vault of bones. Soon, they came to the first one made up entirely of skulls. Stacked in perfect order. All the eyes staring outward. Some of them were missing a jaw, some had gaping holes as if the person had died from a vicious kick to the head. As he stared at the rows of black eye sockets, he kicked something on the ground beneath him and heard a crunch. He looked down and saw he'd destroyed a skull that had fallen out from the wall. Corbin jumped back, feeling sick to his stomach.

This time his escort didn't bother saying anything, but instead gave him a shove forward.

Corbin swung his right fist with everything he had. It was all adrenaline and fear, a desperate act to escape the clutches of whatever madness lay at the end of the tunnel. The punch connected with the man's jaw exactly as he wanted. There was a flash of pain in his hand and a satisfying *crack* as the man's head snapped backward.

He expected the man to drop to the ground. Or at least stagger back a step. Corbin cocked back his throbbing right hand to deliver a finishing blow.

Only the man didn't stagger. Or fall. Instead, the man froze for a second with his head rocked back from the punch, and then slowly lowered it back into place until his eyes were staring right into Corbin's.

"Don't do that again," he said, his voice more amused than angry.

Corbin weighed his options for all of two seconds. The man had absorbed the very best punch he could throw and it hadn't even fazed him. There was no way he was going to be able to fight his way past the hulking guard. He turned and rubbed his hand. "You can't blame me for trying," he said. As he passed through the next arched door and continued through the tunnel, he flexed his hand, amazed that it didn't hurt at all.

He wasn't sure how long they walked. It could have been ten or fifteen minutes as easily as it could have been an hour. He wasn't wearing a watch and it was impossible to mark the passage of time down in the dark, twisting passageways. They passed vault after vault filled with the bones of the dead. In some places, water seeped in through the walls, turning the ground beneath their feet slick and fouling the air. But mostly it was a barren world, meant to be left alone so that the dead could rest in peace.

His escort turned off his flashlight and Corbin stopped. It was hard to say how far ahead Mariyana and her candle were now, maybe thirty yards. Far enough that it felt like the darkness might swallow the flickering light. "You go on by yourself from here," the man said. "Don't stay in one place too long."

Corbin never thought he'd want to keep the man's company, but he felt a stab of panic at the thought of being left alone. "What happens if I stay in one place too long?"

But there was no answer. Corbin backtracked a few steps, reaching out in front of him like he was blind. It was no use; the man was gone.

Corbin tried to control his breathing, suddenly fast and anxious, just like his heart. Prior to that moment he hadn't considered the possibility that they meant to bring him down here, turn the lights off and then let him wander endlessly through the caves until his bones were simply added to the endless piles stacked around him. It was a perfect place to dispose of a body. But if they wanted him dead, he didn't think he'd still be breathing.

Unless they wanted him to suffer first.

The candle still flickered in the distance. Mariyana was on the other end of that flame. Corbin could somehow feel the old woman's presence there, waiting for him. All he had to do was walk toward it. Or he could turn and try to find his way through the maze behind him, see if he could somehow find his way back to the surface before they found him. Then to the police. He would find that Detective

Besson who somehow knew more about what was going on than he let on. Then again, he had no reason to trust Besson. In fact, there was a chance he was on the take and working with the Roma to begin with.

No, if he got out, he wouldn't go to the police. He'd find Margot, somehow, then buy two tickets back to America and make sure she was on the first flight back home with him.

He'd almost made the decision to strike out on his own and try to find his way out, when he heard a sound coming from deep within the vault next to him.

The unmistakable sound of bones moving, one against the other.

25

Besson left the Institut Medico Legal with no more information than he had an hour earlier. The staff there were worthless, unable at first to even locate the surveillance camera videos he demanded. Once they were found, they showed nothing more than four men with their faces covered with tragedy masks, systematically destroying the cameras located in the building.

The three men responsible for security on that night offered up conflicting opinions on which of them ought to have been making rounds at the time of the break-in. Whether they'd been asleep, reading or surfing the Internet for porn, it didn't make a bit of difference. The truth was that their laziness likely saved their lives. If one of them had tried to stop the men from recovering Gregor's body, all that would have happened was that the thieves would have left behind a fresh corpse to replace the one they took.

Still, he'd hoped to turn up something to send him in the right direction. As it was, he was groping in the dark. His superiors in the police department were screaming for answers, especially with the press reporting on the killing. The angle had originally been about a hate crime, a term that Besson found amusing for its understatement. But once word spread of the body being heisted from the morgue, more questions were being asked. And Besson didn't have any answers.

But, while his superior officers were a pain in his ass, they were nothing compared to the pressure from Alexis. He knew one of Gregor's men had been captured. If it were anyone except for Alexis that was questioning the man, then he would not expect the interrogation to yield anything. But he understood how persuasive Alexis could be. He'd seen the man at work before.

It'd been a Russian mobster who had information that Alexis wanted. Besson had arranged for the abduction, and Alexis had made him watch.

Besson thought of himself as a hard man, someone who had been through more than most. But that night witnessing the twisted ways Alexis had made that man suffer still haunted him. Even after the prisoner had given up the information he needed, Alexis continued the torture throughout the night. Finally, after the man's face was gone and Alexis was flaying the skin from his back with a pair of pliers, Besson could take it no longer and he'd shot the man in the head to put him out of his misery. Alexis had stood over the body and whispered to Besson, "No one will be there to do that for you or your family. Just remember that."

It was that threat that kept Besson from turning the gun on Alexis and pulling the trigger. He knew others would fill his place and make good on his promises. And he couldn't let that happen.

He drove north, threading in and out of traffic until the shops and apartment complexes gave way to residential neighborhoods. The area was nice, more affluent than his father would have approved of, but he didn't care. His part of the auto mechanics business gave more than enough cover for the cost of the home. And it would cover the cost of the best private schools for his daughter, Lily, when she was old enough. He wanted nothing but the best for his family. Which meant, right now, that they had to leave the city and run.

When he parked his car, he sat for a minute with the engine still on. The two-story house was more than walls and a roof. It was even more than a home. It was the mirror-image of everything else in his life that was dark and twisted and ugly. Once he walked through the front door, it wasn't just that he was a father and a husband, but he was reminded that innocence and good still existed in the world. That unquestioning love could be as strong as hate. And there were days when he needed that reassurance.

He turned off the engine, climbed out of the car and walked to the side door that led into the the kitchen. Out of habit, he glanced up and down the street to see if anything was amiss. At first, nothing caught his attention. But he slowed when he noticed a white van parked four houses up. Even from that distance, Besson saw that cardboard was taped over the back license plate. He stepped back to the street and ran toward the van, reaching for his gun. Immediately, the van's engine revved and the vehicle lurched forward, tearing away.

Besson slid to a stop, considered following the van, but knew he'd never catch it. The fact that it'd been there only reinforced the importance of getting his family out of town. He sprinted to the house.

"Giselle," he shouted the second he was through the door. "Come on. You and Lily need to get packed." He scanned the kitchen. The residue from lunch was on the counter: parts of sliced apple, lunchmeat, a carton of milk. Lily's chair with a booster seat was at the head of the table, food scattered on the floor all around it. On seeing this, he slowly pulled his gun, his stomach turning over on itself. They had a dog, a little terrier named Charlie, that never let a food scrap hit the floor for more than a second.

He quick-stepped through the kitchen and listened at the door leading to the living room. Hearing nothing, he ran through it, gun in front of him.

"No ... no ... no ..."

In the center of the two-story room, hung by a rope tied to the chandelier, was his dog, Charlie. His fur wet with blood. His tongue lolled out of the side of his mouth.

On the far wall, written in the dog's blood, was a message from Alexis.

"Don't fail me."

That's when he knew. The bastard had taken Giselle and Lily. Hostages to ensure he did his best work.

Still, he raced through each room, calling out for them. Just in case they were still there. He told himself they might be in a closet. Or tied up in a bathroom, scared but all right. But room after room yielded the same result. They were gone.

After looking through the last room, he cried out, not giving a damn if the neighbors heard him or not. He punched the wall nearest him, breaking through the drywall. He hit it again and again, imagining it was Alexis's face.

Then he sagged to the floor, defeated, not knowing what to do next.

26

Corbin staggered back from the movement in the vault. Bones cracked and grated. It was too dark to see where the noise came from, but his imagination didn't need light. It was able to create the horrific detail all on its own. A skeleton crawling through the piles of bones. It had to be.

He shrank away, edging back until he was wedged against the other side of the tunnel. The scraping grew louder, and he knew bony fingers were digging into the empty sockets of the skulls to gain purchase and drag the rest of the skeleton body forward. He shuddered at the thought of it.

But then he heard the squeaking.

He'd missed it at first because of his own heavy breathing, but now that it was closer it was impossible to miss. It wasn't a skeleton crawling through the bones; it was rats. Big ones by the sounds of it. Scampering over the bone-pile toward the bag of flesh that had been dumb enough to deliver itself for their dinner. Corbin shuddered, almost wishing it'd been the skeleton he'd imagined instead.

A thump on the ground right in front of him was enough to get him moving. He took off in a jog toward the candle flame.

He made quick time and caught up to the old woman. She barely gave him a glance, but he thought he caught a smirk on her face. She'd known the rats would come. The choice he'd been given to follow or not hadn't really been a choice at all.

Mariyana picked up a battery-powered lantern from a supply chest embedded in the wall and blew out her candle, putting it in a box filled with them.

"Do you have a lighter or matches with you?" she asked.

"No, I don't smoke."

"No open flames beyond this point."

"Why's that?"

"Paris is an old city. Gas lines leak. Sewer gas takes strange paths through the limestone. There was a problem ten years ago. Now we are more careful."

Corbin imagined a city utility worker sent down into the cata-combs to troubleshoot a gas leak. Whoever drew the short straw for the assignment would take one look at the job and then spend the day hiding out in a coffee shop above ground. The report would be no leak was found; must be somewhere else in the line.

He followed Mariyana's lead and took one of the lanterns and switched it on.

"What do you know of my people?" she asked.

Do you mean the Roma or you sick bastards that call yourselves the Tacho R'asa? is what he wanted to say. Instead he said, "Not as much as I should. And what I know are mostly stereotypes and clichés."

"You mean the gypsy woman with the scarf and the eyeliner. The shuvihani with the crystal ball?"

"Something like that."

"I do like to wear scarves. But I don't have a crystal ball. I prefer to look into a bowl of still water to discern the future." She let that hang in the air for a few seconds before laughing. "I kid you. Just some fun."

Corbin felt a surge of warmth through his body, the emotions surging in him again. God, the sudden love he felt for this woman was overwhelming. An image came to him of Mariyana in her twenties, on a grassy hill, sitting on a blanket with the wind pushing back her black hair. She smiled at him in pure invitation, then lay back on the blanket, one knee cocked up so that her dress fell open just enough to show the inside of her thigh. In a blink the image was gone and he was back in the tunnel, longing to be inside her.

He knew it wasn't real. His mind was clear enough to reason that out. In reality, this woman was dangerous. A monster, if she was anything like Gregor. But even knowing that didn't change the way he felt toward her. Real or not, it felt good to care about someone so much again. It'd been so long since he felt love without it being laced with bitterness and pain that made the sensation almost too much to bear.

The old woman reached out and touched his forearm. It felt like a lover's caress and his knees nearly buckled. But she whispered something under her breath, something in a cadence that reminded him of a prayer. "*Tutti sutti misto. Tutti sutti misto.*" When she was done, the emotions pulled back, receding until he could barely sense them.

"Better?" she asked.

He nodded, wondering at what had just happened, knowing that there were layers to the woman holding his arm that he would never be able to understand.

"Gregor is a man of great appetite. The blood in you gives you a sense of him."

"What did you just do?"

"I told him to quiet down so we could talk." She let go and continued up the tunnel. When he didn't follow immediately, she waved him forward. "Come. Linger too long and the rats grow bold."

Corbin's skin crawled. Imagining a black wave of rats climbing all over his body was enough to prod him forward.

"You were telling me about the Roma," he said, wanting a distraction from the idea of rats chewing his flesh, a madman's blood in his body and whatever fate waited for him at the end of the tunnel.

"No, I was asking what you think you know about the Roma."

"I know you're often called gypsies but that you don't like the name."

Mariyana shrugged. "It bothers some, not others. I don't care either way. But do you know how the name gypsy came into use?"

"Not really."

"We came from Northern India, all of the tribes. Westerners, who have no sense of history, think we came from Romania. One has nothing to do with the other. Romania is a terrible country with no heart, no passion. How can people think we came from such a place?"

"The name?" Corbin said, knowing he was being a smart ass.

"They might as well think we all came from Rome if that's all that matters. It's a ridiculous idea. We came from Northern India, migrating a thousand years ago."

"Why did your people leave?"

"There are myths. My favorite is about the Sasanian king, Bahram Gor, of ancient Persia. He hated that the poor in his kingdom could not afford music so he appealed to the king of India to send him ten thousand musicians so that his people could be entertained. The king of India knew the Roma were the greatest musicians and would bring honor to him, so he sent ten thousand on the journey. When they arrived, each was given an ox and a donkey carrying seeds and tools to grow crops. Bahram Gor's wish was for the Roma to grow their own food and play music for free throughout his kingdom. A year later, the Roma returned to the king, dying of starvation. They'd eaten oxen and donkeys at great banquets and then eaten the seeds as well. The king was furious and cast them out of his kingdom. The king of India, so embarrassed that his gift was a failure, forbid them to return home. That began the great diaspora through Europe and then the New World."

"I'd never heard that story before," Corbin said.

"The full account is in the ancient text Shahnameh, written around the turn of the first millennium."

"Is it true?"

"No, of course not. The Romani say that lies are more believable than truth, but this is not one of them. The Roma didn't migrate for another six hundred years. Probably a drought or something mundane. But it is a good story."

Despite the fact that he was there against his will and the old woman could very well be ready to have him killed within the hour, he found himself liking her. And this time the feelings were his own and not the bizarre aftereffects of Gregor's blood.

"You were telling me why gypsies," he prompted.

"In the middle ages, when the migration truly took place, the people in Europe believed we'd come from the northern part of Egypt. One version had it that we were exiled for having sheltered the infant Jesus when Mary and Joseph were in Egypt fleeing Harod's decree. Rubbish, of course. But makes a good story."

"Yes, but I still don't ... wait ...they thought the Roma were Egyptians. Gyptians."

"Gypsies. That's human history for you. The uneducated masses make a mistake, they're too lazy to pronounce an entire word, and my people get called gypsies for centuries."

The sound of running water rose ahead of them. "What's that?"

"Paris sewer," she said. "The only place the sewers penetrate the catacombs. A cave-in from a hundred years ago."

As they approached, he saw a dark opening in the tunnel wall with debris on either side of loose rock. Metal fencing covered it and large metal signs in multiple languages warned of danger. Metal piping formed a door in the middle of the fenced hole but an enormous padlock hung from it. Corbin took a look through, shining his light back and forth to take it all in. Just like the catacombs themselves, Corbin had skipped on the tourist tour of the sewer system. He was mad now that he'd never done it. The tunnel was an enormous brick arch with walkways on either side and a swift flowing river of black water down the center. It smelled off, but not foul. He thought he smelled a whiff of gas, but it might have been in his head from his guide's warnings about gas leaks. The water was mostly storm drainage from what Corbin remembered from the tourist brochure he'd read. Bolted onto the walls were modern pipes and conduits that he guessed were electricity, natural gas and water.

"This way," she said. "This is what I wanted to show you. It's why you're here."

Corbin turned and saw her standing in front of a pile of rubble, a cave-in completely blocking the tunnel. It was the only thing someone coming through the metal gate from the sewer would see other than the tunnel from which they'd just come. He was about to ask where they were going from there until she pressed a round stone low on the wall and then pressed the side of the tunnel. A large section slid open with a grinding sound and she ducked through. He glanced back at the opening to the sewer, thinking about what he wouldn't give for some bolt cutters.

Then again, part of him wondered whether he would use them or not. He wanted to know what was through the hole in the rock wall. What was it that the R'asa were hiding down there? What were they protecting? It didn't take the squeaking of hungry rats to get him moving this time. He wanted answers, and he knew they were only going to come from moving forward. He ducked his head and entered the hole in the wall.

Deeper into the labyrinth, he thought. *Deeper into madness.*

27

The tunnel continued for another hundred yards on the other side of the hidden door, only now heavy cables lined the walls. Corbin figured that it was electricity being ripped off from the utility lines in the sewer. He hadn't seen the cables outside the secret door so he assumed they were underground out there. That way an over-achieving utility man couldn't find the splice and follow the line into the secret passage.

Red light glowed at the tunnel's far end. Corbin couldn't help but think of all the movies he'd seen as a kid where the bowels of hell were depicted in exactly that way. Only it was worse than any movie because the way was still lined with the skeletons of countless dead piled one on top of the other. He was anxious about what lay ahead in the red glow, but at least Mariyana's voice kept his mind occupied as they walked, the *other* in him especially hanging on her every word and movement.

"The Roma, disparaged as gypsies from the earliest days, have always been scapegoats. Blamed for the ills of any society they entered," she said.

Corbin remembered Margot saying the same thing. He wondered where she was, hoping she'd gotten away safely and was on a train to anywhere but here. Somehow he knew she wasn't. He knew she was still in Paris. Knew it with a certitude he couldn't explain. The other part of him, the part introduced into his mind with Gregor's blood, seemed satisfied with the feeling and didn't find it odd at all. Corbin shivered at the way checking in with this alternative personality inside him happened seamlessly, almost as if it were natural. There was nothing natural about it, and Corbin mentally noted the danger of forgetting that.

"We were enslaved, persecuted, pushed from one country to another," Mariyana said. "Sometimes we fought back, but mostly we moved on. Or took our revenge in the night when our small numbers could make the most difference. For a thousand years, the Roma were a despised people. Always the criminal. The hedonist. The occultist hurling curses, mixing potions, constructing charms using the dark arts. When the Nazis came with their righteous hatred of the Jews, the Roma were added to the extermination list.

"But not the Tacho R'asa," Corbin said, pride swelling from the other part of him. "You killed more of them than they killed of you."

Mariyana stopped and turned, searching his face as if expecting to see someone else there. She smiled. "Yes, dear. We did. And soon enough, we'll kill them all and have our revenge."

Corbin hated that the words excited him, but the emotion was too strong to beat back. In his head, he was horrified at the idea. But his heart more and more belonged to the other. Emotionally he felt like beating his chest and crying out as if he were running into a battle that very second. Mariyana reached out once again and touched his arm. The second she did, the emotion dissipated.

"So Margot told you of the Tacho R'asa."

"She and Detective Besson."

She hissed at the name. "Besson is known to us. He has his debts to pay." She stopped. They were just short of the entrance to what appeared to be a large open space, glowing red with a throbbing pulse. He thought it might be from fires burning within, but he remembered the rule against open flames due to gas leaks. The pulsing had to be from electric lights with an unsteady power supply.

The archway leading in had a heavy metal door but it was thrown open. Around the edges were two rows of skulls, turned so that they looked down at whoever passed beneath them, a silent, deadly vigil over the secrets on the other side.

"Steel yourself," she said. "Open your mind to what is possible."

Corbin surprised himself. He considered that a day ago he might have shaken his head and backed away. Now, he simply nodded. He needed to see what was inside. Together they walked into the chamber.

The room matched any palace he'd ever seen. It was ornate, detailed with master craftsmanship that overwhelmed the senses. And decorated only with skulls and bones.

Thousands of them. Set into the mortar in swirling patterns, circular designs, intricate shapes made from jaw bones and eye sockets. Even the four pillars supporting the high stone ceiling were covered with skulls.

And in the center of the chamber, between the four pillars, was a rectangular box on a pedestal of skulls, the whole thing draped in black cloth. Corbin flashed to his little girl's funeral. A smaller coffin. Fresh flowers and natural light. But still death, no matter what decorations surrounded it.

But his flash of memory didn't last long. A closer look at the pillars and he suddenly could think of nothing else except for what he saw there.

Each pillar had a man chained to it, an albino with translucent skin and shock white hair.

They were wrapped in heavy metal links as if they might have supernatural strength and try to escape. Only they weren't even conscious, possibly not even alive. They were in a standing position only because of the chains, legs together and their arms splayed wide. *Crucified*, he thought to himself. Each man's arms had a black tube attached to them that stretched the distance between the pillar and the coffin. The tube traveled under the sheet and was hidden from view.

"Are they alive?" Corbin whispered, his voice quavering.

"Of course," she said. "They serve a purpose. They are no good to us dead."

Corbin turned his attention to the coffin. He felt bile rise in his throat, but he choked it back down with his fear. "Is it Gregor?" he whispered.

"Come, you must see before we can talk more."

They walked past the pillars and stood together in front of the raised platform. Standing closer, it reminded him more of a stone sarcophagus than a coffin. The edges were straight but it appeared not to have a lid. The cloth sagged slightly in the middle.

"Pull the shroud back and see the truth of things," Mariyana said.

His body rebelled at the idea, even taking an involuntary step away from the box at the suggestion. He didn't want to; even the other presence inside of him didn't want to pull the cloth back. But his hand still reached out as he shuffled forward and took hold of it, grasping the cloth until he held a handful of it in a white-knuckled fist. He recoiled at the feel of it, wet and hot and sticky.

He tugged and it fell away.

He'd been right, it was a stone sarcophagus, carved out of limestone the same as the cave around them. The top was open and, instead of a body, it was filled with a dark liquid. Small waves rippled across the surface where the cloth had dragged over it, but it was a thick, viscous fluid, and it settled soon after.

He dropped the cloth, recognizing the rich smell of copper in the air.

Blood.

The sarcophagus was filled with hot blood, the black tubes draining the albinos as they hung there, chained to the pillars.

His heartbeat thrashed in his ears and his legs turned weak. Mariyana took hold of his arm to keep him from stumbling away.

As he watched, something rose to the surface. It was like a heavy log rolling in filthy water, finding its balancing point. Only this was no log. This was legs and arms. And then a face.

Blood dripped from bare skin as it rose from the surface. Even in the glow of the red light, Corbin could tell the skin was unnaturally pale. It was swollen and spongey from being in the blood. Even so, the person's identity was unmistakable.

Gregor.

Corbin choked back tears. He didn't know if the emotion came from him or the part of Gregor inside him. He didn't care. All he wanted to do was get away from the body. To run until he reached the surface where the normal world still existed.

But he couldn't turn away. Worse, he found himself drawn closer and closer to Gregor's face, floating on the surface, framed by a halo of dark blood. A death mask to be shown at a funeral. Then Mariyana whispered something behind him. He turned to look at her. Only for a second. When he turned back, something broke inside of him. And he started to scream.

Gregor's eyes were open, lolling back and forth in their sockets.

He was alive.

28

Gregor's mouth gaped open and closed, a dying fish out of water. The blood rose and fell around him with each cycle of inhalation. At the peak of his buoyancy, other parts of his naked body broke the surface of the blood, appearing like pale, white islands before sinking back under on the next breath. Corbin felt a powerful sense of revulsion at the sight, his own emotions and those of the version of Gregor inside of him aligned for once. Neither of them wanted to look at the sight inside the sarcophagus, but neither of them could take their eyes off of it.

"It's not ... how can this ..."

"How can he be alive when you clearly saw him dead?" Mariyana asked. Her voice lacked the strength of only minutes earlier, distant now and tinged with sadness as she stared at Gregor's floating body. "The answer is at the heart of the Tacho R'asa. Who we really are. What we are capable of doing."

Gregor's eyes moved in their sockets, turning toward the sound of her voice. It seemed an instinctive response, like a baby turning toward the sound of his mother's voice.

"Is it really him? Or is his body somehow ... I don't know ... reanimated?"

"It's him."

"But his eyes. He's not aware. He's not able to communicate."

"That is at the heart of it. The body can be fooled easily enough. Bone, muscle, blood, their secrets have long been known to us through the ancient texts and rituals of the R'asa. The blood magic of the albino has this power, but it is not enough. The mind? The soul? These are not so simple to bring back. These require specific conditions to revive. Even when the body lives, the soul can die. But you know this, I think."

Corbin rocked back. "I don't know what you're talking about." But he did. And Mariyana knew it.

"When I touched your arm, I felt the terrible pain inside of you. I felt the way you miss your little girl. It's the despair that you fall through every day the second after you open your eyes in the morning and remember that it wasn't all just some terrible nightmare. Your body lives, but part of your soul died with your child. I understand. I've lost children myself. That pain is unlike any other. If you help me, I can make it go away. I can make you whole again."

Corbin shuddered. His skin prickled into gooseflesh as if a ghost had passed through him. "You can't do that," he whispered. "No one can."

Mariyana pulled a knife from the folds of her dress, a movement so quick and smooth that it seemed like the weapon instantly appeared in her hand. His original fear that he'd been brought down to the caves to be killed hit him like a cold wind, but she didn't approach him. Instead, she walked up to the sarcophagus and held her wrist just over Gregor's mouth. "The Tacho R'asa have the ability to bring back the dead." She ripped the knife across her wrist, opening a vein. Blood poured out, spraying Gregor's face. His lips puckered, seeking out the hot liquid. Mariyana lowered her wrist to his mouth and he latched on like a baby to a nipple, suckling greedily.

As Corbin watched in horror, Gregor's eyes rolled toward him. Only now they focused on his face, fully aware and cognizant. There was a moment of recognition, that micro-expression humans can perceive but not explain. Gregor knew who Corbin was.

"My husband will be returned to me," Mariyana said. "The R'asa will have its leader and our work which is so close to being done can be completed. Without your help, it will take a long time, but we will still do it." She winced but let Gregor continue to pull from her wrist. The pain turned worse, lines appearing around her eyes as she strained to bear it. Then, when she could take it no longer, she pulled her wrist from Gregor's mouth.

The wound was ragged, strips of skin hanging from it. Her hand hung limp as if the tendons and ligaments had been chewed through. Gregor's lips continued to suck and slurp at the empty air. Anger and accusation filled his eyes as he strained to look at Mariyana, but she ignored him. Soon, the vacant stare returned and Gregor's body resumed floating, his mouth open and closing as it had earlier.

"But with your help, I can bring him back faster," Mariyana said. "I offer much for your help." She held up her wrist toward him. Already the edges of the wound were healed. As he watched, skin grew, closing from all sides until the gash was covered. Within seconds, her wrist looked untouched.

Corbin reached up and touched the spot on his head where a cut ought to have been. The dried blood was still there, but no cut. He was already becoming like them. The other presence in him pushed a sense of belonging at him. Of salvation. But he knew it was a lie. It was all a lie. There was no salvation. Not for him.

Mariyana walked to a door in the back of the cave and Corbin followed. She pushed back heavy curtains that separated the caves and motioned for him to look. On the other side were a series of cages built into the walls, each of them big enough for a large dog. Only there were no dogs in them. These cages were for men. Albino men that turned away, shaking, covering their heads as if they might be struck. There were over a dozen of them in his sightline, but the cave curved into the distance and he had no way of knowing how far back it went.

"The power we have amassed is immense," she said. "Our destiny is nearly at hand. The thing you most want is something I can give you."

"No," he said. "I don't want any part of this." He meant the words to come out firmly, a powerful statement of his resolve, but he could only manage a trembling whisper.

"Do you understand what I'm offering you?" she said.

"To be like you. To heal like you do."

Mariyana smiled, a patient expression of a mother slowly helping a child reach a conclusion. "That's only part of it. And I think you understand that."

A noise rose up in his head, like static on a radio. It was the terrible idea that wanted to be heard. An idea transformed into a wall of sound that enveloped and cut through him. He wanted to banish it from his head at the same time he wanted to embrace it. Torn between the two, he simply stood there, hands on the sides of his head, squeezing, not sure if he was forcing the idea out or in.

"You know what I offer," Mariyana said.

A ragged sob escaped his throat and he dropped to his knees. He slumped forward, hugging his arms to his chest. Rocking in place.

"Yes, you see it now," she said, her voice a whisper. "I can do it. I've done it before for others. I've done it for myself. Help me and I will do it for you."

He looked up, barely able to breathe. God help him, he believed her. The man he'd seen so violently killed was alive in front of him, how could he not believe? How could he not agree to do anything she asked now?

"Tell me what I have to do," he said. "Tell me what I have to do for you to bring my daughter back to life."

29

Besson landed a right hook on the man's cheek. The skin split and blood seeped from a new cut. Until then, Besson had landed mostly body blows, attention-getters to help the man clear his head and remember if he had information that needed to be shared.

They were behind a dive bar, in a narrow alley that reeked so badly of garbage and urine that even the prostitutes and addicts refused to use it. The man, a small-time drug dealer named Eduard Landa, was typically a useful informant. The kind of criminal who didn't survive because of his strength or ability, but from knowing everyone else's business. And having a knack for staying out of the way when bad things were happening.

"C'mon, man," Eduard said, his French so heavily accented from the south that Besson had to listen close to understand. "I tol' you everything I know."

"Which was nothing," Besson said. "You can see how that's unsatisfying, can't you?"

He landed another blow to the man's right kidney, pulling the punch a bit. The unfortunate thing for Eduard was that Besson believed him. He likely didn't know anything about Tacho R'asa, Margot Vinci or Corbin Stewart. The man was Romani, and he'd heard of the R'asa the way children had heard of the monsters that lurk in the night, but he wasn't part of that world. Most Romani weren't. But Besson was grasping at straws now so he was on a tear through the Parisian underground, visiting every informant he'd ever used to see if he stumbled across something to placate Alexis. He told himself that the beat-down was just in case Eduard was holding out. In reality, it was a stress release. He couldn't stop thinking about his wife and daughter. And with those thoughts came a desire to hurt someone.

Eduard Landa just happened to be the unfortunate person in front of him at that moment.

"I don't know nothin'," Maurice sputtered, spitting a gob of blood onto the road. "I swear it."

"You swear it?"

"Yeah."

"And you think that's going to convince me?"

"C'mon, man. I ain't done nothin' to you. Why you treatin' me like that?"

Besson shoved the man. Eduard fell to the pavement, rolled and slammed into the side of a dumpster. Five or six rats scurried out of the container, eyes glowing red in the streetlight. Besson took a step toward him, fist raised. He wanted to hurt the man. Beat him until his blood flowed. Not because the man deserved it, but because it was something he could do.

But while thinking of his wife being held by Alexis's animals stoked his anger, it also brought on a sudden sense of shame. She knew who and what he was, there were no secrets between them, but she also knew there was a code to be followed on the street. Violence for the sake of violence led to anarchy in the criminal world every bit as much as it did in the rest of society. She would not have let him take pride in beating this weaker man only to ease his frustration. No, she would have thought less of him for it. A truth that saved Eduard Landa a few broken bones and a trip to the hospital.

"Get out of here," Besson said.

Eduard grunted from the effort of getting to his feet. He moved carefully, as if expecting to be kicked at any second.

"Now, before I change my mind."

The man broke into a run, hunched over, knocking over garbage cans as he went. In a final act of defiance, Maurice raised his middle finger over his head. "Fuck you, Besson," he shouted.

Besson grinned. The gesture meant he hadn't hurt the man that much. Maybe Giselle wouldn't have been too disappointed with him after all.

His phone rang and a look at the screen soured his mood.

"I have no new information," he said, answering it.

"It's because you are too easy when asking people questions," Alexis replied.

Besson gripped the phone tighter. Alexis's presence had always provoked a negative response in him, some animal instinct that said the man was a vile creature that ought to be put out of its misery. But now, with his family under the animal's control, it took all his strength not to throw the phone against the wall.

"I know what I'm doing. I'll remind you it wasn't my men who lost the girl and the American at Notre Dame."

"Men who were trying to recapture them after they were in your custody and simply walked out the door?"

Besson couldn't help his temper. "I'm doing my part. I have half of the Paris police force looking for these two. If you would just leave—" The line clicked. "Hello? Hello?" But the connection was gone.

Besson's stomach heaved. His anger turned instantly into fear. Alexis was unstable. And he had his wife and daughter. Why had he spoken to him like that?

He tried to redial the number but his hands shook and he hit the wrong buttons. As he was about to try a third time, the phone rang in his hands. He took a steadying breath and raised it to his ear.

"I'm sorry. I don't know what came over me. I apologize for the disrespect."

A long silence on the other end.

Besson closed his eyes and rubbed them hard, standing in the street filled with filth. "I'm sorry."

"On your knees," Alexis said, his voice pinched.

"What?"

"You heard me."

Besson looked around the alley. There was no one else there. He lowered himself to one knee and then the other. Shame washed over him, but it was nothing compared to the fear of losing his family. "I'm on my knees," he said.

"Apologize again."

"I'm sorry."

The phone disconnected but he still heard Alexis's voice. "Apology accepted." The albino walked out of the far end of the alley, hood pulled up over his head. Two other Fantômes lingered behind him. Besson lifted a foot to brace himself to stand.

"Did I tell you to get up?" Alexis said.

Besson shifted his foot back so that he remained on his knees. His hate for the man, fueled even more by his pride, had him envisioning every possible way for him to kill Alexis. But he knew that if he acted on his impulse, then the Fantômes would kill Giselle and Lily. He had to take whatever Alexis gave him.

And the smug son of a bitch knew it.

"You look angry, Besson," Alexis said. "You'd think you were used to being on your knees. That's what dogs do, don't they? Beg at their master's feet?"

The other two men laughed. He wondered if he could kill those two without offending Alexis too much. Not likely.

"What do you want?" Besson said. "I'm working. Trying to find the American."

"Yes, you said so on the phone." Alexis reached into a pocket and pulled out a small jewelry box. He twirled it in his hand as he spoke. "My methods have proven more effective than yours. The R'asa we caught didn't know much, but he did give me something interesting."

"What's that?"

"They want the girl. It's all they care about. She's a direct bloodline of Gregor. His granddaughter. The American is nothing to them but a way to get to her."

Besson considered the implications. If she was Gregor's blood, then there was no denying her value. "Maybe. Or that information is R'asa misdirection."

Alexis smiled. "I'm very persuasive. You should already know that about me." He held the jewelry box to his ear and shook it. When Besson didn't ask about it, he looked disappointed. "He also told me that the final revenge of the Tacho R'asa was at hand. That we were all going to soon perish at their hands for our transgressions against them." He swept a hand around him in a flourish. "All of Paris, he said. Maybe the world."

"I assume it's not the first time you've been threatened."

Alexis walked around Besson. "No, but the Tacho R'asa in its entirety is coming here. To Paris. It's a chance to annihilate them all. If they want the woman so badly, then she is the key to getting them."

"Then I'll double the effort to find the woman," Besson said, not giving Alexis the satisfaction of turning to look at him. He kept his eyes forward, fixed on a point off in the distance, thinking of the moment he'd be together with his wife and daughter again. He didn't care about his family history, or his stakes in the various illegal enterprises in Clichy; once he got his family back he was going to get them on a train and leave the country. Maybe try for America. Or Canada. Someplace far away from the Fantômes and the R'asa and their war against one another. But he needed them back safe first.

"You're a good detective," Alexis said. "I am certain with the right motivation you can find one person in Paris."

"Let me see them," he said. "So I can tell them they will be all right."

Alexis held out the jewelry box. "Why would you tell them that?"

With trembling hands, Besson reached out and took the box from the albino's hands.

"Find her. Help me kill all the Tacho R'asa, and not only will I set them free, but you will be free as well. Your father's debt will have been paid, forgiven for his sins for having sold my brothers to the

R'asa. Neither you nor anyone in your family will see Les Fantômes de la Nuit ever again. I swear it."

The offer got Besson's attention. It was what he'd wanted since the burden of what his family owed the Fantômes had passed to his shoulders. The sins of the father ought not to have been the sins of the son, but that predicate held no meaning to Alexis. But this was a way out.

"Don't fail me this time, Besson. The stakes are too high." Alexis strode from the alley, his two henchmen falling in line behind him.

Besson turned the jewelry box over in his hands. It was simple, the kind used for worthless trinkets from a tourist shop. He couldn't imagine there was anything inside that he wanted to see, and he considered tossing it into the trash unopened. But Alexis never did anything without purpose. Whatever was inside, he'd gone through great pains to deliver it to him in person. The information about the importance of the girl, the offer to release him from service completely if the Tacho R'asa were destroyed, both of those things could have been conveyed over the phone. But the box. The box was different.

He reexamined it, still on his knees, trepidation now taking the place of his anger. A sudden premonition of what might be inside caused him to sit back on his heels, hunched forward like a man praying. In fact, it was exactly what he was doing. Praying he was wrong.

But when he opened the box, he cried out, stifling the sound with the back of his hand.

The box contained a single earring. A blue butterfly with a tiny ruby on the wing.

Still attached to his baby girl's ear.

He snapped the box shut, as if doing so would make what he'd seen go away. He removed his jacket and carefully wrapped it around the box. Delicately, like it was made of fine glass, he tucked it under his arm and climbed to his feet, bracing it with his hands like someone might try to steal it.

There was a buzzing in his ears. The world seemed to tilt on its axis. Bile rose in his throat as he pictured his little girl screaming while someone hacked away at the side of her face.

No, he couldn't think of that. Not now. He had to clear his head. Find the girl. Find the American.

But how? He had no play left to make. No informants left to question. He could stake out the man's apartment, but what was the likelihood of him returning there? He squeezed his eyes shut, trying to block out everything except for the problem at hand. How to do what Alexis needed. And how to do it fast.

But all he could hear were his daughter's screams. Her tiny, terrified voice calling his name, begging for her daddy to rescue her.

Besson opened his eyes again, wildly searching the alley as if she might be there.

He had to get a grip. Work the problem. Find a way to get his family back.

The truth was that even if he could think clearly, the options ranged from awful to terrible. If there was an easy resolution, or even a hard one, he would have already done it. If Alexis wanted to push him to desperation, he'd succeeded. But Besson wasn't the kind of man that needed desperation to do the unthinkable. He'd already done all the things which would cause normal men to balk. The problem was that his obstacle had nothing to do with scruples or morality. If he thought killing a room of strangers would return his family to him, he'd do it without hesitation. But it wouldn't help. And he didn't know what would.

He pressed the box tighter against his body, fighting to hold on and finding it nearly impossible as the hopelessness of the situation crashed down on him. He knew what Alexis was capable of doing. A line had been crossed, he felt that, and he didn't know where it would end. And that scared the hell out of him.

Then his cell phone rang. Alexis, it had to be. Fear and anguish was replaced by pure hate.

"You don't touch her again," he said into the phone, his voice sounding distant to his own ears. Hollow and lifeless. "Do you understand me? Hurt them again and I'll hunt you down and kill every last one of you."

Silence on the other end of the line. Then a voice he didn't expect. "Inspector Besson. It sounds like we should meet," Corbin Stewart said. "I think we can help each other bring this all to an end."

30

Corbin hung up the phone and slipped it into his pocket. Besson had agreed to meet him. Alone. No police. He wondered if he was being naïve trusting that he would stick to those conditions, but Corbin thought he would. The outburst when he'd first answered his call had told him all he needed to know. They were two men traveling the same tortured road, doing what they would never do on their own to save someone they loved. The difference being that the inspector's family was likely still alive. The child Corbin was trying to save had been underground for nearly four years.

He walked to the nearest subway station, barely taking stock of the world around him, feeling dazed, even a little drunk. Earlier, while in the catacombs, he'd craved the open sky and fresh air. But that was before everything had changed. Before he'd understood that it was possible to get his little girl back. After that, everything else seemed inconsequential. Everything else was just noise.

To him, the two greatest barriers had already been breached. Whether the task could be done seemed undeniable. He'd seen Gregor's dead body in the alley where he was attacked. And the violence of his death, so many stab wounds all over his body, left no doubt there hadn't been some kind of mistake about his passing.

Professional paramedics had tried to revive him. They'd taken his vitals and declared him dead at the scene. Then he'd lain there for over an hour as the police investigated the scene. He was dead and now he was alive. The task could be done.

From an outsider's perspective, the second barrier may have been the more poignant question. No matter whether it could be done, should it be done? The ethicist in Corbin's head, the inner voice that gravitated to writing fiction as a way to parse the intricacies of human motivation and action, wanted to be heard on the subject. But the rest of his mind drowned it out. Instead, a single thought drummed through his head:

I can bring Rose back.

I can bring Rose back.

I can bring Rose back.

But once he boarded the subway, squeezed in with the rush hour crowd, a different thought rose up inside of him. It wasn't his conscience finally pushing through the cacophony of voices, but something else. This was a strange voice that came with an over-whelming sense of *other*. He knew it from the catacombs, whatever part of Gregor that had come with his blood. The same presence that had shared his own revulsion at the sight of Gregor's weak body floating in the pool of blood. That had wanted to push Mariyana up against a wall, hike up her dress and mount her like they were teenagers again.

Only now the voice somehow blended in more with his own thoughts. It was less and less *other*—and more just part of him.

Hate. It filled him as he looked around the crowded subway. These were small-minded people, scurrying about their pathetic lives without any thought to the litany of atrocities committed in their names. They existed only because of what their forefathers had done on their behalf. Colonized and destroyed entire cultures. Enslaved indigenous peoples. Fought brutal wars for no other reason than because the powerful few above them commanded it. Then sucked from the teat of a modern world bought and paid for with the blood of innocent men, women and children. And yet they didn't even pause to acknowledge it. They did not even have the decency to carry the burden of guilt on their shoulders.

They deserved to die, Corbin thought. All of them. Their arms and legs pulled from their sockets. Their genitals carved from their bodies and shoved into their mouths until they choked. Their abdomens sliced open so that they held their own intestines in their hands as they wept and wailed.

Corbin realized he had an erection from the thoughts, the lust for blood as strong as any carnal desire. The subway car was too packed for anyone to notice, but he didn't care. Let them see. Their time was almost over. His people would be avenged. A thousand years of mistreatment, of butchery, of genocide. It was a blood debt, and he would make them pay for it in full.

The subway slowed as it entered the next station. When the doors whisked open, Corbin felt the other voice release its hold on him. He shook his head as if waking from a daydream, saw the sign on the far wall that read Pere Lachaise and then excused himself as he pushed his way to the door. He made it out and onto the platform just in time, adjusting his crotch, embarrassed by the bulge there. He remembered the raw emotions he'd felt only seconds before, so much anger and hate that he didn't think there was room for anything else. But it felt fleeting now. Like a nightmare that left him covered in cold sweat and shaking, but inexplicably unable to recall any detail of what had terrified him.

Corbin strode to a trash can, leaned over and threw up. He hadn't eaten in hours so he retched up only bile and then dry heaved until his stomach cramped. The hate lingered like the aftertaste of a bitter drink, climbing up the back of his throat so that he breathed it and smelled it. He glanced up at the crowd gathered on the subway platform, all of them ignoring him, and he felt a quick impulse again to kill them all. It was like an electric shock, firing through him with such intensity that he felt the urge to reach out and strangle the man nearest him with his bare hands. But then it was gone. He bent over and heaved again into the trash can.

The inner voice chided him for being weak, but only did so softly, as if not wanting to make it worse.

When he was done, he wiped his mouth and checked his watch. He had to hurry to meet Besson on time. Unless he got him to agree to help him, he'd never be able to meet his end of the bargain with Mariyana. And he'd never see his little girl again.

Nothing was going to stop him from making that happen. Not even the delusional ravings of an old man who thought he could destroy the world.

He quickly made his way out of the station and down the street to the main entrance of the Pere Lachaise Cemetery. While it felt odd to think of a cemetery as a place for tourists on holiday, Pere Lachaise held some notable graves. Moliere. Bizet. Chopin. Oscar Wilde. But for all the brilliance assembled under the cemetery's shade trees, the most visited was Jim Morrison of The Doors. People left coins, bottles of booze, even drug paraphernalia. The ugly part of it was the graffiti on the graves around it with statements like, "I am the lizard king, I can do anything." Not exactly the sophisticated eternal sleep envisioned by the other inhabitants of Pere Lachaise.

But as Corbin walked through the massive entrance to the cemetery, enormous plinths of concrete rising on either side of him like the gates to the Underworld, he had no thoughts of whether the dead were content with their crass American neighbor. He was focused only on one question. How in the hell was he going to get Besson to agree to help him?

The meeting place they'd arranged wasn't far from the the main entrance. While the cemetery was over four hundred acres, the Aux Morts monument was only a five-minute walk down a wide boulevard. There weren't too many people around, mostly tourists with one of the maps sold just outside the cemetery walls showing the locations of the most interesting graves. But he was glad they were there. He wanted a public meeting place just in case Besson had any ideas about grabbing him. Then again, if he showed up with a squadron of police, a few tourists wouldn't help anyway.

He came to the Aux Morts monument, the sculpture that had

captivated him on his one other trip to the cemetery. At first glance, it looked like a small stone temple with a lower level exposed underground and a first level with a platform in front of an open doorway leading inside. On the lower level, there was a life-size statue of a woman cradling a dying man, the anguish of loss stretched across her face. On the higher level, statues of men and women gathered on either side of the door, all lamenting death.

But the image that most haunted Corbin was the two figures standing just inside the door, their backs turned completely to the viewer. Clearly still alive, it seemed to Corbin that they were tempted to follow their loved one into death, or at least they had symbolically turned their backs to the living. It didn't take a degree in psychology for him to figure out that he was projecting his own mental state onto the sculpture, but wasn't that the reason for art to exist in the first place? Even though it was depressing as hell, it was the first place he'd thought of as a meeting place outside the city.

Besson was already there, standing in front of the sculpture with his hands cradling something against his chest. When Corbin stepped up beside him, the inspector didn't turn to look at him, instead staring at the images of pain and loss before him. They stood in silence for nearly a minute before Corbin spoke.

"They have your family?" he asked.

The big man nodded.

"Kids?"

"Wife and my daughter. Age three."

Corbin's stomach tightened. Rose had been five when she died. He wondered if she'd still be five when she was brought to life. It'd been four years, but she couldn't have grown. How could she have grown if she was dead? He wasn't sure why he would have even thought that.

"You were followed here," Besson said. Corbin began to turn, but Besson said, "Don't look. It's better if they think we don't know they are there."

"I didn't know. I swear it."

Besson nodded, slowly, like a man nearly too tired to stay on his feet. "I believe you. The Fantômes followed me here. Maybe they and the R'asa will run into one another among the gravestones and add to the population of this place."

Corbin swallowed hard, picturing the albino men chained to the pillars, their blood draining into Gregor's sarcophagus.

"I'm sorry about your family," Corbin said.

Besson lowered his arms, a small box clenched in his right hand. "I'm going to get them back. And then I'm going to make the Fantômes pay." He turned to Corbin. "If you have an idea of how I can do either of those two things, I'll do whatever you say."

31

Alexis remained in the shadow of the mausoleum fifty yards from where Besson and the American Corbin Stewart stood talking. He had three other Fantômes in the cemetery positioned to prevent the two men from being lost in the labyrinthine walkways of the rambling graveyard. But he had come himself because he sensed the importance of what was happening. A lifetime of effort was barreling toward climax, if only he were fast enough and clever enough to capture it.

As the two men spoke to one another, he wished he was able to hear the conversation. It didn't matter, he supposed. Either Besson was going to be able to convince the American to lead them to the gypsy girl or not. It didn't matter what lies he told the man, or what he agreed to. All that mattered was the end result. If Alexis could get the girl, the R'asa would come for her and, if he was ready, he could finally destroy them all.

It seemed impossible to believe that he might finally be able to finish the long journey his adopted fathers had put him on so many years ago. He wished some of them could be there for the end, but they were all long dead, sacrificed for the cause. The journey to this moment had been long and filled with danger.

Alexis was eight when he'd been snatched from his village by the raiders. They came in the middle of the night without warning, only an eruption of women screaming from the huts nearest the jungle's edge. His mother pushed him into the hiding space in their hut, a small trapdoor in the wood floor that opened to the crawlspace under their home. He hated it down there because it was covered with spiderwebs and insects. Once when the raiders had come he'd been bitten by a snake and fallen ill for three days. His mother had refused to go to the magician in the next village for a poultice, saying he was the reason her son feared for his life every day, so how could she trust such a man to save him?

She was both right and wrong about this. The magician, or witch doctor, was not the reason Alexis was hunted. But it was men worse than him that were responsible. The magician was simply someone who knew the right herbs and plants to use to help with small ailments and who could play the part well in ceremonies and festivals of a powerful sorcerer who could shake the earth like a god when angry. But it was all just an act, even the most superstitious knew it in their hearts. But that didn't mean there were not real magicians in the land beyond them, harsh cruel men who used the dark ways to consolidate power and rule over common people. These were not the warlords with machine guns and roving bands of machete-wielding soldiers, but the men who propped them up, men that administered powerful blessings and curses on behalf of those who could pay for the extravagance. Of these extravagances, there was none greater than the blood of an albino.

Alexis's mother had once taken him to a village that was a two-day's journey from their own where his aunt lived with a wealthy husband. Their hut had four rooms in it, and young Alexis had asked whether his uncle was a prince. All the adults had laughed at him but he didn't understand why. Then two older boys were sent for. They wore odd clothes that covered their arms and legs, and a hood that covered their heads. When his uncle told them to remove their hoods, Alexis saw that their faces were tattooed with wild patterns, covering nearly all of their skin. Their hands were similarly covered.

But their eyes shone bright blue with eyelids tinged with soft pink, and Alexis knew at once the boys were just like him. And he knew that the disguises they wore would never be enough, no matter what the adults told them. Thankfully, his mother felt the same and refused his aunt and uncle's pleas that her boy stay and receive the same tattoos to cover his face.

Then again, if he had stayed, his mother would have lived.

It was only weeks later when the men came. Alexis had climbed into his hiding spot, steeling himself against what waited for him in the darkness. He held a small knife in his right hand, ready if something slithered across his lap or tried to chew his bare legs. He had to remain as still as possible or the raiders would get him, his mother had taught him that. But he wasn't going to let anything bite him again.

"Bring him out, *amayi*," a man's voice said outside the hut. "I know you have him."

Footsteps over his head. His mother leaving the hut.

"You know nothing. My husband and sons are all dead. Leave a grieving woman to her sorrow."

The man laughed. "You have told us this story before, but I know you are lying. Come, I am reasonable. I will pay you for him. Enough to make this village prosper."

Alexis heard the sound of coins. He pulled his knees against his chest and hugged them. He knew the village was hungry. He wondered if empty stomachs were enough for someone to betray him.

"Anyone?" the man asked. "This reward can be yours."

Silence, except for some woman crying. He knew it wasn't his mother. He'd only seen her cry once, over the body of his father, but that had been short and followed by steely resolve. No, the man wouldn't get her to cry.

"All right. I had hoped to make this easy on you. Perhaps the *wamatsenga* of this boy has you in a spell, so I will forgive. But that will not change how this needs to end. Grab her."

He knew instantly who the *her* was. His mother screamed and the villagers cried out in protest. A gun went off and the voices stopped.

"Boy, I know you can hear me," the man called out. "I will not hurt you. I promise."

Alexis knew this was a lie. His mother had told him what the raiders did to boys like him. Drained their blood. Cut them into pieces. Removed each organ carefully for sale. Clipped their finger and toenails. Then roasted bones and ground them into a powder for potions and soup. She told him these things to scare him, she admitted that. But she also told him because they were true. "No matter what happens, you don't come out of hiding. Not ever." She'd made him promise and he'd solemnly done so. But nothing had prepared him for that night.

"Do you not love your mother?" the man cried out. "Must I cut her to get your attention?" His mother screamed, such pain in her voice that Alexis immediately sobbed at the sound of it. "Are you such a *mdierekezi* that you will let your mother die for you? I will give you ten seconds before I cut her throat."

Alexis didn't need ten seconds. The trapdoor was already open. He crawled out and two of the raiders who were searching the hut grabbed him under his arms and hauled him outside. The entire village was there, lined up on one side with the raiders on the other. The man who'd been talking stood between them, a young man, severe, wearing the same uniform Alexis's father had worn when he died. His mother was on her knees. Blood poured down the side of her face. One of her ears was gone.

"There you are." The raiders dragged him closer and then threw him down onto the ground where Alexis curled into a ball. "Just like your uncle promised me." At this, his mother wailed in anger and grief. It was more than Alexis could bear.

He said something under his breath to the man.

"What was that?" he said. "Did you have something to tell me, boy?"

He said it a little louder but not so the man could hear it. The only words he emphasized were *hidden guns* and *let me go*. As he hoped, this grabbed the man's interest. He kneeled to the ground next to him and indicated for him to come closer.

"Are there guns hidden in this village? Tell me where they are and you and your mother can live. I promise you."

Another lie, but then so was Alexis's story about there being guns in the village.

He mumbled again and the man craned forward to listen. His throat beautifully exposed.

Alexis rammed the small knife in his hand as hard as he could into the man's neck. He twisted it, slicing across the windpipe. A rush of blood spilled over him. The man's eyes bulged and Alexis stared into them, wanting the man to see his face as he died.

And then everything went crazy.

The raider behind him saw first what had happened. He raised his gun, but then shots fired from somewhere else, puffs of red exploding from the man's back. His gun shot wildly, dead fingers on the trigger, one of the bullets hitting his mother in the back of the head. Alexis reached for her, but missed as she fell to the ground. He went numb, standing outside of his own body as a halo of dark blood spilled out from his mother's wound.

But then one of the raiders had him, a knife at his throat. Hot pain laced across his neck and the side of his head, but then an explosion sounded so close to him that his hearing shattered into a high-pitched hum. He spun, dizzy, and saw the raider's face was gone, a crater of blood and bone staring back at him.

He turned in a circle, confused. There were other men in the village now, killing the raiders. And they looked so strange, and yet so familiar. He dropped to his knees, holding the slash across his throat as if that would keep his blood from spilling out. Darkness crowded in from all directions, limiting his vision. Just before he fell unconscious, it occurred to him what made these new men so remarkable. They were all albino. Just like him. What he didn't know then, was that together these men were to become his fathers and then, as he reached manhood, his brothers. Then, finally, they were to become his followers on his quest to destroy all those who had hunted and sold his people.

At heart, he was still eight years old and all he wanted was to avenge his mother who died trying to protect her only remaining son.

The path had been a long one, filled with terrible things he'd had to do to reach his goals. But no worse than what had been done against his people, something that he always reminded his young fighters when they were first asked to do something that violated their conscience.

While the R'asa was their objective now, they had started the journey first killing the witch doctors that trafficked in albino flesh and bone. Then they followed the money and killed those who used the powders and poultices, moving into the cities and targeting powerful and wealthy men. Sometimes collateral damage was necessary. Children, women, crowds gathered in public areas, no one could be spared if their death moved their cause forward. He reminded his men that there were no innocents in the world, only degrees of guilt and complicity.

Then he had learned of the R'asa. They were an absolute evil, and their particular atrocity against his kind made destroying them a cause not only worth killing for, but one worth dying for.

As he watched Besson and the American walk deeper into the cemetery, he wondered whether it was possible the long journey from his village might soon be coming to an end.

He pulled out his phone, eager to do something to hold the ghosts from his past at bay. "M'akiwe," he said into the phone once his second-in-command answered. "I want you to assemble all the Fantômes. Every single one. The final battle approaches."

"What of the two guarding the policeman's family? Should I have them kill the hostages and then join us?"

Alexis watched Besson's back as he walked away from him. "Have one of them stay to guard them," Alexis said. "But bring me a finger from the woman in case the inspector needs more prompting. Her finger with the wedding ring still on it."

Alexis hung up the phone and followed Besson and Corbin, wondering again what exactly they were talking about.

32

Corbin caught a flash of movement between the gravestones to his right and fought down the urge to look. Besson had told him he could get them out of the cemetery and lose their tails in the process. Since Corbin didn't even know how many men were watching them, he was resigned to following his lead.

"We need Margot," Besson said. "I have all the men I could get looking for her. Flagged her as a person of interest in a terror cell so all the alarms would go off."

"And?"

"And I'm here meeting you, aren't I?"

Corbin saw movement again, this time to his left. "I can find her," he said plainly, not really knowing the truth of the statement until he said it out loud.

Besson stopped. "Where is she?"

"She's in the city still, that I know. Besides that, I just feel like I can find her."

"Keep walking," Besson said. Once they turned down a row of marble mausoleums replete with pillars, porticoes and lavish funerary statues, he whispered harshly. "You *feel* like you can find her? That's what you have for me?"

Corbin probed the sensation he had in the back of his mind. Mixed in with all the dark bitterness and hatred was a pulsing sense of a female presence. He'd thought at first that it was the Gregor part of his mind obsessing over Mariyana, but he didn't think so now. It still came from the intruder inside of him, but he somehow knew he wasn't sensing Mariyana. It was Margot. He could feel her. He knew when he was getting closer or farther from her, like the game he used to play with Rose, calling out colder or warmer as she searched for the last Easter egg hidden in their backyard. She'd worn the prettiest dresses, with her hair––

"Hey," Besson said, poking him hard enough in the arm that he stumbled sideways. "Wake up."

Corbin caught his balance and rubbed his arm. "What the hell was that?"

"You wandered off. Your eyes were open but you weren't home."

Corbin looked around. They were at the end of the long row of imposing gravesites. He glanced over his shoulder with no memory of walking the last twenty yards.

"Where'd you go?"

"Doesn't matter," Corbin said. "I can find Margot. Can you make good on getting us out of here?"

Besson looked him over, the same expression on his face when he'd interrogated Corbin back at the police station. "There are things you're not telling me."

"Can we agree that goes for both of us?" Corbin said. "Tell you what, let's not assume each other are fools. If we do that, maybe at least one of us will survive this whole thing."

The big man grinned, a reaction that seemed so out of place on his somber face that Corbin thought maybe he'd gone too far and pushed him over some unseen edge. But a small chuckle followed it and it seemed genuine enough.

"So help me, I'm starting to actually like you. It's going to be a disappointment if I have to kill you at the end of this."

"Let's hope it doesn't come to that. One thing is certain, we can't do what we need with both the R'asa and the Fantômes following us.

Can you get us out of here? Is there a secret passageway or something?"

They turned the corner next to a dilapidated mausoleum with the roof caved in. Not too far from them was a small entrance gate, just wide enough for a single car to pass through the tall stone pillars. Three policemen stood near a checkpoint, smoking and chatting as they waved tourists through.

"Nothing that complicated. I parked on the Rue des Rondeaux just for this purpose. Come. And don't say anything."

As Besson walked up to the men, he pulled out his badge and spoke in rapid French. The policemen snapped to attention, tossing their cigarettes to the ground. Corbin tried to catch what he was telling them but it was too fast. Seconds later, Besson waved him through the checkpoint while he was still barking orders to the men.

Once they were out in the street, Corbin asked, "What did you tell them?"

"That some assholes were defacing graves and taking souvenirs. They needed to fully search anyone who comes through."

Corbin turned and saw the policemen lower a parking lot arm across the entrance and put out their hands to slow down the two R'asa men jogging toward them. Corbin stutter-stepped and nearly tripped as it occurred to him that the two men might decide to put up a fight and kill the policemen to get through. But they stopped, looking past the checkpoint at Corbin. Behind them, masked by the shade of the trees lining the walkway, were the Fantômes, glaring at both the R'asa and Corbin.

"What the hell are you doing?" Besson asked. He already had the door open to his car and had one foot in. "Get in."

Corbin ran to the car and slid in. The car's huge motor roared to life and Besson swerved out of his spot, cutting off a flatbed delivery truck. The truck's driver dodged left and blared his horn, but the road was too narrow. The truck hit a parked car and the back skidded out until it was nearly touching the stone wall of the cemetery. Corbin swiveled in his seat to see the driver waving his arms inside the cab and hammering the truck's horn. No one seemed hurt and the road was effectively blocked for anyone to try to follow them.

"I'm guessing you've done this before," Corbin said.

Besson took a corner hard and hit the gas. The tires chirped as they flew out of the small side street and into a roundabout. It was only once they were on the main road heading back toward the city center that Besson began to drive like the devil wasn't chasing them.

Besson said, "I just made the men who have my family very mad. You'd better be able to deliver the girl. And I mean right now. Or so help me, you're going to wish the Fantômes had caught you."

Corbin closed his eyes. He didn't blame Besson for threatening him. He knew what it was like to have everything he loved whisked away in one moment. Whether kidnapped or stage four cancer, it didn't matter. The long and short of it was that Besson's core was being attacked. More than that, it was likely about to be destroyed. Just like Corbin's had been.

But you don't have to suffer anymore.

You get your daughter back.

Your Rose.

We've done it for others, Mariyana will do it for you.

Corbin opened his eyes and was surprised that they stung with tears. He pressed his fingers against them as if concentrating, hoping that Besson hadn't noticed.

"Which way do I go?" Besson said.

To his surprise, Corbin knew the answer to that question. He *felt* where he needed to go. Some kind of internal compass that pulled him in a direction if he just allowed it.

"Well?" Besson asked.

Corbin pointed down the street to their right. "Turn here. Just follow my directions and I'll take you to her." It was only the first part of the plan, and not the part he needed Besson's help with. After they got Margot, he had to deliver her and as many of the Fantômes as he could to Mariyana. And that would require that Besson bring Alexis to him.

You're doing well, boy.

Do as you're promised and you'll see your daughter again.

"Shut up," Corbin said to the voice in his head. Only he said it aloud. Besson cast a look in his direction, but then directed his eyes back to street. Corbin thought he caught a glimpse of something in the look. Suspicion? Fear? He couldn't be sure.

Watch that one close, the voice said. *He'll try to stop us.*

They sped through the streets heading into the center of Paris. Both he and Besson were searching for a way to save their families. But the voice was right. Only one of them could be successful. And once that was clear, Besson would try to stop him.

When he did, Corbin was ready to kill him.

33

Margot pulled her hair taut and cut it only a couple of inches from her scalp. She let the long strands fall into the sink, piling up with the hair she'd already cut. Once she was done, she reread the instructions on the box of hair dye and then went to work finishing her transformation. The chemicals reeked and made her eyes water, but she knew that if she had any chance of avoiding capture, she had to make a dramatic change to her look. She'd considered a wig, but she worried that might actually draw more attention to her if she wore it wrong. While she waited for the hair dye to do its work, she thought through her options.

She'd been a fool to come back to Paris. Even with the meeting with Gregor a year before and the promise that had been made there, she ought to have just kept away. It was her own stubbornness that had done it. That and a pop psychology self-analysis that said she needed to face her fears and not run from them like her mother had all those years ago when she'd escaped to America. Margot had always thought her mother a coward for not taking a stand, even if the odds were impossibly against her. What a damn-fool idea that had been. Her mother had been right all along. Running was the only option.

Margot was under no illusion of the type of danger she was in. She had not only her mother's stories about the Tacho R'asa, but her own memories as well. She'd been eight when her mother had fled and her father had paid the price of their escape with his life. What she remembered had the feel of a nightmare. Disjointed scenes that floated up against each other, snippets of conversations, smells that evoked complicated emotions of fear and euphoria and panic all at once. It was hard for her to separate out what she'd actually witnessed with her own eyes and which things just seemed that way from her mother telling her the same stories over and over until they became solidified as fact in her mind. Even so, there were a few memories that she was certain were her own.

The ritual sacrifices were seared in her mind. And the orgies that followed: the naked bodies of every adult she knew, all of them writhing on the cave floor together, soaked with blood, limbs and genitals rubbing and thrusting, the room filled with moans. She remembered thinking the floor was covered with a single, writhing organism, and it had terrified her. She'd never participated, wasn't required to, but in her nightmares she was sometimes back in that cave, as a grown woman, and dozens of hands reached out and dragged her into the pile of bodies. Hot blood splashed over her, the metallic taste of it in her mouth. And she rolled and twisted with the others. The nightmare wasn't that she was forced to join in, but that, in the dream, she always wanted to. She craved the feeling of belonging, of being part by sharing her body even as she took what she needed from those around her. Whenever she awoke, trembling and covered with sweat, she was plagued with guilt and self-loathing for wanting it.

She knew from what she'd seen and from the few stories her mother had shared that the R'asa was depraved. An abomination. It made her longing that much more disturbing.

One memory in particular lingered with her, the same event that pushed her mother over the edge and sent her running from her tribe. It was another ritual night. The vats of blood were prepared from the farm in the catacombs. Margot didn't work in the farm so she only saw the product, not the process. It was like people buying meat in antiseptic, shrink-wrapped containers at the market and never having to step foot into the slaughterhouse. The mind disconnected the end product from origin, so that part never disturbed her.

But that night, her grandfather had brought something special for his people. After consulting the ancient texts, he announced he'd discovered a new way to reach a higher level of enlightenment. That they would all reach it together in the orgy that night. Even as a little girl, she remembered being excited at the idea, feeding off the buzz in the cave and the adults whispering among themselves. Her excitement ended when five little boys, kids her own age, were brought into the room. They weren't R'asa; they were just regular boys from the outside. Four of them stared dully at the crowd, obviously drugged, but the fifth was in a panic. Whether he wasn't susceptible to whatever drug he'd been given, or if the little troublemaker had managed to spit it out, Margot never knew. All she knew for certain was the sheer terror on the boy's face as he looked out over the crowd of people in the cave.

Margot saw her mother push her way toward the platform with the boy, take Gregor by the arm and whisper into his ear. She swore to her daughter later that she'd begged Gregor not to do it. To let the boys go. But he pushed her aside and signaled for the ritual to begin. Margot huddled against the wall with a handful of other young girls, wanting to leave, but unable to take her eyes off the boys as they were tied to the wall on the far side of the cave. Once the orgy reached its peak level of intensity, Gregor's voice filled the cave with words Margot did not understand. Then, one by one, like they were candles on a table, the boys were set on fire. Margot had heard their screams a thousand times through her life. She heard them in nightmares, inside the sound of an ambulance siren, buried in the whistle of a teapot. The screams came with her and her mother to America, and she was sure that they would always be with her no matter where she ran.

The timer on her phone beeped and she went to the small hotel sink and rinsed out the hair dye, careful not to discolor the skin on her forehead. She had to assume Besson would have an alert out for her by now. If the police were looking for her, a smudged forehead showing a quick dye-job would likely bring some unwanted attention. She mopped up the water with a towel and then looked at her reflection in the mirror.

The girl that looked back at her had short, blonde hair that stuck up in tufts in all directions. She brushed it through, adding some product to give it form. In a minute, she had it looking decent. A little 80s punk-rockish, but believable as a fashion statement. Regardless of her hair color and the leather jacket and jeans that completed her new look, it didn't change the absolutely terrified look in her eyes. She slid on a pair of glasses. That solved the problem of other people seeing she was scared. She only wished getting rid of her sense of terror was just as easy.

She stuffed her other clothes into a small backpack along with the makeup she'd purchased at the store. After being chased through the streets of Paris, she hadn't dared return to her hotel, choosing instead to check in to this dingy place, only a step above a youth hostel. Now she just had to decide the best way to get the hell out of the country.

As she left the room, she considered her options. Catching a plane was tempting. A direct flight to Heathrow, a quick stop at her apartment to collect her things and then another flight back to the States. She wondered if the stop in London was even necessary. What really was there for her? Even her prized photos of her mom and dad were safely digitized and stored on the Internet. No, she wouldn't even need to stop. She'd fly straight to New York, or maybe Boston. Go lose herself in New England, up where people knew how to keep to themselves and not ask a hundred questions of every new arrival. She'd restart and rebuild her life under a different name.

The thought brought her to a stop in front of the elevator, just as she reached out to press the button. It was the first time she'd played things out that far in her mind. Her old life was through. The job. Her friends. The apartment in London. Gone. There was no escaping it. Not with the R'asa hunting her down for God knew what purpose.

Damn you, Gregor. You promised me I would be left alone.

But then, what value ought to be placed on a promise made by the devil?

She pressed the elevator button and waited as the ancient contraption wheezed and clicked into motion in the bowels of the building, her mind still searching for a way out. The airport was too risky. If Besson had gone as far as contacting Interpol, then she'd be stopped at passport control. But that was true if she took the train through the Chunnel back into England, because Britain didn't share the same open borders as the rest of Europe. The movies always made it look so damn easy for the heroes to fly back and forth to wherever they needed to go. Too bad she didn't have a pile of fake passports and a bag of money. That would have been helpful.

Italy then. She'd rent a car and just drive. Even if they tracked her down to the car rental location, she'd be long gone before they figured that out. Except cars all had tracking devices on them with the navigation systems and onboard Wi-Fi. A rental car would just turn her into a blinking dot on a screen for them to follow. She was back to the train then. A multiday pass would enable her to change trains whenever she wanted to help cover her tracks. And her new look might not fool someone she knew who saw her in person, but it would likely make it hard for them to spot her on the CCTVs that recorded every movement in all train stations in Europe.

She pressed the button again, thinking she could have done the four floors by stairs two or three times over by then. If the stairs hadn't been filled with junkies and prostitutes saving the hourly rate on the regular rooms.

Now that she had the semblance of a plan, she wanted to get out of there. Because the longer she waited, the more guilt she felt. Especially about Corbin. The poor guy was knee-deep in it now, and it was all her fault. She'd tried to help him, but he'd been so difficult about it. Still, she felt responsible. He could have escaped when the R'asa and the Fantômes were chasing them down, but he'd sacrificed himself so she could get away. And she was repaying him by sneaking away on the first train out of town.

But the guilt ran deeper than that. She knew the true depravity of the Tacho R'asa. She knew exactly what they were capable of, and she'd done nothing about it. How many people had died over the years because of her silence? How many other little boys had been burned alive in the midst of a blood-drenched orgy to heighten the effects of the ritual?

How could she do nothing? Wasn't inaction the same as complicity? She'd been plagued by the Edmund Burke quote her entire life: *The only thing necessary for the triumph of evil is for good men to do nothing.*

She didn't consider herself necessarily *good*, but she wasn't part of the evil of her birth and blood. If she were good, she would have long ago found some way to shine a light on the R'asa and expose them. But she'd been too scared. Too ready to accept her mother's mantra that the past ought to be left alone.

And for this, she was ashamed.

Then stay and fight.

The thought surprised her, not so much for the idea behind it, but because it came to her as a man's voice. As if it were spoken aloud right next to her ear.

The elevator door reached her level and slowly opened.

On the other side stood the man whose voice she'd heard. Corbin Stewart.

34

Besson checked the rearview, eyes scanning for anything out of the ordinary. He knew Alexis had eyes everywhere in this city. As did the R'asa. He would have preferred to find somewhere underground to park his vehicle rather than waiting on the curb next to L'Avion, the worst of the dilapidated motels in the red light district. He felt too exposed, but there was nothing he could do about it. Corbin had promised it would only take two minutes, and it'd already been ten. He hated when plans got shot to hell.

He knew the motel well. Like everyone else who wanted to make detective, he'd put in his time working the streets when he joined the force. L'Avion was an easy place to visit when a guy needed a quick collar. Pimps, dealers, johns, pros, it didn't matter much. They were all just a checkmark on a file somewhere, regardless of what law they'd been breaking. Bringing a few of them in through the week showed the higher ups that you hadn't been sipping coffee all day while watching the tourist women walk by in their short skirts. Even if that's exactly what you had been doing. L'Avion, The Airplane in English, lived up to its name. Whoever was there got transported either through a drug high, a romp with a cheap whore, or a police wagon down to the station.

So what was Margot doing there?

Then again, Besson's own men would never have thought to look for her there. They'd distributed a fax and email to the regular hotel chains, asking for a phone call from the front desk if someone fitting the description checked in or out. Besson leaned forward in his seat and glanced up the building. Eight stories of crime. He supposed it was as good a hiding place as any. Perhaps this woman had more experience with this sort of thing than he realized.

He was still unnerved by the way they'd arrived at the location. True to his word in the cemetery, Corbin had directed him right to the spot. Eyes closed as if listening to spoken instructions only he could hear, Corbin whispered the directions. *Left. Right. Straight for a while. Now left.* When his eyes opened and he pronounced that they'd arrived, they were at the back of L'Avion. He'd pointed up to one of the higher floors.

"She's up there," he said.

"How do you know?"

Corbin had shrugged. "I just know. And, to be honest, I don't want to think about how I know. Drive us around the front."

Besson had done as asked, and then waited patiently. But he'd also reached some conclusions about how Corbin had pulled off his little parlor trick. And made a decision on what to do about it.

He picked up his phone and placed a call. It rang four times before someone picked it up.

"I'll be coming soon," he said. "He's not going to be easy. You'll need a few guys to hold him."

"We will be ready," said a voice.

Besson began to say more, but the line went dead. He looked up and saw Corbin and a woman he didn't recognize step out from the motel doors. His first thought was that he'd found a prostitute with information and brought her along. But as they got closer, he realized his mistake. It was Margot. The bleached out, short hair, biker clothes and heavy makeup had fooled him, and he'd had the benefit of expecting to see her walk with Corbin. His guys on the lookout for her wouldn't have stood a chance.

Corbin opened the back door for her and they both climbed in. The door was barely shut before Besson pulled away from the curb.

"Corbin said you can be trusted," she said from the backseat. "Is that right?"

"I should ask you the same question," Besson countered, trying not to give anything away with his eyes. "I'm not the one wearing a disguise."

"I'm not the one helping Les Fantômes, a bunch of sadistic murderers."

"That's rich coming from a member of the Tacho R'asa. If you think for a second that—"

"Enough," Corbin yelled, loud enough that they both fell silent. Besson switched lanes and then took a right down a secondary road. "I told you, the Fantômes have his wife and daughter."

"That's great. So he hands us over and he gets his family back?"

"They sent my daughter's ear to me in a box," Besson said, keeping his voice flat, not trusting that he'd be able to get the words out without losing it. "Alexis knows I will never forgive this. They are going to kill my wife and my little girl. No matter what I do for them." Margot rocked back in her seat. Besson glanced up at the rearview and met her eye.

"Our interests align," Corbin said. "I have a plan, but I need Besson to bring the Fantômes along for the ride."

"And in return?" she asked.

"In return, if the plan works, Alexis and all the Fantômes die and his wife and daughter go free," he said.

"We're talking like a one-in-a-million chance we can pull this off, right?" she asked.

"It's better than the hundred percent certainty that Alexis will kill my family," Besson shot back. "I know him. My family is dead unless I get to him first."

"His allegiance isn't with us, but it is against the Fantômes," Corbin said. "That will have to be enough."

"I still think it's a mistake," she said. "How do we know he's not taking us to them right now? I saw him on the phone when we walked out. Who were you talking to?"

Besson liked this woman. He realized he'd expected her to be cowering and timid, overwhelmed by the danger she was in. Instead, she was bold and aggressive. And smart. She looked at him with cold contempt. And he knew he deserved it.

"I'm not taking you to the Fantômes," he said gently. "On that, Corbin is correct. But I'm not taking you where he expected to go either."

"What the hell are you talking about?" Corbin asked.

"There's something you need to do before we can go any further. Someone you need to meet." He cocked the hammer back on his SIG Sauer and showed it to his passengers. "And I don't want any complaints."

35

C orbin clenched his teeth together until his jaw ached. He'd known trusting Besson had been a risk from the beginning. But he thought the promise of rescuing his family was a strong enough incentive. Obviously, he'd been wrong.

The cost of his mistake struck him over and over like a whip scourging his flesh. Bile rose in his throat. His limbs shook. Besson didn't understand. If the chance of getting Rose back slipped through his fingers, it'd be like losing her all over again. Corbin couldn't handle that. Even with the insanity he'd been subjected to over the past two days, losing his daughter again would put him in a padded cell. Or have him sucking on the end of a shotgun, his toes fumbling for the trigger.

"We had a deal," Corbin snarled.

Besson didn't respond, which made it all the worse. He just drove as if he were alone in the car.

Corbin clawed at the doors. Locked. And he couldn't manually override the controls. He beat his hands against the glass until his palms stung, the panic rising. Margot pulled on his shoulder, and when he twisted around he had the bizarre impulse to bite at her like an animal. She backed away from him, eyes wide with shock.

"There's something wrong with him," Margot said.

"I know," Besson said, taking a corner hard.

"You don't know shit," Corbin said, leaning forward. Images flashed in his head of what he should do next. Lunge for the gun. Or for Besson. Maybe grab Besson's face and gouge the man's eyes, forcing his index fingers into the sockets up to the middle knuckle.

Kill him or you'll never see your little girl again, the voice inside him shouted.

"Shut up!" Corbin yelled. "Just shut up and let me handle this."

When he looked up at Margot, the shock on her face registered that he'd said the words out loud. He hadn't meant to. It was supposed to be only in his head. All in his head.

"I've got to see her ... don't you see? This is my chance ... I have to get her back ..."

"Who?" Margot asked. "Get who back?"

"Almost there," Besson said from the front seat.

A buzzing sound rose up all around him. The world vibrated, washing out their voices.

"He's gone pale. Sweating." It was Margot talking, but there was an echo to her voice. Even so, she sounded concerned. "Was he sick before?"

Then he felt like something picked him up and tried to snap him in half. Every muscle in his back spasmed. His legs thrashed.

"Oh shit, I think he's having a seizure. What am I supposed to do?"

Corbin heard the words, but they were distant and tinny, like voices on a weak radio band barely audible through static. His mind churned, confused at what was happening, panicked by the idea of losing Rose again, reeling from Besson's betrayal.

But then a single thought rang out in his head, silencing everything else.

Kill him.

Corbin rebelled at the idea. It wasn't his voice that had said the words, so it couldn't have been his thought. But it felt so right, so much like truth. A command with the certainty of scripture behind it. The longer it lingered, the more it seemed the only obvious solution.

Kill him.

What about the gun? he asked in his mind.

The voice came back quickly with its answer.

Do you forget my gift to you? My blood is in your blood. You will heal. Fear nothing.

Kill him. Do it for me.

Perhaps without the last two words, Corbin might have launched himself at Besson, absorbing a gunshot at worst and forcing the car into a crash. But the words, *for me,* sparked something inside of him. He called out the demon inside him by name.

Gregor.

In answer, a sheering pain exploded inside his head. He felt like one of his eyes might have popped out of its socket and was dangling out of his head on the end of a strand of bloody nerves. He even fumbled his fingers up the side of his cheek, ready to grab it and shove it back home.

But there was no eye there. Just pain unlike anything he'd ever endured.

Attached to the pain was the insatiable need to kill Besson.

"Help me, Chey," he heard himself scream, his voice sounding impossibly foreign to him. "Together, child. We can kill him."

Pain flared through every muscle and they all seized together in a massive cramp. He cried out and he felt Margot's hands hold him down. Where their skin touched, it scalded him like she was a creature made of fire. He bucked and shoved her back.

The car squealed to a stop. Neither he nor Margot had seat belts on and they flew forward and then smashed backward.

When Corbin twisted his body into a sitting position, his first thought was that he'd completely lost his mind.

As he watched, the world pulled away from him like a rubber band being stretched out. He was still in Besson's car. Still in the backseat. But the distance between him and Besson stretched out until it seemed like he was forty or fifty feet away. The front seat was only a pinprick of light in the distance. Everything else around him was black, like he was looking through the wrong end of a telescope, the image at the end impossibly small and far away.

He supposed the thing ought to have scared him, but it didn't. In fact, he felt a strange sense of comfort, as if the darkness was a blanket put there by a kind stranger. He remembered the same feeling in those months after Rose died. The cool, sweet darkness the drugs and the booze provided, that refuge in a world where his little girl wasn't dead, where she hadn't wasted away before his eyes until she was a skeleton with thin, pale skin, where she hadn't squeezed his hand and asked him to let her die so the pain would go away.

Somehow he knew that all he had to do was close his eyes and even the postage stamp-sized scene of the car interior could be gone. If he just stopped fighting, he could let Gregor, or whatever part of Gregor that had crawled into him through his blood, take over. And he wouldn't have to worry about anything.

He felt the promise in that. Felt that maybe Gregor was a better choice to run things for a while anyway. If the cost of seeing Rose alive again was to deliver what Mariyana needed, then who better to get it for her than Gregor?

Margot's voice rose up around him like a windstorm raging in his head. "Fight it. Stay in control."

Don't listen to her. Give me control so I can kill him.

It's the only way you'll see your daughter again.

Give me your body. Give me permission.

Before he could do anything, a searing pain exploded on his cheek. He traveled down the black corridor in a rush, reentering the brightness of the real world with such speed that he thought he might throw up.

He looked up just in time to see Margot rear back for a second slap. Something in his eyes must have changed because she stopped in mid-swing.

"He's back," she said. "You're back."

Corbin gasped for air like someone just coming up from water. He was disoriented, but only for a second. The dark shadow rose up again inside his mind and a cold shiver passed through him. He knew that shadow, and he feared it.

"Knock ... knock me ..." He couldn't catch his breath.

"What? What is it?"

"Knock me out," he said finally.

Margot had a bewildered look on her face, but then Besson leaned in from the front seat, the butt of the SIG Sauer cocked back and ready to strike.

"Best idea you've had all day."

"No, wait," Margot shouted, but it was too late. Besson's hand came down. There was a flash of pain, and then everything went dark.

36

In the nothingness, a presence waited for him.

Corbin's eyes were open, but the darkness was so absolute it didn't matter. Even without his sight, he knew the thing was there. He knew it in his bones the way you feel a storm approach from over a horizon.

Wind whipped up around him. A howling rose from above.

"Show yourself," he shouted.

The wind grew, whistling past him, harder and harder until he had to lean into it to keep from falling. The sounds of the storm were all around him now, but something had changed. It wasn't only wind. It was the sonic force of thousands of voices, hundreds of thousands. Screaming. Wailing.

Within the cacophony were individual sounds. Voices filled with pain and terror.

Then there was something next to him. Not only did he sense it there, but he smelled it. A wave of putrescence, like decayed meat and rotten blood. He gagged but nothing came up as he retched. "Open your eyes," a voice hissed in his ear. It sounded like it could be Gregor, but he wasn't certain.

"They are open," he shouted. The wind picked up intensity. Debris hit his face. Clumps of dirt and leaves. He sensed the thing circle around him. It occurred to him that he needed to run. That if he didn't run, he was going to die right where he stood. But no matter how hard he tried, he couldn't make his body do what he wanted. He bucked and kicked, but his legs wouldn't move.

"I mean truly open them," the voice came. It was Gregor. He was sure of it now. "See the world as it could be. See it as it should be."

Even though he knew that his eyes were already open, assaulted by the wind and debris, he suddenly understood there was another layer available to him. A second set of eyes. These were the ones the voice was talking about. Slowly, he lifted the lids as he was instructed, awash with an incredulous feeling that he'd had this extra set of eyes his entire life and had never noticed them before.

Harsh red light poured in. He held up a hand to block it.

"Open them!" Gregor boomed.

A gust of wind violently spun him around and he opened his eyes wide. At first, it was like looking directly at the sun and he thought the light would burn right through him, leaving two perfect, round holes gaping in the back of his head.

But his new eyes adjusted. When the pain ebbed, he saw what Gregor's true plan really was. In the vision, a wasteland of pain and death spread out in front of him. An army swarmed through the streets of Paris, killing everything in its path. Fires burned. Blood ran in rivers. The chaos and the violence roared through the streets like floodwater, devouring everything. But it was the sight of the soldiers that made him think he might lose his mind. That made him wish the light had burned out his corneas and blinded him. He wanted to shut his eyes, but somehow he knew the vision would still be there if he did.

"Now you understand," Gregor shouted next to him. "Now you see my destiny."

He turned to look at Gregor, mustering the courage to confront him. To tell him he was insane. But when he turned, the words caught in his throat.

It was Gregor next to him, but not as he'd seen him before. The skin was flayed from his body, exposing the meat and blood and bone. His groin was a grotesque area of hacked flesh, oozing a black fluid. But it was the face that made Corbin's throat constrict until he thought he might never breathe again. The skin here hadn't been neatly peeled back like on the rest of his body. Here the flesh was torn in ragged lines as if clawed over and over by an animal, or with a butcher's hook. One of the eyes was gone, leaving only a straggle of connective tissue protruding from the socket. The other eye bulged out, next to the hole where there was once a nose, staring at Corbin with manic intensity.

"I will do it," Gregor said, pointing to the landscape in front of them. "I will avenge my tribe. And you will play your part if you want to see your little girl again."

"No," Corbin said. "I ... no ... I won't ..."

"Daddy!"

The word cut through him. Every other emotion blinked out of existence as pure love and the absolute pain of losing that love filled him. It wasn't just the word. It was the voice. The voice he thought he'd never hear again.

"Rose! Baby, I'm here," he cried out. "Where are you?"

"Daddy!" This time the voice was scared. It was the voice from the other room when a nightmare had woken her up. The voice when she thought she was alone in the house even though he and Heather were in the next room. When Heather had explained to her how sick she really was, and she'd turned to him as if he could make it go away. "Daddy. I'm scared!"

Then he turned and saw her. He clutched his chest as a thousand blades of ice plunged into him.

She was in a hospital bed, the same one she'd died in. But she wasn't in the hospital gown and she didn't look sick. Her blonde hair flowed to her shoulders. Her blue eyes twinkled as if she knew a secret no one else did. The bedsheet was off and she wore a yellow dress with little blue flowers. Her favorite dress. The one they'd buried her in.

She turned to him, tears streaming down her cheeks. "Daddy, it hurts. Make it stop. Pleeease. They're coming for me. They always come for me."

He strained to run to her, but he couldn't move. "Who, baby? Who's coming?"

Then, to his horror, dark shadows appeared around the bed. They wore tattered doctor's coats and surgical scrubs, ripped and covered with dirt and filth. What was under the clothes was worse. Emaciated limbs, like corpses found after a year of decay. Skulls with shrunken eyes that inexplicably glowed red. Jaws that opened and shut like possessed dolls.

"Leave her alone!" he screamed.

But they weren't going to leave her alone. They set upon her, pinning down her arms and legs, ripping her pretty dress from her body, showing her raw skin, red from the radiation therapy burns. The ghoul-doctors stabbed her arms with IV needles, blood spurting into the air from the punctured veins before being attached to bags of poison to pump into his little girl's body. Rose fought back, she always fought, until the very, very end when she'd quietly asked him if she could please stop. But this wasn't the end, it was the brutal middle. The part where Rose screamed and pleaded, begging her mom and dad to stop letting the strangers hurt her. As she kicked and shrieked, clots of her hair fell out, piling up around her neck. More and more fell off, until she was bald again. Her cheeks sank in. Her eyes turned hollow. Corbin tried with everything he had to go to her, but he couldn't. He was helpless. So fucking helpless.

"Why did you let them do this to me?" she said. "Did I do something wrong? I'm sorry. For whatever I did, I'm sorry."

His body heaved with sobs, tears obscuring everything. "You didn't do anything wrong. I'm sorry, baby. I'm so sorry. Daddy's going to make it right again. I promise."

He blinked and she was back in her yellow dress again. Her complexion pink and alive. Blonde hair back in place.

But there was still something wrong. Her eyes still held on to his, terrible panic in them.

"They're coming for me again, Daddy. They always come for me."

The ghouls came again. Reaching out and ripping her dress. Descending on her like vultures on carrion.

That's when he knew. He was face to face with his daughter's afterlife. Locked in eternal torment, an endless cycle of the torture that had killed her.

"I'm going to make it right again. I promise!" he shouted, trying to get her to hear him above the sound of her own screams. "I promise."

Gregor's face was in front of his own, blocking his view. The putrid smell of his black flesh cutting into his senses. "Then keep your promise to me. No matter what happens."

Something slapped his face and Gregor vibrated like a television transmission going out.

"Keep your promise."

Another slap across the face and suddenly he felt like he was thirty feet in the air, looking down into a hole at Gregor and his little girl on her hospital bed.

"Rose!" he cried out, just as a wave of water crashed over him.

He sat up, sputtering and gagging. Disoriented, he swung around, but strong hands held him down.

"Easy," Besson said. "You're all right."

Corbin tried to pull in the loose strands of the million thoughts going through his mind. He was soaking wet. Besson held an empty bucket which explained that. He was in a dark room with old stone walls. It was musty, like a cellar. Margot stood against the wall, looking at him with questioning eyes filled with undeniable sadness. He wondered what part of his vision he'd acted out loud for everyone in the room. He was about to ask her when he noticed Margot's hands were tied in front of her.

He wanted to demand from Besson what was going on, but the images of Rose in her bed washed back over him. He crumbled from the inside, like a hollowed-out thing suddenly unable to support its own weight. Bent over at the middle, he sobbed just as he had at his little girl's bedside a lifetime ago. The day he'd said good-bye to her forever.

No, not forever. He had a way to bring her back. He'd made a deal.

A woman's voice spoke up from behind him. It rasped and slithered through the air like a serpent.

"But a deal with the devil," she said, "is no deal at all."

37

Corbin turned to see the source of the voice. Standing by rough hewn stone stairs that led from the room above, stood a nun. She was ancient, bent over and hunched so that she had to crane her neck upward to look at him, a posture that reminded him suddenly of the first time he'd seen Gregor in the alley. One of her bony hands gripped a walking stick while the other teased divine favor out of a rosary. Her garb wasn't noteworthy, just the simple black habit made of serge fabric pleated at the neck and draping to the ground. A white coif covered with a thin layer of black crepe. A silver cross hung from her neck. Corbin wasn't Catholic, so he had none of the associations some had with nuns, both good and bad, but as he watched the woman cross the room toward him, a shiver passed through him.

She smiled as if acknowledging her effect on him. "Did you hear me?"

He didn't answer. All he could do was stare into the woman's face. It was wrinkled and blotchy with age, yet the beautiful woman that was once there was clearly evident. High, proud cheekbones. A slender, inquisitive face. Eyes that shone as if with a fever. He understood viscerally that this woman possessed power to be reckoned with.

"My name is Sister Agnes," she said. Her English was nearly perfect, only a trace of a French accent on the vowels. "I am a friend."

"I've heard that from a few people recently," he said, glaring at Besson. "I thought we had a deal."

"Like you have one with Gregor?" Besson asked.

On reflex, Corbin looked at Margot, but she wouldn't meet his eye. Somehow she knew too.

The old nun clucked her tongue at Besson as if scolding a child. "Just as you have an agreement with Les Fantômes de la Nuit," the nun said softly to Besson. The man looked away, embarrassed. "There is no innocence in this room."

"Except yourself, I suppose?" Margot said, finally speaking up.

The nun threw back her head and laughed. It was deep and throaty, as if two layers of bass had been added to it from some hidden speakers in the room. It didn't belong to the body in front of them. Each instinctively recoiled from the old woman.

She smiled at Margot. "No, I'm afraid we are a company of sinners here. Myself included. Myself most of all, perhaps."

"Why are her hands tied?" Corbin demanded. Any fogginess was clearing as he pieced together their situation. He spun on Besson. "Are you handing us over to Alexis?"

Besson began to answer, but Sister Agnes held up her hand. Surprisingly, the big man remained silent. The nun didn't seem surprised at all by his obedience.

"I can help you, if you'd like," she said softly. She tapped the side of her head. "I know what's going on in there. I know what you saw before you woke up."

"How could you possibly——"

"She's not in that hospital bed," she said. "Your daughter. She's not there, and you shouldn't believe that she is."

He felt his legs weaken, the image of Rose, the sound of her screams, rising inside him again. "You can't know that. Not for certain."

"The devil knows our weaknesses, child. And perhaps we were born imperfect so he might exploit them. But we're not required to allow him to take advantage." She leaned toward him, her face close to his. "Search yourself. You must know it's true. You saw what the devil Gregor has planned. It cannot be allowed."

Corbin shut his eyes tight and he saw the scenes again from when he'd first opened his inner eye on the glowing red world which Gregor controlled. He'd felt like he was looking at a prophesy. With Gregor standing in the center of it all, somehow Corbin knew it was possible.

"He has the ability to do it, doesn't he?" Corbin whispered, willing to accept that this strange little woman had somehow seen the same vision of Gregor's plan. He felt like knowing what Gregor intended had pushed his sanity to the very edge. Saying it aloud might just send him all the way over.

"Are you talking about his revenge on the world, or his promise to raise your little girl from the dead?" Sister Agnes said, her voice stern as if reprimanding a boy caught stealing from the Church poor box.

From the wall behind him, Margot stifled a groan. Corbin felt a wash of guilt, but also panic that he was about to lose his chance to save his daughter. If they knew, they wouldn't follow him back to the catacombs. Besson wouldn't deliver Alexis and the Fantômes, albino blood Gregor needed for his final plan. Margot would run again. Gregor needed her blood so that he could be restored.

"No ... no ... you have it all wrong," he stammered. "I don't really believe ... I was playing along so ..."

"You can't lie," Sister Agnes said. "I can see in you and through you."

Corbin felt that terrible shadow rise up in his mind. The world dimmed as if the lights had been turned down. Gregor's presence pushed forward and a stab of pain shot right behind Corbin's eye as the voice exploded in his head.

Don't listen to her. She's as blind as her dead God.

Kill her. Kill her with your bare hands.

Or you'll never see your daughter again.

"I can help you," Sister Agnes whispered. "But you have to ask me to."

Kill her!

Sink your teeth into her neck and rip out her throat.

"I've got ... Rose ... she needs me ..." Corbin looked over the nun's shoulder at Margot. She was pressed up against the wall, her tied hands to her mouth. Body shaking. "You don't understand. I can get her back."

"Daddy?" The voice came out of Sister Agnes, but it was a voice he knew in an instant. A voice he once was able to pick out of a crowded room filled with screaming kids. But now the only screaming was in his head as the last scraps of sanity were stripped away. "Daddy, it's me."

Corbin fell to his knees, suddenly without energy to stand, barely enough to breathe. The shadow inside of him retreated, cowering. "You're fooling me," he said. "Somehow you ... you know her voice. Stop it. It's too much."

"Daddy, it's me. It's your Rose."

Corbin's body convulsed in a choking sob at the name. There was no way the nun could have known the name. But still he didn't want to believe. He steeled himself against it. "Ms. Agnes said you're sad. She said you needed my help so you don't do something bad."

Corbin somehow managed to lift his head. He didn't want to see his daughter's voice come out of the old woman, but he had to see if it really was her. He had to see whether he saw his sunshine somehow in the nun's eyes.

"Oh baby," he cried out when he looked. It was her, it was his little girl. With a thousand years of time he couldn't have explained how he knew, but he knew. "I love you, honey. I miss you. Every day I miss you."

"I miss you too. And Mommy. But it's nice here. I'm all right."

He caught movement against the far wall. It was Margot, hands to her face, tears streaming. Besson's mouth hung open, and he made the sign of the cross. Corbin turned back to Ms. Agnes, somehow seeing his daughter staring back at him from inside the woman's eyes.

"I'm going to come get you," Corbin said. "I'm coming for you, and we can all be together again. Me, you and Mommy. OK?"

Sister Agnes reached out an old, liver-spotted hand, but Corbin knew it was his little girl reaching out for him. He took her hand and held it.

"I don't want to come back," she said. "I know more than you now. People who come back are … are … wrong." He felt a shudder pass through the nun's body. "Promise me, Daddy. You won't let them bring me back. You have to promise me."

"I can … I can't promise … I miss you … I can't …"

"Please, let me stay. Promise me."

Corbin couldn't. Promising meant he would lose her all over again. He shook his head. He remembered the pain too clearly from the last time. The way his world rotted and withered around him afterward. The black, empty hole he'd carried with him. How everything lost its flavor, its texture, its promise. In the end, there was nothing but the pain and, later, the loneliness that came after he'd chased away everyone else in his life. He couldn't do it. Not again. "I'm going to bring you back. I'm going to fix this," he said.

"If you bring something back to life, it won't be me. And it won't be life," she said. "Do you love me?"

"Of course."

"Then you have to leave me here. Anything else hurts me. And it will hurt you too."

"But what if––"

"Daddy, I've seen it too. I know what he plans to do. And besides …" the old nun smiled and Corbin swore it was Rose's smile. "It's so beautiful here. I want to stay. Please. Promise me."

Finally, he nodded. A simple gesture, but one that took every bit of his strength. His body shook and tears ran freely. "I promise," he whispered. "I promise to let you rest."

"Thank you, Daddy," she said. She patted the top of his hand, a gesture he remembered doing to her a thousand times in the hospital. Only now he was the one who felt like he was dying.

He clutched at her. "I don't know what to do now," he said, choking on the words.

"Yes, you do," she said. "You stop him from winning. The one inside you. Ms. Agnes can help. You can trust her. I've seen her on the inside."

He bowed his head and nodded. "I love you, Rosebud," he said.

"Because I'm your boo-tiful sunshine."

"Yes. For always."

The woman's hand pulled away and he let it slip from his. When he looked up into the nun's eyes, his little girl was gone. He wrapped both arms across his stomach to brace himself. Margot stepped toward him, but Besson held her back.

"She's at peace, Corbin. You heard the child," Sister Agnes said, her voice once again her own.

Corbin closed his eyes and rocked back and forth, letting the pain of losing his little girl wash over him and then through him. It came at him in torrents, but he held on. Just barely.

He felt the nun's hand on his shoulder. When he looked up, she smiled at him.

"Will you let me help you?"

The shadow in him screamed and cursed, but Corbin was numb to it. He nodded once. "Get him out of me."

She stood up in front of him, her shoulders square, jaw set. "You need to prepare yourself," she said, the gentle tone replaced by something half steel and half menace. "This won't be pleasant."

38

Margot sat in a kitchen chair, drawing on her cigarette. A yell came from the cellar door and she tried to ignore it, but her hands trembled the next time she lifted her cigarette to her lips.

"Can I have one of those?" Besson asked, walking into the room.

She slid the pack across the table to him as he sat down. He pulled out a smoke, lit it and took a long drag. He sighed as he exhaled through his mouth and nose. "Haven't had one of these in ten or eleven years. Not sure why I ever stopped."

"So you wouldn't die?"

Besson laughed. "I guess so. Mostly it was Giselle, my wife. She wanted me to stop. So I stopped."

"Simple as that?"

"She didn't ask nicely," Besson said. "You've never met my wife," he added, sliding the pack back across the table.

Margot pulled another out, lighting it with the butt of her last one. She rubbed her wrists where the bindings had chaffed her skin. She still wasn't happy about Besson tying her hands when they first arrived. He'd apologized for the precaution later, but it still grated on her. At least he'd removed them once Corbin and the nun had asked them to leave the basement. That had been over an hour ago.

She nodded toward the cellar door. "Where'd you find her?"

"That's a long story."

"I doubt it."

Besson's eyes narrowed. "Why do you say that?"

"Any story can be short if you figure it out. People only say it's a long story when they don't want to talk about something."

"How'd you get away from the Tacho R'asa?"

"It's a long story," she said, giving him a weak smile. "See how it works?"

Another cry came from the cellar. The door rattled like a wind had blown up from the room below. A puff of dust blew out from under the door as if the house had just exhaled. Besson and Margot both stared at it for a beat, but when the door remained closed, they turned back to one another.

"Are you sure she's all right?"

Besson laughed. "I'd worry about Corbin." He leaned forward and took a deep breath. "There was a woman in my neighborhood, years ago. She says a demon is in her head, telling her to do terrible things. Most people ignore her, but even then I lived in a world where demons existed and the dead could walk again, so I paid attention. I visited the house the next day and found the door open. I go in and the front room is littered with corpses."

"Her family?"

"Dogs. Some cats too, but mostly dogs. It was like she'd rounded up every pet in the area and then taken a knife to them. All of them were gutted, their organs piled into the corner. And that's where the woman sat. Playing in them like a child. Laughing the whole time." Besson blew a cloud of smoke and stared at it for a few moments as if contemplating its shape. "I was raised Catholic, so I went to Father Simone at my church telling him that a demon had taken possession of the woman. He laughed at me, calling me an idiot for believing in such things."

"The Catholic Church recognizes demons and exorcisms."

"Many priests feel it is a hangover from a more superstitious age. They're embarrassed by it."

"So you found Sister Agnes instead."

"No, she came to me. She never told me how, but I suspect she has ears throughout the city listening in churches and confessional booths on her behalf. She told me that nuns cannot perform the rites of exorcism, but that she knew rituals older than those of the church. I didn't believe her. Not really. But I had nothing to lose. So I brought her to the house.

"As we approached, we heard terrible wailing coming from inside, a sound unlike anything I'd ever heard before. There were people in the streets, but not too close to the house. This was an immigrant community, mostly African. As we walked through the crowd, I saw talismans and charms from the old country. Many of the elders stepped back from Sister Agnes as she walked by, making signs with their hands to ward off evil.

"For her part, she never slowed down. We walked side by side through the crowd, but then she took the lead ahead of me, up the steps and straight into the house. The animal bodies were stacked in a circle in the middle of the room, so many of them that the circle came up to my waist. The woman stood in the middle of the circle, naked and smeared with blood and organs. She smiled when we walked in, her wails finally stopping. And then ..."

Besson stopped and smoked his cigarette. Margot let him be, seeing that he was having difficulty telling the story. But as the silence grew longer, she worried that he meant to simply end the story there. "And then what?" she finally prompted.

"It's a long story," he said, his expression half grimace and half smile. "Hours later, we emerged with the woman. Every inch of my body was bruised. Sister Agnes cradled a broken arm and had her leg bound where it'd been ripped open. But when we came out, the woman's husband ran to her. She looked up and called him by name in her own voice. The crowd didn't cheer, but they closed in around the man and wife, surrounding them and pulling them away from Sister Agnes."

"They still didn't trust her? After she helped one of their own?"

Besson shook his head. "They knew, just like I think you know, there's something different about her. Something inside of her that's not quite ..."

"Human?"

Besson pursed his lips and thought. "Not the right word, but close, I think. He snubbed out his cigarette butt and gestured whether he might have another. She slid the pack across to him. "I feel like there is something else bothering you," she said.

Besson shrugged. "I worry about having an ally who is willing to fight against her own kind."

"They are not my kind," Margot said. She glared at the pack of cigarettes, as if thinking about snatching it back from him for asking the question. "My mother fled when I was eight. My father paid the price for our freedom. Who are you to judge me? A man who bows down before those animals Les Fantômes? Evil comes in many forms, Inspector Besson. I'd say a man who abuses trust for his own ends is one of the worst kind there is."

Besson didn't take the bait. He remained calm, contemplative even. "I do what I do for my wife and daughter. I did Alexis's bidding to protect them, nothing else. Now that he has them, and because I know he will kill them no matter what I do, I'm willing to risk everything on this crazy idea your friend has. My reason for being here is clear. What's yours?"

She didn't answer right away. There was no accusation in the man's voice, no malice. Only curiosity. She leaned back in her chair, realizing it was a fair question. One worth answering, if not for him, then for herself. "I want to sleep without nightmares," she said quietly. "I want to live without the guilt of knowing what the R'asa does and not doing something to stop it. Is that a good enough reason for you?"

"No," Besson said, pushing the cigarettes back to her. "But that doesn't matter. It just needs to be good enough for you."

The door to the cellar opened and they both jumped. Sister Agnes walked out, a thin smile on her lips. She said nothing, but walked to the table, pulled Margot's cigarette from her hand and took a long drag.

"It is done," she said.

"Where is he?"

"Here," Corbin said, coming up the stairs. His shirt was soaked through with sweat and his hair stuck out in all directions.

"You look like shit," Besson said.

Corbin went to the kitchen sink, turned on the faucet and drank mouthful after mouthful of water. Margot stood and handed him a towel. As he took it and dried his mouth, she grabbed a knife from the counter and sliced his forearm.

"Damn!" he shouted, glaring at her. "What the hell are you doing?"

She watched blood trickle from the wound and drip down his arm. He covered it with the towel but she yanked his hand down. He looked like he was about to object again, when it must have occurred to him what she was doing.

He held up the small surface wound for them all to see. The seconds ticked by and still the blood beaded up and slid down to his elbow, some even dripping onto the floor. Finally, Margot was satisfied. "Sorry," she mumbled, handing him another clean towel. "Just had to be sure."

Corbin covered the cut and dabbed at it. Ms. Agnes motioned for him to get her a drink of water.

"It was only a small part of a spirit, a mere fraction given in blood," Sister Agnes said. "But it's power ... it was like nothing I'd seen before."

Corbin turned to Sister Agnes. "Those things I said to you down there. I don't––"

"It wasn't you," she said. "And, to be honest, the threats weren't particularly creative. I've been through worse, Mr. Stewart."

"But thank you. For this. For Rose."

Sister Agnes smiled. "I didn't have much choice in the matter. Your daughter's spirit was very strong. She was going to speak to you whether I invited her in or not." She ground the butt of her cigarette into the ashtray on the table. "I believe the three of you have business to discuss. I will leave you as that part is none of my concern."

"But we could use your help," Margot said. "Someone with your abilities––"

"My abilities are very specific, my dear," the old nun said. "And not what you need."

"Margot's right," Corbin said. "You know what we're up against. You know the evil both the R'asa and the Fantômes represent. You won't help us?"

Sister Agnes crossed the floor to him, her hunched, tortured gait making it several long seconds for her to make the transit. Once there, she took his hand in her own and squeezed it. "There are others I'm meant to help."

"Coward," Besson said. The word came out like a projectile, and Sister Agnes flinched. "How can you turn away from this when you know what we face?"

Sister Agnes turned to him. Margot expected to see anger on her face but instead there was only sadness. "Because whether I come with you or not," she said, "you're going to fail. And when you fail, I'm afraid you're all going to die."

39

Alexis looked impatiently up and down the deserted alley. The phone call from Besson had been cryptic, as if he'd been standing near people whom he didn't want overhearing their plans to meet. That annoyed him. How hard was it to steal away to a quiet space to speak freely?

It also made him suspicious, which was why he had armed men hidden in the windows around them.

Ever since he'd taken the woman and little girl hostage, Besson had been erratic. Alexis considered that kidnapping the man's family might have been a tactical error on his part. Once this was over, the man would hold a grudge. He would never be able to trust Besson again. There would always be the child without an ear and a wife missing a finger clouding their relationship.

He felt the bulge in his pocket where he'd put the wrapped up finger to give to Besson as a present for taking too long to find Margot Vinci. At least Besson could serve a purpose for a while longer. Until Alexis ran out of body parts to deliver.

He was frustrated things had progressed so slowly. After years of effort and planning, he felt like the great battle was nearly at hand, the final confrontation with the Tacho R'asa. But things had stalled,

and he sensed the opportunity fading. He couldn't let that happen.
He'd sacrificed too much. Seen too many of his friends die in the
service of their mission.

And killed too many innocents for it all to have been pointless.

This was the time for him to take risks, even if those risks meant
his own death. He always expected that his journey would end with
his own sacrifice to the cause. When he was a younger man, he'd
been tough and certain that it was an honor to die for the cause, a
privilege granted to those only with the greatest purity of heart. As
he'd ascended to leadership, he'd learned to recognize this idea for
what it was: necessary propaganda for those young men under him to
look death head-on when it was required. Still, some of the old teach-
ings remained in him and he saw death, especially one necessary to
annihilate the R'asa, not as something to dread, but a worthy end.
Surely, if the option presented itself, he preferred to live. There were
things he wanted to do. Places to see. A life to live outside of his
mission, if it came to pass that he could vanquish his enemies.

Then again, there would always be an enemy. Perhaps not one
with a depth of evil equal to that of the R'asa. Not one with the direct
personal connection to him and his people. But his homeland was
replete with atrocities. Men did not need the supernatural to be evil;
demons came in military uniforms, in the guise of warlords with AK-
47s and even machete-wielding child soldiers. No, there would be no
lack of enemies if he survived the coming battle. But Alexis didn't want
to think about that. He just wanted the final confrontation to begin.

Besson's car pulled slowly around the corner of the deserted alley
and came to a stop. The engine remained on, and Besson didn't get
out of the car for several long seconds. Alexis squinted, trying to see
what the man was doing behind the wheel. He seemed to be staring
at him, eyes fixed in an expression Alexis couldn't read. He wished
he'd brought one of his hostages with him for the meeting. The man
might need a reminder of what was at stake if he acted rashly.

The door opened and the big man climbed out. Alexis relaxed.
Besson looked to be broken. His swaggering step was a slow shuffle.

His shoulders hunched forward. As he came closer, flanked by two of the Fantômes who had their guns trained on him, Alexis saw the dead expression in his eyes. This look he had seen many times before in his adversaries. Absolute defeat.

"What took you so long?" Alexis said.

"I did as you asked. I have both the Americans, Corbin and the woman, Margot."

Alexis felt his heartbeat quicken. He looked over the man's shoulder at the car. There didn't appear to be anyone in the backseat. "Where are they?"

"I want to see my wife and daughter," Besson said. "I want to see that they are still alive."

Alexis raised his hand to strike and Besson cowered, turning his head but not raising a hand to protect himself. Liking the reaction, Alexis held his hand back. "You disappoint me, Besson. This was not the arrangement."

Besson dropped to his knees. "Please. Just let me see them. Corbin wants to work with you. He and the woman have a plan. It might just work."

"I don't need their plans," he said.

"Isn't it better to have them actively trying to help instead of running scared?" Besson said. "Even if you just pretend to be following their plan, you'll have better captives. Kill them after, I don't care. But you have to consider the opportunity here."

"I don't *have* to do anything," he said. "Just like I don't *have* to keep your family alive. Or you for that matter."

Besson dropped his hands to the street, bowing before Alexis. "Please, I'm asking you. Let me see them. Even if I look in a window just to see they're alive. That's all I ask."

Alexis smiled, enjoying the sense of power that swelled in his chest. "The proud Maurice Besson, groveling at my feet. I have to admit, I never thought I'd see this."

"I beg you."

"No, I don't think you are begging. Do you think he's begging?" he asked to the two men behind Besson. They laughed and shook their heads. "They don't think you're begging either. Try harder."

Besson hesitated, and Alexis thought for a second that the man's pride had caught up with him. If it did, it was only for a second. The man lowered himself until he was prone on the pavement and then crawled forward, sliding on his chest and stomach until he was at Alexis's feet. "Please. Please. I beg you."

"Bark like a dog," Alexis said. The men chuckled, enjoying the show. "I've always known you were a dog. Now I want to hear you bark like one."

Besson complied, making whimpering, barking noises.

"Louder!" Alexis said.

Besson barked louder as the men laughed. Finally, Alexis nudged him with one of his feet. "All right. Get up." Besson climbed to his feet, not bothering to wipe the dirt from the front of his suit. "I'm a reasonable man. I'll grant you a visit. But like you said, they will not see you. A look through a window. If you try to alert them that you're there, my man will cut off your wife's breasts. Understand?"

Besson nodded.

5"Good. Now," Alexis said, "tell me about this plan the American has. And how we're going to use it for our advantage."

40

C orbin pushed the curtain back and glanced out the window. Besson had been gone for over an hour, longer than he'd expected. He wondered whether waiting in the house was a mistake.

"Any sign?" Margot asked.

Corbin shook his head and slid the curtains back. He sat back at the kitchen table where a mounting pile of cigarette butts had built up in an ashtray. Margot lit another and offered one to him.

"No thanks. Those things will kill you."

She grinned. "If the gang of psychopathic albinos or the ancient sect of gypsy blood cultists don't get you first, right?"

"Something like that."

They sat in silence for a while, the only sound Margot's periodic exhalation of long streams of smoke.

"Do you think this will work?" he finally asked.

She shook her head. "No, not really."

There was no hesitation to her answer, and it took him by surprise. "Then why are you still here?"

"I've been sitting here asking myself the same thing. You have no idea how hard it's been to put all of this behind me. To build a normal life when I knew this is what existed back here."

"But still you came back to Paris," he said. "You didn't have to."

She glanced away as if being caught in something. "I know. But guilt isn't always from doing a thing. Knowing evil exists and doing nothing about it eats at you."

"Is that why you came back? To fight back?"

"Not even close," she said. "That makes me sound like I was brave. I think I hoped to prove my mother wrong. Over time, I thought my childhood memories were too fantastic to be real. Fictions of a little girl's mind fed by her mom's delusional paranoia. Ghost stories about the demons living underground in Paris? I mean, come on. When I first came back, I hoped it was all a lie. Or at least some kind of exaggeration. Maybe some weird cult that my parents had caught themselves up in. But nothing like their stories."

"But then Gregor contacted you," he prompted.

"On the first day I was in Paris. Like he knew I was coming."

Corbin thought about how he, with only a bit of Gregor's blood in him, had been able to sense exactly where she was. He imagined Gregor's sense must have been even more acute. He thought about explaining this to her, but decided against it.

"What did he say to you?"

"That he forgave my mother for leaving. That I had a family waiting for me. That I could choose for myself whether or not to return."

"You make him sound like a decent guy."

She shuddered at the table. "When I met him, memories came flooding back. Specific memories in the catacombs and the blood rituals. All pretense that perhaps my mother's stories were wrong or that my own memories were somehow exaggerated were gone the minute I sat down with him."

"But he let you leave."

She nodded. "I wasn't certain that he would. But he told me that his family wasn't held hostage, especially the last of his direct blood-line. He predicted that one day I would come back from the world and choose to join them. Perhaps when I was ill. Or if I had sick child who doctors could no longer help. I would return, he predicted, when I needed my family most."

"But now they need you," he said. "You understand why, don't you? You know why they want you so badly?"

She took a drag off her cigarette and the ashes fell. "They're bringing him back to life. Direct blood must be used. You didn't have enough of him in you, otherwise you wouldn't be sitting here with me. Your blood-drained body would be floating through the sewers of Paris right now."

Corbin saw headlights outside the window and got up to investigate. "That's a pleasant thought," he said, spying through the curtains at Besson's car pulling up. A second vehicle pulled in behind him.

"I'm not going to let them use my blood, though," she said. "If it comes down to it, I'll kill myself before I let that happen. You don't know what these people are capable of. What Gregor's end goal is."

"I think I have a pretty good idea," he said, trying to block out the vision he'd seen while Gregor's blood had boiled in his veins. "Revenge. On a massive scale."

"It's more than that," Margot whispered. "He wants punishment. For all the abuse done to the Roma over the centuries. The mass killings, the bigotry, the scapegoating, all of it. It doesn't even matter that the Tacho R'asa has been disavowed by the Roma, he seeks revenge for all of them. He blames the world and he will have his pound of flesh."

"And so he plans to set the world on fire," he said. "When he was ... inside me ... I saw his plan. I know what's at stake here."

"Then you know we may both need to die in order to stop him. Are you prepared for that?"

Corbin felt like he ought to turn and look her in the eye, but he couldn't bring himself to move away from the window. An ice bath cascaded down his back as he watched the pale men climb from the vehicles, Alexis among them. He flashed to the blood-soaked night in the alley, a night that felt like years ago when it had only been two nights before. So much of what Corbin knew about the world had changed in that little amount of time. Still, he felt like he knew evil when he saw it, and Alexis fit that bill. The saying came to him that the enemy of his enemy was his friend. He thought it might be just true enough to get the manpower he needed to make a move against Gregor.

The problem was that the enemy of his enemy was a murderous psychopath. As the men entered the house, Corbin just hoped his plan would work and that both Gregor and Alexis would get the gruesome deaths they deserved.

"Yes," he said, surprised at the sense of clarity he felt. "I am willing to die to stop them."

"I'm starting to feel like that's the best case scenario," she said. "But it's more likely that crazy nun will be right. We'll die *trying* to stop them."

Corbin shook his head, finally turning back to her. "That's not good enough. We have to win. And we will. Trust me."

Margot barked out a short laugh, but saw he was serious. She snubbed out her cigarette and reached for her pack. She shook it and then crumpled it in her hand and tossed it aside. "Out of cigs. Can't smoke so might as well save the world."

They both stood as the door opened and Besson and Alexis strode in.

"Might as well," Corbin agreed.

41

C orbin stepped back as the two men entered the room. The reaction made him feel weak, but it was an involuntary reaction. Alexis's pale, scarred face unnerved him, especially when the man's red-rimmed eyes bored into his, looking him up and down as if he were meat on a hook.

"I don't sense the filthy blood of the Tacho R'asa in you," he said. "Besson was telling the truth. The Catholic witch drained it from you." Alexis's nostrils flared and he turned his attention to Margot. "But the air in here still reeks of gypsy scum."

Corbin stepped between Margot and Alexis, but she didn't need his protection. She walked around the kitchen table, her eyes flashing with anger.

"Did you come here to insult me or to kill Gregor?"

"Maybe I came to kill you," Alexis said, licking his lips as his right hand appeared from under his clothes holding a curved knife.

"What point would that serve?" she asked, her voice sounding unsure for the first time.

Alexis rotated the knife in his hand. "My understanding is that you are Gregor's direct bloodline. If they are trying to raise up the bastard, they will need your blood to do it. If I kill you, then Gregor can't rise."

"If you kill her, you lose the chance to kill the Tacho R'asa," Corbin said. "Every single one of them."

Alexis kept his eyes on Margot. "Besson told me you have a plan."

"I do," Corbin said. "I've been to where they're hiding. I've seen where your people are imprisoned."

Alexis spun toward him. "Enslaved, you mean. How many?"

"Of the R'asa? I don't know."

"No, you idiot. How many of my people?"

Corbin thought of the men chained against the pillars, IVs draining their blood so that it might sustain Gregor's floating body. Then the back room where the others were stored. How far back could that room go? How many of the albino men were in those cages?

"Fifteen? Twenty maybe?" he said. "It was hard to see."

The muscles in Alexis's neck twitched and the scar on his face turned a deep red. "That many still alive?"

"There are more than that," Margot said. "They're bred. Like animals."

Alexis twisted his body toward her, his lips curled back in a grimace. But he must have read the disgust on her face because he seemed to bring himself under control. Through clenched teeth he asked, "How many?"

"I was only a child ..."

"How many?" he snarled.

"Over a hundred," she said. "And that was twenty years ago. Who knows how many there could be now."

Corbin tried to process the number but he couldn't fathom that many people held underground. Born in captivity, a lifetime spent in the dark, fed scraps of food, without any idea of an entire modern world a few hundred feet above their heads. A hundred men, women and children raised only for their blood to be harvested for Gregor's grand vision of revenge and punishment.

He saw Alexis was also having trouble absorbing this new fact.

His mouth moved as if uttering a voiceless prayer. He put his hands to his mouth, murmuring into them. The sound rose louder and louder until his hands moved up, over his head, hands curled into claws. He wailed in a guttural cry that froze Corbin in place.

The sound was so filled with pain and hurt that Corbin felt a pang of empathy for the man. But he quickly remembered the horrors the man had committed, both the ones he had witnessed and the ones Besson had told him about. There was no redemption for such a man.

The door to the kitchen burst open and several of Alexis's men ran into the room, weapons pulled. They came to a stop, confused to see their leader standing alone and apparently unharmed. Alexis fell silent, his cry winding down like a machine grinding to a halt after running out of fuel. One of the Fantômes, a tall beast of a man with a swirl of tattoos on his neck, looked at Margot suspiciously as if she were the cause. He carried a wicked-looking hooked sword and raised it in her direction.

"No, M'akiwe," Alexis said. "That's not necessary."

The big man lowered the weapon, but remained tense, looking at each of them in turn. Sizing them up. Ready for a fight if one was in the offering.

"My plan," Corbin said cautiously, "will give you a chance to free those people. But we'll need a lot of help to pull it off."

Alexis seemed distracted, staring at the floor. Corbin wasn't sure if he was even registering what he was saying to him.

"Will you help us?" Corbin asked.

Alexis raised his head. "No, but I will take the woman now. I have my own plans of how to use her to get to Gregor."

Margot shifted uncomfortably, but Corbin raised his hand to settle her. "That would be a mistake."

"Why's that?"

"How many years have you spent fighting the R'asa? Small victories here and there, but no progress. I've been to their lair. I've had Gregor in my head. I know things you don't. I know a way to get them all. At one time."

That got Alexis's attention. He glanced over at Besson as if looking for some sign that he was being played. "And you can deliver this? How?"

"I know of a weakness," he said. "A blind spot that you can use to threaten them. With that threat in place, you can bargain for the release of the people they have trapped there."

"What's the weakness?"

"Are you in?"

Alexis rubbed his neck, his fingers absently tracing the line of the jagged scar. "You don't want to tell the weakness because you think I'll get rid of you and use it myself."

"No, you need us."

"Why?"

"Because the R'asa aren't stupid," Corbin said. "They're on alert. I made a deal to bring Margot to them. You need me to do that to get them to let down their guard. We'll be the bait, but it's going to take your people to set the trap. Some of them will die in the process."

The prospect of death for his men didn't seem to faze him. "What's in it for you, Besson?" Alexis asked. "What's your part in this?"

"I figure once the R'asa are all dead, then you'll give me back my wife and daughter and then get the hell out of my city. If I die trying to help you, you'll let them go anyway. They wouldn't be any use to you."

Alexis shrugged. "Maybe I would. If you died serving me, that is." He turned back to Corbin. The expression on his face was the same Corbin remembered from the night in the alley as he'd gutted Gregor. Pure animal fury.

"This is the final battle I've spent my entire life preparing to wage," he said. "I've already assembled my men. But if this plan doesn't work, you're the first person I kill."

42

F our hours had passed since Alexis and Besson had left the small
house to prepare for the assault. They had listened to his plan
with varying reactions. Besson thought it impossible. Margot thought
it horrific and sure to fail. Only Alexis remained silent through it all,
asking only a few clarifying questions along the way. Once Corbin
was done, with Besson and Margot clearly thinking he was insane, he
turned to Alexis for his opinion.

"My men can do what is needed," he said. "We have the expertise,
but we'll need some time to get the right equipment and stage it in
the correct areas, but it can be done. We've searched the catacombs,
though. Several times. Can you be sure of the location?"

Corbin reached out for the computer tablet Besson had produced
from his car and brought up a map. "The section of sewer I saw, it had
signs on the wall with the street names." He pointed to a spot on the
tablet screen. "They blocked off a large section of the catacombs with
cave-ins, then created secret passages for access. Your men may have
searched the blocked passages and given up."

"Why do we need such a complicated plan?" Besson said. "We
have the element of surprise. Guns and an ambush would be as
effective."

It was Alexis who answered. "Have you ever put your foot down on a floor covered with cockroaches? Lift your foot and you'll have killed only a few. If twenty of my men charge in with guns and knives, we will kill more than a few, but not all." He pointed to Corbin. "No, this is the plan we must execute. If it fails, we will still stomp our foot down and kill as many of the insects as possible. But the American's right; if there is a chance to destroy them all, we must try."

They'd gone through the plan several more times, making adjustments to timing, talking through possible points of failure and how they would respond to those. Alexis received a phone call and nodded as he listened to the speaker on the other end. "I have confirmation the sewer line at that point has what we need. The question is whether you and this gypsy whore can pull off your part."

Margot, silent through most of the planning, didn't hesitate to answer. "The weakness in this plan is relying on you and your gang of freaks."

"Margot," Corbin said, trying to dial her back.

"No, I'm serious. What you're suggesting is complicated. These assholes only know how to slice people up. What makes any of you think they can handle this?"

Corbin and Besson turned to Alexis as if acknowledging that it was a fair question. Alexis glared at them, but he answered. "My men have varied skills. They live and work in the daytime world. Indeed, some of them have very specific expertise in this field. If there is failure, it will not be because of my men."

Corbin looked to Margot. She didn't look convinced, but she also didn't challenge him again. After that, they'd broken up the meeting, Corbin and Margot staying behind while Besson and Alexis made the necessary arrangements. At first Corbin had enjoyed some quiet to reflect on the decision they'd made, but as the sun sank lower in the sky, the apprehension had started.

"I've searched the entire house for cigarettes," Margot said, coming back into the kitchen. She'd disappeared into a back room for a couple of hours to sleep. By her still-haggard appearance, he doubted she'd been successful.

"Too risky going out," he said. "All we need is for one of us to be spotted by the R'asa."

"I know," she said groaning. "But it's almost worth it."

Corbin grabbed a bottle of wine from the counter and two coffee cups. "I did find this."

"Finally, some good news. You're nicer than I am. If you'd left me alone for a couple hours, there'd be an empty bottle on the table."

Corbin pulled the cork and it popped out with a satisfying *thunk*. He examined the cork but only out of habit. There could have been vinegar inside the bottle and he'd still have taken a drink. He poured into one of the coffee cups and handed it to her.

"Fancy," she said, some of her playfulness coming back. "This is some second date. Is this where you take all your girls?"

"On a hunt for a blood cult in the underground caves of Paris? Yep, works like a charm." He poured his own drink.

"You don't go on a lot of third dates, I take it."

"Not one."

"A toast?" she said, holding her mug.

He held up his coffee cup, surprised to see a cartoon smiley face plastered on its side. It seemed an odd way to toast to the annihilation of their supernatural enemies, but odd appeared to be the new normal. "To our next afternoon sitting at an outdoor café together."

She smiled. "Cheers to that."

They drank, deep and long. The wine was decent, not great, but it didn't matter. A little liquid courage was just what the doctor ordered. He refilled her mug. This time she sipped it.

"Do you think maybe we're making a mistake? That maybe we ought to go to the authorities?" she asked.

He felt the gentle warmth of the moment slip away. "The police?"

"Police. Interpol. FBI. I don't know. Anyone."

"And tell them what?"

"The truth." Corbin gave her a sidelong look. "OK, not the truth. Something like the truth. Maybe that there's a terrorist cell plotting attacks and they live in the catacombs."

"And how did you get this information, Ms. Vinci?" Corbin said in a deep voice.

"I ... I ... I'm sleeping with one of the group. He told me everything."

The answer caught him off guard. The image of her in bed with anyone was enough to make him lose his concentration. It took him a second to get back in character. "What's this guy's name?"

"Which guy?"

"The terrorist. The one you're sleeping with."

"I'd make something up. The point is, let's say I'm really convincing and they believe me. Wouldn't they have to go check it out?"

Corbin sipped his wine. As much as he'd like to get out of the task ahead of them, he knew she was reaching for straws. "Even if someone believed you, which is a big if, do you think they'd call out the army or something? No, they'd send down some poor schlub and his partner to check it out. And what would happen to them?"

"But––"

"Or even if they got really serious and sent the SWAT commandos down there with machine guns and grenades, do you think they'd get them all?"

"No, they wouldn't," she said. "But they would find the people trapped down there. Scatter the Tacho R'asa. Get them on the run. Once they saw what they'd been doing down there, the police would hunt them down, right?"

Corbin wanted to agree with her. He wanted nothing more than to pick up the phone and make all of this someone else's problem. But even Besson had said he wouldn't be able to convince a force of any size to go underground without proof of some kind. There was no easy way out. They were the solution.

And his little girl had told him to help. Begged him to stop Gregor. There was no way he was backing down now.

"If we don't end this, they'll never stop coming for you," he said. "This is the chance to end it forever. To stop Gregor from completing his plan."

"Tell me what you saw when Gregor was inside your head." She leaned forward and grasped his hand. The move caught him off guard and he felt his face grow hot. "You said you had a vision of his grand plan. What was it?"

He shook his head, trying to shake the image that came to him. "Nothing. Just the wild thoughts of a madman. It wasn't real, not like a memory. It was a wish. A dream."

"Describe it to me," she said. A shudder passed through him. She must have felt it in her hands because she clasped them more tightly. "Tell me."

The door flew open and in walked Besson. Margot withdrew her hands quickly, looking self-conscious. Besson looked back and forth between them like a parent catching two teenagers making out.

"We're ready," he said. "The Fantômes may be a group of deranged psychopaths, but they delivered tonight."

"And your wife and daughter?" Corbin asked.

"I saw them. They are terrified but alive." The big man's voice choked up as he spoke. "I didn't get to talk to them."

"Because that was our arrangement," Alexis said, strolling into the room. "I kept my word to you." He turned to Corbin. "And now it's time for you to keep yours."

Corbin looked at Margot. She took a deep breath, then drained the last from her coffee mug of wine. "What the hell," she said. "Let's do this."

He tried to think of something brave to say. Or at least something witty like in a 1980s' action flick. But nothing came to him. He was too paralyzed with fear. He simply nodded that he was ready, and they all left the house together.

He knew the next few hours were going to be filled with death, he just hoped that he and his new friends weren't part of the body count.

43

It wasn't hard to get captured by the R'asa. Corbin and Margot were let out of Alexis's car on the Pont Neuf and they crossed over to the Ile de la Cite and the looming structure of Notre Dame. Though alone, they both knew they were being closely watched by the Fantômes for any sign of betrayal.

Corbin reached down and took Margot's hand as they walked. He hoped it came across as a gesture of support. In reality, his nerves were so on edge that he needed the reassurance of her touch just to keep walking forward. She may have felt the same way herself as she slid her fingers between his and squeezed tightly. They walked through the square in front of the cathedral, still filled with tourists even in the off-season. The cathedral was illuminated so that it looked even more regal than it did by day.

"If I'm going to die in the next few hours, this is as good a sight as I could imagine to end with," Margot said.

Corbin pulled her closer. His impulse was to say something comforting about how neither of them were going to die, but they both knew the risks ahead. The chance of success was low. But the chance of success and one or both of them getting out alive was abysmal.

He followed her gaze up the length of the tower nearest them, relishing as he always did the immutable beauty of the cathedral. "Yeah, it's not a bad way to go." Then a thought occurred to him, one that surprised him that he hadn't thought of before that moment. "When this is over, if it ... you know, somehow works out ... I'd like to ..."

"I'd like that too," she said.

He smiled and held her hand more tightly. "Good. That's good."

She nodded to her right. "Here they come."

Corbin scanned the crowd, but saw nothing at first. Seconds later, two men with dark complexions and jet black hair appeared, striding toward them. He squeezed her hand as they approached. The first one grabbed Margot roughly by the arm and yanked them apart.

"Hey, easy," Corbin said. "We came looking for you."

The second man took hold of his arm, painfully digging his fingers between Corbin's bicep and triceps. "Move," he rasped in his ear.

Corbin did as he was told, following several paces behind the man guiding Margot through the crowd. They quickly picked up two more escorts, making it three on Margot and only one on him. It was clear who the more valued prize was. He just hoped that meant they would handle her carefully. A rough shove between his shoulder blades told him he could expect no such special treatment for himself.

They were marched toward a waiting white van and the door slid open as they approached, revealing two more of the R'asa waiting for them inside. Margot was forced into the van and a bag put over her head. He planted his feet, and turned as if looking for a way to run.

"What do you think you're doing?" his R'asa escort asked.

"I delivered the girl. That's all Gregor wanted. I'm done. You're supposed to let me go."

"Funny, no one told me about that deal. Now get in the van." The man grabbed him by the back cuff of his shirt and, nearly lifting him off the ground, dragged him the last few steps. As they pulled the bag over his head and he felt the van speed away, he tried to relax. Alexis's men were already creeping through the catacombs and accessing the sewers to the spot he'd given them. It was all part of the plan.

Even so, he was so nervous that it took all of his focus to keep from throwing up.

The van ride was less than ten minutes, about the same as the last time, so he was hopeful they were taking them through the same entrance. As he was pulled from the van, he called out to Margot to make sure they were still together.

"Yes, here," she said, her voice stronger than he expected. It made him feel guilty for being terrified.

They walked them down several flights of stairs, and he felt the air grow cool and dank. When they removed the bag from his head, he was standing in a familiar narrow stone passageway with a lime-stone floor.

"Let's go," a man grunted behind him. "Gregor's none too pleased this took as long as it did. Best not to piss him off any more by taking our time."

Margot, standing ahead of him, turned enough so that they caught one another's eye for a split second. He saw the fear there and he knew his face carried the same look. Everything was going exactly as they'd planned, and still it was terrifying. He just wondered how he'd feel when the whole plan went to shit, as it inevitably would. The old saying came to mind: The greatest battle plan is made obsolete by first contact with the enemy. The enemy was all around them, and there was only a short hike through the catacombs to come face-to-face with the evil they'd come to eradicate. And already he was having doubts about his plan.

The only thing he knew for sure was that it was too goddamn late to turn back now.

"Move," his escort said, giving him another shove. There was a sharp pain in his side. He looked down and saw that the man was holding a knife to his rib cage. "And try anything like you did last time and I'll slip this into you. Gregor wanted to see you alive. He didn't say nothing about having all your body parts attached. Keep that in mind. Now go."

He did as he was told and walked forward, following the R'asa man ahead of him, catching glimpses of Margot over the man's shoulder. Every time they passed an open passageway that led off the main artery they followed, he tried to casually glance down to see if there was any sign of the Fantômes. They'd gotten a head start, lying in wait, but he didn't know if any were following their path, creeping in the passages alongside them.

Once he thought he saw the barest movement of shadow at the end of a tunnel to his right, but he couldn't be sure. The fact that their escorts seemed unconcerned made him believe that the Fantômes had gone undetected so far. It would only take one mistake on their part to warn the R'asa that the ambush was being set. If that happened, he wasn't sure what his next move would be. He just hoped it didn't come to that.

As before, the passageway led them to a skull-lined entrance to the catacombs. The man in front of him stopped and he heard him say something to Margot, but it was in a language he didn't understand. Whatever he said worked because Margot continued forward. Corbin realized she was entering a world that had existed only in the nightmares of an eight-year-old little girl. He worried that seeing everything again would be too much for her to bear. So much of their plan called for her to keep her wits about her. He wondered if he'd asked too much.

Soon, they reached the cave-in where the metal fence blocked the path to the sewer system. Corbin grew anxious as they approached, thinking that if the Fantômes were to make a mistake, if there was a place where they might be discovered, this was it.

But they passed by without incident. The man in front of Margot engaged the hidden mechanism and the door swung open. Once they were all through, the stone door slid shut with a grinding finality that sent a chill up his spine.

Soon, the air changed again. Mixed in with the musty smell of the piles of ancient bones on either side of him was something new. It was rich and metallic, something he could taste in his mouth as he drew the air in. Even without Gregor's presence inside of him, he knew what it was: blood.

They entered the large chamber where he'd last seen Gregor to find it completely transformed. First, it was filled with people. Men and women dressed in old-style clothing, the men in pants with wide legs, cinched at the waist with rope belts. Shirts with billowing sleeves. Some with embroidered jackets with fine, elaborate stitching. The women wore floral print dresses or wide pleated skirts and blouses. It looked like a Hollywood version of a group of gypsies. All that was needed were some painted caravans and a sign for crystal ball readings.

The crowd fell into a hush when they entered. Slowly, they parted in front of them as they walked farther into the room. Some spit on the ground at Margot's feet. Others made strange signs with their hands that he didn't recognize, but it didn't take a genius to know they weren't signs of friendship.

Ahead, Corbin saw the pillars made of skulls that were now, like the rest of the room, illuminated by glowing red lights, pulsating from the irregular power supply so that the room felt like the inside of a beating heart. The two albino men, the blood bags that had been draining into Gregor's sarcophagus, were gone. In fact, the sarcophagus looked to also be gone. On closer inspection, it had simply been transformed. There was a stone cover over it serving as a solid base for the throne that sat upon it. And throne was the only proper word for the object resting there.

Metal twisted through bones and skulls to create a wide seat with a high back that rose to the height of a man standing. The skulls were positioned so that they all looked at the occupant of the throne, signaling that nothing else mattered except for the man sitting there. But that wasn't enough to make the throne stand apart. As he watched, the skulls twisted within their metal cages. Jawbones rose and fell as if trying to speak. Or scream. Skeletal fingers flexed and pointed. Somehow, impossibly, the bones were alive.

As terrifying as the sight was, the man sitting on the throne drew away his attention. It was Gregor, out of the sarcophagus, but barely more alive than the last time he'd seen the man gasping like a fish in his bath of blood. He was hunched over and pale. His hair thin and grey, pasted against his spotted skull. A crown of thin gold perched precariously on his head, tilted to one side so that it rested on one of Gregor's shriveled ears. He lifted his chin only inches off his chest and his beady eyes glistened with phlegm as they tried to focus.

Once they did, a thin smile came to his lips, cracking the skin. "Chey ..." he rasped.

"Grandfather," Margot said, bowing her head in supplication.

Mariyana stepped forward from beside the throne, dressed more formally than before in a black dress and head scarf. Corbin wondered if it would prove to be her attire for her husband's triumph or for his funeral.

The old woman walked toward Margot who stood alone in the center of the room, arms crossed over her chest as if that might somehow protect her.

Mariyana looked her over once, her expression unreadable. Then, with a suddenness that took him off guard, she reached out and embraced her, pulling her to her breast like a mother comforting a child who has fallen. Margot was stiff in the woman's arms, but slowly she relaxed and allowed herself to be held. The old woman spoke steadily in a hushed voice, her eyes closed as if it were only the two of them in the world.

Then she pushed Margot back gently, took her hand and led her toward the throne. If Corbin had known what the old woman intended to do, he never would have let it happen.

44

Corbin watched as Gregor lifted his head only slightly as Margot approached. He looked so frail and weak that Corbin wondered if he was witnessing the limit of whatever supernatural force they'd used to bring him back. That he was alive at all was nothing short of a miracle, or perhaps the more apt word was abomination. Corbin stood, mesmerized by what was happening in front of him, but fighting a building panic. For their part of the plan to work, they needed Gregor to wait before he tried to use Margot's blood. Ten minutes was all they needed.

"Chey ..." Gregor said again. One of his hands lifted off the armrest of his throne. The sleeve of his shirt fell back, exposing a thin, emaciated limb. His fingers curled into a fist and then his index finger slowly extended until it pointed at her.

The air in the room appeared to freeze. Nothing moved.

Gregor's tongue bulged from behind his cracked lips, wetting them. When his voice came, it was like a gunshot in the room. A single word:

"Mine!"

Mariyana produced a blade from some hidden spot in the folds of her dress. In a blur of motion, she slashed Margot's wrist.

Margot screamed. Every voice in the room rose in unison, crying out in celebration.

Corbin lunged forward but was held back by his guards.

The old woman cupped her hand over the wound, but blood spurted through her fingers.

The next instant, Gregor was off his throne, moving in quick, jerking movements like a scarecrow brought to life. He lowered himself to Margot's wrist and clamped down on it, sucking hard, nostrils flared.

Corbin froze. Every pop culture image of a vampire draining its victim of blood flooded over him. He felt somehow outside his body, like he was watching everything play out on a screen. It had to be, because thinking that this was real was too much to bear.

The crowd around him cried out even louder, swaying together as if in some kind of collective ecstasy.

But, above it all, he heard Margot scream again. It shook him out of his stupor and he lunged forward, thinking to make a run at Gregor. To knock him off her. To stop the horrific slurping sounds of Gregor drinking down her blood.

He had barely taken a step before a blow struck him aside his head. Pain exploded, first at the point where the punch landed, then again when he hit the ground. Someone was on his back, holding him down, increasing force the more he struggled to get up.

The tempo of the crowd noise rose, building to a climax.

As much as Corbin wanted to shut his eyes, he couldn't help but look.

Margot's body was limp now. Arms flailing on either side of her as Mariyana continued to hold her up. Her head lolled back and he saw her eyes flutter, rolled back in their sockets so that only the whites were visible.

Mariyana moved her free hand and placed it on Gregor's head, pushing him gently away. She leaned down and spoke directly into his ear. Softly at first so that it looked like a lover coaxing a partner in a sex act. But then she adjusted her grip, grabbed his hair and yanked him backward.

Gregor detached from Margot's wrist with a loud gasp, as if coming up for air after a deep underwater dive. The cut on Margot's arm was ragged and torn, blood pouring from the wound. The old woman produced a bandage and wrapped it expertly around the gash. Gregor tried to push her away, mouth open, searching again for the opening. But Mariyana held him back.

"You'll kill her if you drain her completely," she said. "Be wise. There is no other source for you."

Gregor spun around and walked away from the two women, walking up the pile of crushed bones towards his throne and adjusting the gold crown so that it was positioned properly on his head. The room fell silent.

When he turned, Corbin couldn't believe the transformation.

Gone was the gaunt, frail skeleton of a man that had been there only minutes before. Gregor stood tall and poised, his flesh full, his face that of a younger man, middle-aged instead of the ancient version Corbin had first seen in the alley. Black hair hung down to his shoulders. Gregor flexed his arms and legs as if trying on a new piece of clothing, grinning broadly. Then he snatched a knife from his side and held it up to the crowd, shouting, "Tacho R'asa! Opre Roma!"

The room responded, taking up the cry. Those who had weapons thrust them into the air. Any who did not, shook angry fists over their heads.

Gregor held up a hand and the sound slowed and then stopped. The men closest to Corbin turned to stare.

"My people are disturbed by your presence," he said. "You'll forgive them. We're on the cusp of settling our score with the human world. To them, you seem an easy place to start."

"We had a bargain," Corbin said, trying to hide the tremble in his voice. "I expect you to honor it."

"Honor?" Gregor said, walking down from his throne. "How can you speak of honor? Where was honor when the Roma were being hung from trees, accused of crimes they could not have committed? Or shipped to concentration camps because of the blood in their veins? Or, even today, persecuted as animals, spit on and forced to beg for basic dignity?"

"That wasn't me."

"It was you," Gregor said, raising his voice to address the crowd gathered around them. "It was always you and your people. Since the days of diaspora, through history and to today. You subjugated us, cast us out, treated us as no more than animals. Your kind did this. Sins that are not forgiven. Retribution that is long overdue. And now punishment has finally arrived."

Cheers erupted again. As it went on, Corbin saw that Margot was conscious now. She sat on the ground, leaning against the throne. Dazed but alive. He tried to make contact with her, but her eyes were unfocused, staring into the distance, unseeing. Perhaps that was a blessing.

Their part of the plan was off-track, but the others were still out there. It didn't mean they couldn't stop Gregor. Only that Gregor was stronger now, which would make him harder to fool. Corbin drew in a deep breath as the reality of his position set in. He thought of Rose, and her voice asking him to help stop the evil men here. There was a comfort to that. Knowing that there was an existence of some kind waiting for him after death. And that Rose would be there. Proud of her dad for helping others. For being brave enough to stand up to evil where he saw it.

As long as Gregor's plan was stopped, then it was worth the sacrifice.

"Friends," Gregor said. "The time has come to change the world." The crowd roared in delight. "We've harvested the blood of our prisoners and performed the sacred rituals. But, as you all know, we need more."

"Les Fantômes," the crowd murmured.

"Yes," Gregor said. "The albino blood we need can be found in our old friends, Les Fantômes. And they have been kind enough to bring themselves here for our use." Gregor looked right at Corbin. "Even now, they think they prepare an attack against us, but they walk into a trap. And, soon, we will have them all."

Corbin turned his head, not wanting Gregor to see his reaction. He made eye contact with Margot. She was more alert, but still sagged against the throne. She shook her head when she saw him staring, then closed her eyes again.

"Disappointed?" Gregor said to Corbin. "You can't think that you'd be able to fool me so easily."

"H ... H ... how did you know?"

"A mutual friend," he said, waving a hand toward the crowd. "I think you know this man?"

The crowd parted and Corbin groaned as Besson made his way over to him.

45

"You son of a bitch," Corbin said to Besson.

If the man felt any sense of guilt for the betrayal, it didn't show on his face. He looked the same as he had the first night he'd questioned Corbin at the police station. Calm, controlled and smug because he knew he was the one in the position of power.

"Don't hold it against him," Gregor said. "This man has been an enemy for many years. Helping the Fantômes. Not as a believer in their cause, but because of the risk to his family." He waved a hand toward the others in the cave, many who were now filing out of the doors in the back of the cave toward where the slaves were kept. "This is my family. There is no end to what I'm willing to do to protect them." He placed a hand on Besson's shoulder. The big man flinched, a movement Gregor either didn't notice or simply ignored. "I cannot fault a man for something I would do myself."

"How could you do this?" Corbin said. "The Fantômes still have your family."

Besson shook his head. "I made my deal with the R'asa once I convinced Alexis to let me see them. Gregor's men followed me there."

"And once he left, we easily slit the throats of the Fantômes, and gathered his wife and daughter. They are safe, back in their home where they belong."

"What have you done?" Corbin said.

"Nothing more than what you'd originally planned to do."

"Bullshit."

"You were going to sacrifice Margot to save your daughter. Even though you knew exactly what these creatures wanted her for."

"Careful," Gregor whispered. "I've already forgiven a great deal from you. Call me creature again and I'll have your family disemboweled in front of you."

Besson went silent, bowing his head in submission. "I'm sorry. Forgive me."

A cry rose from the far side of the cavern, the same direction from which Corbin had entered. "Our new guests are here. If Alexis is among them, then there is nothing to forgive. If he's not, then ..." he wagged his finger from side-to-side.

The crowd surged forward, pushing along a knot of men, hitting and kicking them as they passed. Corbin immediately recognized the dark clothes and hoodies of the Fantômes. In the front was Alexis, his face crazed with rage and anger.

"Quiet," Gregor called out, and the crowd did as he commanded.

Corbin took the opportunity to try to get Besson's attention, but the man was purposefully looking away from him. He turned to watch Alexis, wondering what the man would do.

"Hello, Alexis," Gregor said, looking over the collection of the dozen men behind him. "Thank you for bringing you and your men tonight. We need all the blood we can get."

"I remember taking your blood last time we met," Alexis snarled. "I should have ripped out your heart and cut off your head."

"That would have done the job," Gregor said. "But, as you can see, my lovely wife and granddaughter have nursed me back to health. Along with quite a bit of blood from some of your kind." Alexis charged forward but two R'asa men on either side grabbed his arms. A third dropped a rope around his neck and pulled tight, just enough for Alexis to know it was there. Gregor sidled alongside him. "Did you really think you could kill me? Do you think I'm just a man who knows a bit of dark magic from the old country? That I would be like the villagers you used to slaughter by the dozen?"

"I've never taken you for anything other than what you are," Alexis said.

"And what's that?"

"A demon from hell," Alexis said. "One that needs to be returned to his master."

Gregor smiled, seeming to like the conversation. "We've both served the same master. Can't you see that? How many innocent men and women have you killed? How many of those did you torture? Sometimes not because you needed anything from them, but only because you needed their screams to sow fear in all who heard?"

"You are a devil. Unnatural. An abomination."

"And yet it's the blood in your veins that carries the power I need for my work. So who is unnatural? Who is the abomination?"

Alexis looked caught off guard by the argument. "W ... we exist ... we are only as we were created. It took a monster like you to twist that into something terrible. And now you raise my brothers like animals in cages."

"Brothers?" Gregor smiled. "Not just brothers. Sisters too. Nearly two hundred of your kind at last count. Bred here for this glorious day when I can exact revenge on the world for centuries of belittlement and persecution."

"They are innocents. I've come here to release them."

Gregor laughed and the men nearest him followed his lead. "Release them? Well, you're a bit late for that."

"What do you mean?"

"Their suffering ended only a few hours ago."

Alexis stared him down, unable to say a word.

"I took their blood, but it wasn't quite enough for my plans. The dozen you brought will be a welcome addition."

Alexis threw an elbow to his left, catching the man holding that arm off-balance. He grabbed the rope around his neck, and piked as hard as he could. The man flipped over and landed on the ground in front of him. Alexis immediately stomped on the man's head with his boot, crushing it.

The man on his right loosened his grip in surprise just enough that Alexis tore away from him.

Alexis launched himself at Gregor, teeth bared, hands ready.

Midair, he slumped suddenly and then arched his back with a paralyzing scream.

A sword stuck out from his abdomen.

The hilt firmly held in Gregor's fist.

Alexis's eyes were wide, but still he stared with pure hatred at Gregor. Inch by inch, he pulled himself along the length of the blade until it appeared, blood-soaked, out of his back.

"Die, you monster," Alexis said. "I want to see you die."

"Sorry," Gregor replied. "But I will live forever. And you're going to live long enough to see what I've done."

With a jerk, Gregor pulled out his sword. Alexis clutched his wound, but, with a snarl, he still tried to lunge at Gregor. His legs gave out and he went sprawling on the ground. Gregor sneered at him.

"And to think I believed you to be a worthy adversary. You're nothing but a common street thug."

Blood trickled from Alexis's mouth and he groaned. But as his body shuddered, he turned to Corbin and a blood-covered smile appeared on his lips. Then all energy left him and he sagged to the ground.

Gregor turned and gave Corbin an odd look, as if piecing something together.

A R'asa man walked up quickly to them. "We're ready," he said.

Gregor remained staring at Corbin, a single eyebrow raised. He looked back from Alexis to Corbin and then Besson. Corbin's stomach tightened. He prayed his face hadn't given him away.

Finally, Gregor turned to the man waiting for him. "Assemble everyone. Even the outer guard. Every member of the Tacho R'asa. All of the True Tribe deserves to be at our moment of triumph." The man turned and jogged away to implement his orders. Gregor nodded at Alexis. "Pick him up. That stomach wound won't kill him for a while. I want him to see the new world I'm going to create."

Corbin and Besson did as they were told, hefting the albino up from the ground, each of them supporting a side.

"What are you going to do?" Besson asked.

"I'm going to raise the dead," Gregor said. "And watch them inherit the Earth."

46

The world was a gauzy cloud, layers of veils that shifted and rubbed against each other. Margot blinked hard, trying to clear her vision and pull herself together. She knew something important was happening, but she couldn't remember what it was. But she needed to remember. It was essential that she did. But whenever she thought she'd found an edge to hold on to, it slipped away.

All she knew for certain was that her arm hurt. A dull ache now, but there were echoes of real pain from not long before. Mind-shattering pain. Agony that made her feel like shattered glass.

She focused on a row of skulls imbedded into a wall. Empty eye sockets staring at her. Mouths open like they knew what she was meant to remember and would tell her except for the unfortunate loss of their tongues.

Then her vision was clear and she was running through the catacombs, rows of bones flashing past her. She was alone, sprinting and laughing. Free from the others. Free from her parents who never let her roam alone when they were underground.

Her parents. They would be worried about her if she was gone for too long. They were always so serious. So concerned that she might see something she wasn't supposed to. She was eight years old and had seen pretty much everything. She'd even seen adults naked. Kissing with their tongues. But she didn't care. She'd seen it a hundred times on television anyway.

A noise came from the passageway ahead of her. This was some-place she'd never gone before. Not because she'd been specifically forbidden to go there, just in general terms she wasn't permitted to go anywhere. Whenever she threw a fit and demanded to know why they even brought her if she wasn't allowed to do anything, her parents always grew quiet. The kind of quiet when she knew she'd stumbled across something the adults didn't want her to know about. Probably a fight put on hold until they were alone.

The sounds coming from the passageway were frightening. Low groans of suffering. The wailing of a woman crying. The *chink chink* of someone striking metal with a hammer. It was unlike anything she'd heard before. Even without knowing what it was, she under-stood immediately that it was something she wasn't meant to see. And that made her walk faster toward it.

The first person she saw was a woman her mother's age. She had the physical appearance of the people she'd met with African heritage. Tall, with strong shoulders, a face characterized with full lips and nose that gave her a proud, almost regal expression. She was naked from the waist up, exposing full breasts. On one of these, suckled a baby so small that it might have been born earlier that day. But what made Margot stop and stare was that the woman and baby were white. Not like she was, or her mother, but totally without color. Margot had seen an albino person before out in the world. She'd gawked and received a slap on the bottom and a scolding from her mother about manners. But she'd never seen something like this before.

The woman's short, kinked hair was a light yellow, perhaps only that color from the lantern burning nearby; her skin so pale that it was nearly translucent. Even in the dull light of the cave, Margot could see twisting blue veins crisscrossing her torso and stretching down her arms and threading through her breasts. The baby reminded her of one of those fish in the pet store, the see-through kind where the tiny organs are visible to the naked eye. It was wrinkled and swollen, like a dead thing fished out of a river. But it wasn't dead. It suckled urgently and the woman didn't disturb its meal even with Margot's arrival. The woman's eyes were a pale blue but seemed to capture every bit of light around them because when they turned on her they shone with hatred unlike anything she'd ever seen.

Margot tore her eyes away, ashamed to have intruded on the woman's nakedness and moment with her baby. She knew she should turn and run back in the direction she'd come. But she didn't. Instead, she walked farther into the cave.

Metal cages were bolted into the limestone walls around the circumference of an enormous cavern. In each of these was a single man or a man/woman pair, locked in a tiny rectangle only barely large enough to stand inside. They were all albino like the woman she'd first seen. Most of them ignored her presence, but others, maybe sensing her discomfort, pushed arms through their cages, reaching out to her. It frightened her and she began to cry. More of those caged took notice of her and they all reached toward her, calling for her to help them. Even though they spoke in a foreign tongue, she understood.

Help us. Help us.

And then she saw the tubes coming from each of the cages. Thin, plastic lines hooked to machines, terminating in plastic bags hanging on metal poles. She knew what she was looking at. A student at her school had gotten sick, so they'd all gone down to the hospital and the parents gave blood. The red bags bulged with it.

She stumbled backward, suddenly scared and mad at herself for being so foolish to be standing there. For being so naughty to ignore her mom and dad's warnings to never wander off. She wanted to get out of there. Wanted to forget she'd ever seen the people in the cages.

She ran into something behind her and stopped.

She slowly turned, fear clamping down on her. Somehow she knew what stood behind her even before she turned. She felt a warm gush between her legs as she wet herself.

"Chey," Gregor said. "You shouldn't be here."

She backed away from him, as terrified of him as she always was. But more now because she knew she was in trouble. She'd seen her grandfather punish people before. She didn't want that. She just wanted her mom. But she wasn't there. It was just her and her grandfather.

"You shouldn't be here," the voice came again, only this time it was a different man. A kind voice, filled with concern. "You need to get to a hospital."

She blinked hard and the world came back into focus. She was in the same cavern filled with cages, only there were more of them now. Stacked one on top of the other. And they were empty. She knew the man holding her up, telling her to go to the hospital as if they could just walk out of the cave if they wanted. Corbin. That was his name. And he looked so worried about her.

But she was worried about the cages. Why were they empty? Where had all the people gone?

Then she turned and saw what had happened to them.

And started to scream.

47

The scream caught Corbin by surprise. One second Margot was barely conscious, sagging against his body, her breath coming in ragged bursts. The next she was fully awake, eyes staring at the far wall of the cave, screaming in horror at what she saw there.

He pulled her to him, trying to calm her. She stopped screaming, but it turned into a low whimpering as she clutched to his chest. "I ... I should have ... I should have done something ..."

He had no words to comfort her. She'd told him she knew about this place as a child, but had always thought maybe it was something she'd made up. A horrific construct from the things she saw as a child conflated with images from the Holocaust, slave ships and other images of human deprivation. But that had just been a way for her to wash away the guilt of knowing the place existed and not doing anything to stop the atrocity. The people here had been real.

And now they were all dead.

The end of the cave was stacked with bodies, naked, even more pale than the Fantômes. From a lifetime underground. From being drained of every ounce of blood.

Men, women and even children lay tangled in a monstrous heap, limbs flailed in all directions, faces locked in expressions of pain and terror.

Barrels lined the walls of the cave in front of the empty cages and Corbin knew what was in them. Blood. The fuel for Gregor's final solution.

I should have done something.

The same guilt wracked him. What could he have done differently over the last day? What if he'd gone to the police? Or the US embassy? They probably would have laughed at him. Maybe detained him for his own safety. But maybe they might have done something. Maybe all those people would still be alive if he'd had more courage.

I should have done something, wasn't good enough.

He had to do something. The plan was still operational. The only difference was that the threat of destruction he'd planned to use to get the albino slaves out safely was now potentially a way to get Margot out alive.

He swore to God that if the rest of the plan fell apart, then he would die trying to kill Gregor. And he wouldn't make the same mistake as Alexis. He'd chop the bastard's head off to make sure he didn't come back this time.

He searched the crowd and found where R'asa guards held Alexis. The man was on his knees, head slouched down, unmoving. Corbin thought that perhaps the knife wound had been more severe than he'd thought, but then he saw the man's shoulders jerking and he knew he was sobbing at the sight in front of him. At his failure to help his people. Corbin's own guilt perched on his shoulder like a ravenous bird. He could only imagine the weight on Alexis.

"Can you walk?" he whispered to Margot.

"Not yet. But give me a minute. My head's clearing."

He took her hand, the one with the bandaged wrist. Minutes before it'd been totally limp and as white as a sheet of writing paper, drained of blood. Now it was pink and fleshy, and she flexed it open and closed on his fingers. Slowly, he reached up for her bandages, but she flinched.

"What are you doing?" she asked.

He didn't answer her, but quickly pushed back the wrapping.

The wound was healed.

She stared at it dumbly, not quite believing what she saw there. With her other hand, she rubbed the red flesh carefully, pressing against it as if testing thin ice. She looked up at Corbin.

"How is that possible?" she asked.

"Gregor took from you, but he gave as well. It happened to me too. If you feel something, like a presence inside you, it's him. And you have to tell me right away."

She nodded, pushing the bandage back into place as if she were embarrassed by how it had healed. "I'm feeling stronger with each minute," she said. "What are we going to do?"

Before he could answer, Gregor's voice soared over the crowd. "My family, come to me. Come and listen." The R'asa fell silent and pressed forward. Corbin and Margot were on a slightly elevated part of the cavern so he had a good view across the assembled masses. There were at least a hundred people there, maybe more. He just hoped Gregor's order to bring all the members of the R'asa in for his big moment had been carried out.

Because he knew something Gregor did not. As planned, only half of the Fantômes had allowed themselves to be captured.

Besson hadn't betrayed them. In fact, he'd played his part exactly as planned.

It had made perfect sense that he might betray both Alexis and Corbin in order to save his family. When Besson had approached him, Gregor accepted the offer and now Besson's family was safely at home. Where Gregor had miscalculated was that Besson had no interest in simply changing masters. He wanted freedom.

Besson had been executing Corbin's plan the entire time. Alexis and half of his men being caught had been necessary to pull off the next stage.

Corbin hoped the other half of the Fantômes proved as brave and committed as their leader. As Gregor began to speak, Corbin found it hard to keep a smile off his face. The trap was set and the R'asa didn't have a clue.

"We gather here today," Gregor said, Mariyana at his side, "as the survivors of centuries of ill-treatment. For hundreds of years our people, not only the Tacho R'asa but all of the Romani, have wandered the Earth without a home. Persecuted, hunted, punished. Simply because of the blood in our veins." He pointed an angry hand toward the ceiling. "The world above us wants to believe such things are resigned to history, the sins of a different generation. But the abuse continues. Perhaps now we are called refugees. Or immigrants. Forced to live segregated from society in camps or barrios or ghettos. Regardless of label, they see us as less than they. As animals that ought to beg for scraps at the master's table." He lowered his hand in a fist. "That ends now."

The crowd erupted in cheers and howls. Men beat their chests as if preparing to charge into battle. Corbin realized that was exactly the mindset Gregor was trying to create. He was about to declare war and he needed his soldiers ready to fight.

Corbin saw Besson slide through the crowd toward him and Margot. If there were R'asa assigned to guard him, they'd fallen off their duty, likely caught up in the rapture of Gregor's speech. He made eye contact with Corbin then looked at the rear doors of the cavern that led back to the room with the throne. Corbin followed his gaze and saw that once outside the ring of the crowd, there seemed to be no one guarding the way out.

"Come on," he whispered to Margot. "Get ready to move."

"My family," Gregor called from his spot in front of the group, his voice pitched higher. "I have done my best to shepherd you for these long years. And I have been imperfect in my position. But I have led us finally to this moment. The moment when we will avenge the injuries done to our people. And we will do it in a way that will make the world finally understand our true power. The gifts that we might have given freely to the world had it chosen to embrace instead of oppress us. Our power will rewrite what they understand about the natural world and make them tremble when they hear the name Tacho R'asa."

The crowd began to chant, "Tacho R'asa. Tacho R'asa."

Gregor held up his hand and the room fell silent again. He pulled the sheet away from the table in front of him. On it were a pile of catacomb bones, topped with four skulls that faced the crowd. Gregor ran a hand over them, caressing the contours of the skeletal remains.

"We needed an army to fight. And after all these years of raising the stock we needed, we have a blood harvest great enough to execute our plan." He picked up a silver cup from the table, thrust his hand into it, and then raised it over his head, blood dripping down his forearm. "The rituals have been performed, the ancient words have been spoken, our army is ready to be brought to life."

He flicked his fingers at the bones, spraying them with blood. He dipped his hand back into the cup, scooping out a handful and splashing it across the table.

The room was silent.

Corbin, Margot and Besson were as enthralled as the rest, unable to tear their eyes away. A sense of dread spread from Corbin's stomach like tendrils of ice. He felt Margot slip her hand into his and he clung onto it.

Then the bones on the table started to move.

48

Corbin didn't want to believe his eyes. It was the vision Gregor had shown him when he'd been in his head. He'd hoped it was just an old man's fantasy, not something that could ever exist in the real world.

But there, in front of them all, was the proof that it was real.

The pile of bones moved closer together, as if they were made of metal and a massive magnet had been turned on to energize them. Then, always touching, sliding and grinding against one another, the bones reoriented themselves beneath the skulls. Parts of anatomy Corbin knew well were the easiest to spot. Long femurs, some of them broken in half but fusing together when they touched, fit into hip girdles. Tibia and fibula connected, rotating in place as if to test range of motion. Rib cages formed. Dozens of tiny bones, phalanges that belonged in the hands and feet, danced through the twisting pile, migrating along the newly formed arms and legs to their correct positions. Vertebrae snapped together like children's building blocks, finally attaching one by one to a skull.

Then the first complete skeleton swung its legs off the edge of the table, balancing there as if ready to teeter back into a worthless pile. The crowd hung silent in anticipation.

Gregor waved a hand in its direction. "Rise," he said.

The skeleton did more than asked.

It leapt from the table, jumping through the air and landing in front of Gregor's face.

This was no frail thing. It moved with purpose, balanced and solid. The skull cocked to one side, as if evaluating Gregor.

Then it raised a bony hand, clenched it into a fist and struck out at Gregor.

Gregor didn't flinch. The skeleton's fist stopped with only a thread's-width distance away from Gregor's cheek. It tried a second time, its jaws moving open in a silent scream. But it stopped short once again. Gregor smiled.

"Whoever you were in life, you are one of the Tacho R'asa now," Gregor said. "And you may not injure one of the True Tribe."

Three more skeletons rose from the table. One was missing the bones for its left arm, but had a hand attached directly to its shoulder socket. The other two were complete and moved with the same intensity and determination as the first. They ran at the nearest living thing and attacked.

Each time, the skeletons froze just before impact.

"We have to leave. Now." Besson had taken advantage of the room's complete attention on the skeletons to maneuver directly behind Corbin and Margot. Hearing his voice broke Corbin out of what felt like a spell cast over him. Every part of his mind had been locked up in bearing witness to the impossibility in front of him. And the single fact that kept rolling through his head.

There are six million skeletons buried in the catacombs.

Six million!

He tugged on Margot's arm. She flinched, coming out of her thoughts with a panicked look. "If we can, we need to go. Right now."

Gregor's voice rose behind them. "These are the first," he intoned to the crowd. "But the army we need slumbers all around us. The same people who oppressed us will now do our bidding and attack and destroy their own descendants. In these long corridors filled with the dead, we shall finally give rise to the instruments of our vengeance."

He waved them forward. The crowd surged, grabbing blood-filled bags and holding them over their heads. Corbin watched as one of the R'asa took a bag to the bone vault on the wall nearest him. The man threw it into the gap between the top layer of the bones and the limestone ceiling.

"No one's watching," Besson hissed. "Now's our chance."

Corbin tore himself away from the terrible sight in front of him. He spun around and saw that Besson was right. The path between them and the back wall was open. On instinct, he sought out the only other person who might be aware of the opportunity to escape. Alexis.

The man was still on his knees but his head was up now, staring at the pile of bodies of the albino slaves. In front of the stack of carcasses were the ten men he'd led into the cavern to be captured with him as a part of the ruse. All of them had been hung upside-down from meat hooks, their throats slit. A bucket beneath each of them gathered their blood.

"Leave him," Besson hissed. "It's what we wanted."

"We need to make sure he can do it," Corbin said. "That he can finish this."

As if sensing their eyes on him, Alexis slowly turned to look at them. Even though Corbin knew the man was a monster and that all the Fantômes had committed horrific atrocities, it was impossible to see that tear-streaked face and not feel a pang of sympathy. His eyes were glazed, as if staring out into some far distance, shocked to a point that comprehension failed.

Still, as his eyes settled on Corbin, he slowly raised his right hand and opened it ever so slightly. Something silver flashed there and Corbin knew exactly what it was.

"Okay. Let's go," he said.

The moment they turned toward the back wall, keeping low to the ground, a cry rose from the crowd. His heart nearly stopped as he thought the sound was for them. But a quick look over his shoulder dispelled that fear. But replaced it with something worse.

The vault of bones into which he'd seen the first bag of blood hurled was alive with motion. The air was filled with a sickening *clack clack clack* of bones rattling, moving, reorganizing.

One-by-one, full skeletons climbed out from the pile. Sometimes with such violence that bones snapped as they shoved their way through.

All around the room, members of the R'asa were throwing blood bags into other vaults. Others, their backs bent from carrying heavier bags, left the room to go to other passages filled with the bones of the ancient dead.

Six million are buried here.

Margot tugged on his hand so hard that he nearly stumbled. Corbin turned away from the dozen skeletons behind him and ran toward the rear exit alongside Margot and Besson.

A R'asa spotted them and shouted in alarm, but he was drowned out by the excitement of the crowd. Besson smashed a heavy fist in the man's stomach. When the man bent over from the blow, Besson's knee met the R'asa's head with so much force that he was out cold before he hit the ground.

Corbin and Margot ran past him, ducking into the next room. They immediately began coughing and hacking, their eyes tearing up. It was a good sign that his plan was working, but also a worry that they only felt the effect in that room and not in the main cavern.

The other Fantômes were there, the ones Alexis had left hidden when he pretended to have been surprised and captured by the R'asa. They looked bizarre in their loose black clothing and full-face gas masks. The man nearest to him raised a sword over his head and was about to strike when he recognized him. He stopped mid-swing.

"I have a message from Alexis," Corbin said, recognizing the man from the safe house. M'akiwe was his name. The bodies of several R'asa lay on the ground around the man. Not all of the patrols had been stopped during the ceremony, but whoever had entered this room had not been allowed to leave.

"What is it?" M'akiwe asked, his voice muffled from the gas mask.

"Alexis says the glorious end is here," Corbin said. "He commands all the faithful to join him inside to finish the Tacho R'asa once and for all."

It was hard to read the man's expression through the gas mask, but Corbin thought he saw him smile. For a zealot, it was the perfect message.

The man waved for the others to follow him. They lifted the heavy, commercial hoses at their feet and dragged them forward. There were three different hoses and all of them reached through the door and into the next room.

Corbin watched with a mix of pride and horror at what he'd done.

It was working. And that meant they had to get the hell out of there.

"Faster," he shouted at the others. There was no way to know if they had seconds or minutes left. "We have to make it to the sewer."

They sprinted down the passageway, avoiding the hoses the Fantômes had stretched down the length of it. Corbin tried not to think what would happen if they were too late.

The bodies of three R'asa sentries were stacked up in a pile at the secret entrance. That explained how the Fantômes had been able to drag the hoses into the tunnels.

"Through the gate," Besson said, pointing to the metal fencing separating the catacomb tunnel and the sewer.

Corbin glanced over his shoulder. There was no sign of anyone chasing them. For the first time since being captured he allowed himself a moment of optimism. They might just make it out alive.

But when Margot grabbed the gate and yanked, that hope disappeared. The gate was locked.

Corbin threw his weight at it, but the metal chains holding it closed didn't move.

"Shit!" he shouted. The fence went to the ceiling. There was no way over it.

"There," Besson said, pointing to the hoses snaking under the fencing on the left side.

Corbin ran over to the hoses and saw that the metal had been cut through, then lined up perfectly to give the appearance that it was still intact.

"Help me," he said.

Besson and Margot grabbed the fence and together they bent it back until there was an opening large enough for them to crawl through.

They ran into the sewer. Corbin barely had time to register the impressive pumps the Fantômes had been able to set up. He was no engineer, but any doubt he had about whether their plan was going to be effective seemed suddenly unfounded. But that created a different set of problems.

"We have to jump in," he shouted.

They all looked down at the dark, brown sludge. Water runoff and raw sewage. Judging by the smell, mostly sewage.

Margot pointed to the walkway alongside the channel. "Maybe we have time. We can find an exit and climb out."

A loud *thump* sounded from the tunnel behind them. Wind ripped past them, being sucked into the catacombs.

"Jump!" Corbin shouted. "Now!"

49

Alexis knew the numbness in his abdomen that had spread to his legs meant that the wound was bad, most likely fatal. Normally that would be bad news, but he considered it a blessing he couldn't feel the pain. There was no way he was leaving the cave alive. No reason to suffer in his last few minutes on the planet.

The real risk was passing out. He felt drunk, swaying as if rocking on a boat only he was on. Wasn't that fitting? Hadn't he always been alone in the world? Even when surrounded by his own loyal men. Even, as a child, housed in the barracks with the other soldiers, he'd never been one of them. He was destined to die as he'd lived since his mother had been butchered in front of him: scared and alone.

He'd watched Gregor on the rock platform and cursed his name. And then when the first skeleton had come to life, he cursed the god that had allowed such a thing to be possible.

Now the R'asa were in a frenzy, all of them grabbing bags of blood from the front of the room. The blood of his people. All of them dead. There were his men, hanging upside down in front of him. He'd known most of them since they were just children. They'd followed him for a lifetime, and their reward was to have their bodies desecrated by their enemy.

Beyond them were the men and women stacked like firewood against the wall. There were so many that he felt unable to comprehend the sight as a self-defense mechanism. They were all bred for their albinism and the supposed power in their veins. The men and women who Gregor had raised from birth in the dark tunnels of the catacombs like common rats. People Alexis had known existed but had failed to save.

He clutched his fist tight and swore he would not fail to avenge them.

He'd caught the eye of the American, Corbin, for only a few seconds. But they'd both known what must be done. Alexis had a nagging feeling that the man had worked all of this out in advance. That Corbin's plan from the beginning had been the destruction of both the Tacho R'asa and Les Fantômes de la Nuit. When he saw the rest of his men run into the back of the cave, he knew he was right.

The American had played him perfectly, getting him to bring all his men into the fight. Even convincing him to surrender to Gregor as a way to get the man's guard completely down so that his other men could complete their work. Corbin had been playing three-dimensional chess, and Alexis had missed the most important moves.

As more and more skeletons pulled themselves from the bone vaults all around them, he saw that it didn't matter. Had he been offered the choice of martyrdom to slay his enemy, instead of being tricked into it, he would have taken the duty as an honor.

Gregor strode across the platform and jumped off it with the limberness of a young man. He walked through the crowd of his people waiting for their chance to gather up their own bags of blood to bring more of the dead back to life. The animated skeletons filled the empty spaces. Many stood next to the vaults, waiting for a newly formed skeleton to reach out from the bone pile, so they could grab on to their extended arms and pull them out as if they were being born into the world.

Darkness crowded the edge of Alexis's vision. His head felt impossibly heavy but he fought to keep it raised. He bit the inside of his mouth until it filled with a gush of blood, the pain clearing his mind just enough to focus a little longer.

That's all I need. Just a minute or two.

Gregor held his arms out wide and walked toward him. "Look at this," he said. "This would not have been possible without your people. In a way, you share this victory."

Alexis managed to look up at him. He tried to spit at the man, but he succeeded only in producing a dribble of blood and saliva that ran down his own chin.

Gregor laughed. "I didn't expect you to understand, but this is what greatness looks like, Alexis. This is what revenge looks like."

"No," Alexis said. He turned his head just enough to the back wall so that Gregor followed his line of sight. He waited as the man looked, nearly missed it, but then froze as he realized what he was seeing. Alexis held up his hand to show Gregor the lighter he held there. "Those hoses have been piping gas into these chambers for hours."

Gregor held up his hands. For the first time, there was fear in his eyes. "Don't ... just let me ... wait ..."

"This," Alexis said, "you evil, arrogant bastard, is what revenge looks like."

He flicked the lighter and the whole world caught on fire.

50

The fireball blasted through the fence and destroyed the pumps. It spread left and right, hungry for more oxygen. Its fiery brethren, numbering in the hundreds, were on the same quest, burning everything in their path through the winding catacombs. Destroying. Consuming. Eradicating.

The fire that had traveled to the sewer was more fortunate than that in the caves. While back there the fire could only feast on the flesh of the R'asa and the bones of the undead, the flame here found a much more satisfying source of fuel. Once the hoses used by the Fantômes had disintegrated, it ran into something better than flesh. Even better than oxygen. Natural gas.

If seen in slow-motion, the barest of distance would have been evident between the wall of flame and the mouth of the gas main where gas jettisoned into the air. Then a single line of combustion worked its way across the barrier, atom by atom, spreading with exponential chaos and unpredictability. Then, in a chain reaction occurring faster than any camera could catch, the fire did as it was meant to do. It proliferated. And it destroyed all in its path.

51

E ven under the layer of heavy sewage, the heat was incredible.
Corbin held Margot as they pushed to the bottom. Then the
world shook and he was thrown to the side, smashing his shoulder
into the rough wall of the sewer channel. He almost gasped at the
pain, but self-preservation took over. Sucking in a lungful of water
would have killed him. Sucking in the sewage would have made the
death miserable.

He lost Margot. There was no sense in opening his eyes, so he
flailed around searching for her. Nothing.

Then the first rock hammered into him from above.

It hit his thigh, deadening it.

The roof was caving in from the blast.

Instinctively, he wrapped his arms over his head and tried to get
as deep as possible. He just hoped the current was fast enough to
carry them out of the danger zone before the entire place collapsed.

Or before he ran out of breath.

With all the motion and in his panic, he was already choking on
the stale air in his lungs. He'd read an article once about free divers
who held their breath for ten to fifteen minutes. The point of the
piece had been that the body thinks it's going to die from a lack of

oxygen far earlier than it actually will. That the key was to ignore the alarm bells the body was ringing and just keep going. He'd been under the sewage for less than two minutes and his body was already telling him he was in real trouble.

And it was making it hard for him to ignore.

He swallowed convulsively, as if the pockets of air in his mouth were going to save him. His lungs burned. It felt like his head was pumped full of blood and that it might pop like a giant tick if he didn't rise to the surface and breathe.

Another rock slammed into him, this time square in the middle of his back. It pushed him deeper and, for a horrifying second, he thought it might pin him there. But it rolled to the side and he was free.

And dying of asphyxiation.

Choking sounds emanated from his throat and echoed in his head. He couldn't last any longer. Even if the air was on fire above him. Even if breaking the surface to draw in a breath meant sucking fire into his lungs so that he burned alive from the inside-out, it didn't matter. Another second and he'd be dead under this layer of urine and feces anyway. He had to breathe.

He clawed for the surface, kicking with his legs, until he broke into the open air.

Even though he knew it was likely the most putrid, stench-ridden breath of air he'd ever taken, no single inhalation had ever tasted so sweet.

His lungs swelled with oxygen. And no fire.

He reached up a hand and wiped the thick coat of sewage from his eyes. The channel was half the width in this part of the sewer and so the current was twice as fast. He treaded in the brown water until he faced in the direction he'd come.

There was a bend in the sewer here, so all he could see was an orange glow in the distance. The sounds of rocks crashing into the water and onto the concrete walkways still reached his ears, but from what he could see, the structural damage hadn't extended to where he was. But with the low voltage maintenance lights flickering off and on, it was hard to tell.

"Corbin! Help!" Margot shouted. He spun around. She was downstream from him, next to a large floating shadow. Besson.

Corbin swam toward her, trying to keep the sewage out of his mouth. He reached her and saw that at least Besson was floating on his back. "There's an access ladder. Work toward it."

They pushed the big man's body to the right side of the channel where a little cutout held a metal ladder. The task was easier said than done as the current kept trying to rip Besson's body back into the channel. The man was dead weight and it took every ounce of their strength to hoist him out and onto the concrete walkway.

Margot was the first to act once he was laid out. She checked his air passage for any blockage then started on CPR. Corbin crawled forward and felt for a pulse.

"He's alive," he said. "Keep going."

Margot pumped his chest. Besson coughed and Corbin rolled the big man on his side just as he vomited up a vile mix of sewage and bile.

Margot rocked back and pushed away from them until she found a wall to lean against.

Corbin caught her eye. "We did it," he said.

Besson groaned but sat up under his own power. He wiped his face with his hands, but they were as dirty as his face. Corbin pointed at him. "You missed a spot."

It was a stupid comment, but under the stress of the moment, he couldn't resist. Besson chuckled, and then the three of them laughed together, a strange sound that had relief and tears and joy all wrapped in together. It only lasted a few seconds before they fell quiet, as if some silent agreement had been reached for them each to digest what had just happened to them, what they had survived.

Margot closed her eyes, a faint, satisfied smile on her lips. Corbin watched her and smiled too. Partly because they'd stopped Gregor and managed to rid the world of the evil Fantômes. But that wasn't all of it. No, something else had happened to him.

He'd fought to stay alive.

And while it seemed like a natural human instinct, the will to survive was something that had gone missing since Rose had died. He realized that for the first time since losing his little girl, that he didn't just want to survive, he wanted to live again. He wanted to find a way. And perhaps this strange woman with whom he'd shared the most bizarre adventure of his life could be part of that journey.

He was watching her face closely when her smile suddenly disappeared. Her eyes squinted as if she were concentrating very hard. Then her eyes popped open and they were wild, like an animal waking to find itself in a trap.

"What is it?" he asked.

"It's Gregor," she said. "I can feel him inside of me."

"From the blood," Corbin said, remembering the way her cut had healed. "The same thing happened to me. We can fix it. We can get Sister—"

"No, you don't understand," she said. "I can feel him, not because of his blood. It's because he's still alive."

52

The service exit wasn't hard to find, but it took all three of them to break the door that led outside. They lost their balance and tumbled out in a heap onto a patch of grass in a park. Corbin was the first to his feet and helped the others up.

"Lean on me if you need to," he told Besson. "But we have to move fast. We need to find Gregor before he gets away."

They were in a small park in a residential neighborhood. Sirens filled the air. Screams came from what sounded like the next street over.

"Don't worry about me," Besson grumbled, pushing himself harder. "I'll keep up."

Margot led the way. Corbin recalled the feeling he'd had when he'd felt the draw of Margot's blood when he'd tried to find her. It was deep and instinctual. He knew it would be pointless to ask Margot where she was taking them. She didn't know, but she'd be able to feel what direction to take them.

When they turned the corner, they all stopped in horror.

Huge sections of the street had caved into massive sinkholes. Flames shot up from the underground, sending columns of black smoke into the air. The ground was covered with broken glass as every building and car window in sight had been shattered. People ran in all directions, in whatever their personal interpretation of *away* was. In a city rocked with terror attacks, *away* was the only safe bet.

"Oh my God," Margot said. "We did this."

"We had to," Corbin said, believing the words even as his stomach turned over on itself. He scanned the area desperately, looking for any sign of fatalities. He didn't know what he'd do if he saw a kid sprawled out on the pavement. But, miraculously, there didn't seem to be any. Some of the sinkholes had cars in them, but he didn't see anyone struggling to climb out.

"There," Besson said. "Do you see it?"

Corbin looked where he pointed. It was one of the deeper holes, covered with smoke that glowed from the fire burning beneath it. Within the smoke, Corbin thought he saw movement. People crawling up the steep incline of the caved-in street.

"Survivors," Corbin said. "We need to help them get out."

Margot grabbed hold of his arm and held him in check. Besson hadn't moved.

"What are you doing?" he said.

"Those aren't survivors."

As Corbin turned, the nearest shadow broke free from the smoke. A skeleton from the catacombs scrambled on all fours, looking like a bizarre spider out of a nightmare.

Another broke free. And then another.

"Holy shit," Corbin said, looking around for a weapon. A stick, a rock, anything. He spotted a piece of rebar sticking out from the ruined sidewalk and ran to it. He pulled on it, but it was imbedded in the concrete, impossible to move.

"Watch it!" Besson roared.

Corbin looked up just as one of the skeletons launched itself through the air, jaws snapping. It landed on him with surprising force, knocking him over.

He pulled the skeleton into a bear hug, trying to take away its ability to use its arms and legs against him. The skull was right next to his face as the body twisted and writhed in his arms. Jagged broken teeth snapped inches from his cheek.

He cried out as the skeleton bent its leg at an impossible angle to use its bony feet to scratch at the meat on his thighs. It fought like a wild animal, struggling to get free from Corbin's grasp.

The thing was stronger than him. It was only a matter of time before he lost the fight. He strained, trying to rotate the skeleton's body to get it into a chokehold. Corbin cursed himself for never wrestling as a kid. Who would have known the skill would have come in handy one day battling the risen dead?

The thing's snapping jaws inched closer and closer. Corbin realized the trap he'd fallen into. If he moved his arms to reposition his grip, even for a second, the teeth would sink into him. All he could do was push back. But his arms were getting weaker and weaker. The skeleton seemed to sense its quarry was nearly done struggling because it shifted weight back for a split second before leaning in for a final lunge.

Corbin closed his eyes and shouted at the top of his lungs, expecting to feel his cheek ripped from his face at any second.

Instead he heard a crunching noise and the skeleton's body rocked to one side.

Corbin opened his eyes just in time to see the thing lift its head to see what had struck it, only to have its skull knocked clean off its body. He watched it soar through the air, bounce once off the pavement and then fall into a sinkhole.

Corbin pushed the headless skeleton body off of him and scrambled to his feet, expecting to see Besson there.

It was Margot. Holding a three-foot-long metal pipe in her hand.

He was about to thank her, but he didn't get the chance. She dropped to the ground, her hands to her head.

"What is it?" he asked.

But she didn't hear him. She couldn't, because her screams drowned him out.

53

"What is it?" Corbin said. "What's wrong?"

Margot's scream turned into a high-pitched whimper. Both of her nostrils bled. He held her up to see her face, and her eyes fluttered open to show only white.

"Corbin," Besson said, walking up next to him. He held a heavy stick in one hand and a skull with a dangling section of spine in the other. "Just when you thought shit couldn't get any stranger."

Corbin looked down the length of the pavement that had sunk into the hole, forming a kind of ramp. At the end of it, walking steadily as if out for an afternoon stroll, was another skeleton.

Only this one carried a crown balanced on its head.

It was Gregor, only the flesh had been burned from him so that he looked like any other of the catacomb skeletons.

"How can that be?" Corbin whispered.

"You still don't understand," Margot said next to him, her voice deep and coarse. Gregor's voice. "I can't be killed. I'm a god."

As the skeleton version of Gregor continued its march toward them, Corbin bent down and picked up the metal pole Margot had used. Besson tossed the skull he'd been carrying aside and took a two-handed grip on his stick.

"Some god you are," Corbin said. "You couldn't even save your own people."

The skeleton reached the end of the ramp and jumped down the last few feet, landing with more balance and grace than the other skeletons had. This was clearly a different beast.

"That's true," Gregor said, his words still coming out of Margot's mouth. "But I will avenge them."

Gregor ran at Corbin and smashed into him. Corbin got in one swing of his metal pole, but it glanced with no effect off Gregor's raised forearm.

Corbin sailed through the air and landed flat on his back, knocking the wind from him. Bony fingers wrapped around his neck, squeezing so hard that he thought his windpipe would crush in on itself. He hit Gregor's head, his knuckles turning bloody from hitting against bone. But it did nothing to loosen the grip around his neck.

Then something hammered against Gregor's skull. Besson with his stick.

But even with a direct hit, Gregor hardly budged.

Next to him, he heard Margot screaming. "Die! Die! Die!"

Just when he thought he would pass out, a massive weight seemed to climb onto his chest. It was there one second and gone the next.

He gasped for air, his hands kneading his throat as if that would somehow help the oxygen find its way in. Rolling up on his knees, he saw Besson on the ground wrestling with Gregor. When the stick hadn't worked, the big man had just jumped on the skeleton's back to peel him off.

Corbin grabbed the metal pole and struggled to his feet.

Besson screamed and Corbin saw bright red streaks soak through the shirt on his back. Gregor's fingers were sharp as talons.

With a cry, Corbin charged, his pole lowered like a spear. He worried that he might hit Besson by accident, but he knew he couldn't hold back.

Besson was swinging Gregor around just as Corbin made contact.

The pole crushed into one side of Gregor's rib cage, shattering the thin bones there, then exited the other side. Perfectly impaling him.

Margot screamed in both pain and frustration, matching the movement of the skull's jaws. Gregor detached from Besson, rolled over and then stood with the pole sticking through its body.

Besson got to his feet and took a position next to Corbin.

"You are fools," Gregor said. "You cannot kill what's not alive." He gestured to Margot. "But my resurrection is guaranteed. My blood lives."

Besson picked up a heavy and jagged piece of concrete from the ground. He turned, and before Corbin knew what he was doing, Besson was standing over Margot, rock held over his head.

"What if I bash her brains in?" he said. "What will that do to your plans for resurrection?"

Gregor's skeleton tilted his head to the side, regarding Besson. But it was Corbin who shouted at him.

"What are you doing?" he shouted. "Don't you touch her."

"Don't you see? It's the only way," Besson said. "She's the only blood he has left. If she's dead, it's over. He has to stay as this *thing* forever."

There was a crash behind them as part of the street caved in further. It left a section of pavement teetering over the edge. A geyser of flames spit up from below.

"Don't let him kill me, Corbin," Margot whimpered. It was her voice now. "I don't want to die. Please."

"I have to," Besson said, emotional now, choking on his words. "There's no other way."

"Please don't," Corbin said. "There will be others here soon. The sirens are near. They'll have to believe us." He pointed to Gregor. "They'll see."

"No," Besson roared. He grabbed Margot by the arm and pulled her away from Corbin as if he were the danger. Gregor turned as he tracked his movement. "This ends now. I've been pushed too far. I've been pushed over the edge."

"Help me," Margot begged. "Don't let him do this."

Corbin was so focused on Margot that he nearly missed what Besson was actually doing. *Pushed too far. Pushed over the edge.* With Gregor's back to him, he was exposed.

With a cry, he ran at Gregor with everything he had. He lowered his shoulder and caught him low in the ribs, lifted him into the air and drove him backward.

Blows rained down on his head and neck as Gregor lashed out, but he ignored the pain. His cry had turned into an animal sound he hardly recognized. He drove his legs, harder, harder. Waiting for the ground to give way.

But then somehow Gregor managed to land a brutal blow with his elbow directly into the side of his head. Corbin's legs buckled and he went down like a power switch had been turned off. His hands took most of the impact with the street, but he smacked his forehead hard enough to open a gash that poured blood.

Groaning, he looked up, wiping his eyes, ready for Gregor to attack.

The skeleton stood fifteen feet in front of him. When Corbin had fallen, Gregor had let go, but his forward momentum had carried him that much farther.

He stood on the section of pavement that cantilevered out over the sinkhole.

"Fall," Corbin whispered under his breath. "Fall now, you son of a bitch."

Gregor seemed to understand the danger he was in. He crouched low to the ground, spreading his weight as if balancing on thin ice on a lake. But after a few seconds of being on the ledge and nothing happening, he strode forward, each step lessening his risk.

It wasn't going to work. The ledge was too strong.

Then a motor roared behind him.

"Watch out!" screamed a voice.

A car rushed past him, barreling at Gregor. Margot hung from the open driver's door, steering the wheel. At the last second, she jumped from the car as it bore down on Gregor.

Gregor crouched low and jumped on the car's hood. He ran up

the length of the car as it passed, onto its roof, then its trunk, and then back off of it and onto the pavement as the car flew out into the sinkhole. Corbin's couldn't believe his eyes. The car hadn't done a thing.

Gregor opened his arms wide, like a circus performer taking a bow.

Then a *crack* filled the air. The pavement Gregor stood on dropped a few feet.

He looked up, and Corbin had the satisfaction of being the last thing Gregor saw before he fell.

The pavement broke away completely, rolling over as it fell into the sinkhole. Gregor disappeared from sight, trapped under the slab. The pavement landed perfectly on top of another slab already at the bottom, smashing into it, pancaking Gregor between the two.

Corbin, Besson and Margot walked together to the edge of the sinkhole, looking down at the slab for any sign of movement.

"Do you think he might ..." Corbin left it hanging. Both he and Besson turned to Margot.

She stared into the pit, focusing. Then she said the words. "No, he's gone. He's finally gone."

54

Corbin waited outside the small house on an old, worn bench in a sun-dappled courtyard. He closed his eyes and faced the sun, moving slightly until he felt warmth on his face. A smooth breeze blew through, filling the air with the sound of a million whispering leaves. It was the first time in the days following the catacombs that he'd been able to have a moment without the terrors of that day filling his head. For whatever reason, he felt at peace. He hoped it was a sign of good things to come.

A door creaked open and a little girl walked out. She focused on the glass she carried with both hands, staring at the liquid sloshing back and forth as she crossed the distance to Corbin. She reminded him of his Rose, years ago but so present in his mind that it could have been earlier that afternoon. He let himself bask in the memory.

"Lemonade, Monsieur Stewart?" Lily Besson said.

"Merci," he said, flashing her his best smile. As he reached to take it from her, he noticed the bandage on the girl's ear poking through the hair she'd carefully combed to that side. He tried not to let his smile waver, but he must have, because the second he took the glass she turned her face so her ear was hidden from now.

The door opened again and Besson and his wife, Giselle, came outside. Corbin marveled at how much softer the big man seemed around her, soft-spoken, polite. The attentive husband who opened doors and pulled out his wife's chair even when eating at their own home. So different from the man he'd come to know over their adventures together.

He didn't know if Besson had always been this way. Having walked the line so close to losing his family might account for it. When he'd asked in a roundabout way over lunch whether her husband was always so kind, Giselle had replied, "Oui, but more now than before." She'd nuzzled into his shoulder, her bandaged hand a reminder of what she'd recently been through. "I hope he stays like this."

Giselle held Lily's hand and walked her to the back of the garden where they had a swing. Besson sat on the bench with Corbin, took a deep breath and let out a long, satisfying sigh.

"It feels like it's over," Corbin said. "For the first time. For me, anyway."

Besson nodded. "For me too. But not over. Not really."

"No, not really," he admitted. The nightmares would always be around the corner of his mind's eye, ready to pounce. He'd been around long enough to know you didn't live through something like what they'd experienced without it leaving a mark. "Lily looks to be handling it well."

"It comes and goes. Sometimes it's like nothing ever happened. Then she'll start crying and nothing you say can get her to stop. We just hold her. And wait."

"Then keeping holding her," he said, thinking what he would give to hold his Rose again, crying or not. "As long as she'll let you."

"We will." They fell silent as the creaking of the metal chains from the swing set mixed with the soothing sound of the trees above them. "I'm sorry Margot didn't come. I would have liked to see her."

Corbin nodded. "Me too."

"I have something for you," Besson said, reaching behind his back and pulling something from his beltline. It was Corbin's leather notebook. "You left this at the station that first night. Thought you might want it."

Corbin took the notebook and flipped through it. "Thanks."

"A word of advice?"

"Sure," Corbin said, bracing himself for an uncomfortable conversation about how to deal with the madness they'd seen together. Or dealing with Margot. Or the void his daughter's death had left in him.

"I looked through that book. You ought to stay a writer, because you are one shitty artist."

They shared a laugh together, warm and comfortable, like two lifelong friends. And that was all they said, choosing instead to enjoy the afternoon and Lily's laughter floating toward them on the breeze until the sun went down and it was time for them to say their good-byes.

THAT NIGHT, Corbin packed the last of his belongings into a suitcase, leaving out a change of clothes for the morning and his shaving kit. The empty apartment looked sad, emptied of all the magazines, newspapers, food wrappers and pizza boxes. He'd removed four bags for the trash and three boxes for the charity collection box at the small church around the corner. Now the place looked as bare as the day he'd moved in.

The notebook sat on the kitchen table. He'd tossed it into one of the garbage bags at one point, but then gone fishing for it minutes later to pull it out. He opened a bottle of wine and sat down, flipping the pages. Despite being images of the most beautiful city in the world, Corbin felt the oppressiveness of his state of mind as he drew them. He relived the wasted days, the sense of hopelessness, the way he'd wished the sun would speed faster across the sky just so that he could be done with another day. He hadn't been living. He'd simply been waiting to die.

Corbin turned the page after the last drawing. There were thirty or forty blank pages left in the book. On impulse, he slid the chair back and crossed the room to his book bag, searching the front pocket until he found a pen. He returned to the table and pushed on the notebook's binding to make it lie flat.

He put pen to paper and hesitated, expecting the wall to rise up in front of him like it had for years. But there was no wall. Only open, infinite space, filled with wonder and tragedy and love. Most of all, circulating around every thought, was hope.

Corbin Stewart wrote.

IN THE MORNING, he woke up on a bare mattress. He was in his bedroom, but he couldn't remember making the trip there from the table the night before. He rubbed his eyes, marveling at the lack of a headache. Then he remembered that his first sip of wine last night had been his only. He'd experienced a different kind of intoxication, a high he hadn't experienced for so long that he'd given up hope of ever feeling it again.

He'd written. Just like in the old days. Written with a fever, with his mind expanding to grasp meaning, to discover purpose and reason. It'd come out of him like it was his pulse. His only fear was that great writing after midnight often turned to ash in the light of morning. With no lack of trepidation, he walked into the main room to read the words he'd written.

He stopped at the door, frozen by the sight waiting for him in the other room.

Margot sat at the table, a suitcase next to her, turning the last page of the journal as she read what he'd written.

"What are you—"

She held up a hand to silence him. She was reading and didn't want to be disturbed. The fact that she'd disappeared for three days and had broken into his apartment and read his journal without permission didn't seem to be up for discussion.

The writer in him battled the man in him that wanted to ask a hundred questions of her. The writer won. He leaned against the door and waited.

Finally, she closed the journal and turned to him. Tears streamed down her face. "It's beautiful," she said, extending the journal out to him. "Just perfect."

He walked to her and accepted the journal back. "Where have you been?" he whispered.

"I've been with Sister Agnes," she said. "I wanted him out of me. Every last part of him."

"You could have told me," he said, shuddering at the thought of what she must have gone through. "I could have been there for you."

"I needed to do it by myself." He turned away from her but she reached out and took his hand. "But I don't want to be alone now."

He squeezed her hand. "Neither do I." He pulled her to her feet and kissed her gently on the lips. She laid her head on his chest, holding on to him.

"What now?"

"Let's unpack," he said. "There's a story here. And I'd like to see how it turns out."

She looked up at him with a mischievous grin. "Well, I can imagine how the next hour is going to go."

"And beyond that?" Corbin asked.

"You're the creative one. You tell me."

He looped an arm behind her back and one under her legs and picked her up off the ground. She gave a delighted laugh. "Should this story be a comedy or a love story?"

"Can it be both?"

"As the lady commands," he said. "As long as you don't laugh too much in the next hour."

"We'll see," she said. "Like you said, a story tends to tell itself if you let it."

"So I should stop talking?"

"I think you ought to."

"Because I can stop talking right now."

"You're still talking."

Corbin shut his mouth, carried her to the bedroom and they began their story together.

AFTERWORD

Thank you for joining me on this journey into the underbelly of Paris and into the darker parts of my mind. I am endlessly thankful that you entrusted me with your time and your attention. I hope I lived up to my side of the bargain and delivered the goods.

Nothing helps authors and books more than word-of-mouth and online reviews. If you enjoyed GYPSY BLOOD, please let the world know on social media and head over to your favorite book site to post a review. Even a line or two helps.

Thank you!
Jeff Gunhus

ABOUT THE AUTHOR

Jeff Gunhus is the USA TODAY bestselling author of thriller and horror novels for adults and the middle grade/YA series, The Templar Chronicles. The first book, Jack Templar Monster Hunter, was written in an effort to get his reluctant reader eleven-year-old son excited about reading. It worked and a new series was born. His books have reached the Top 30 on Amazon, featured in magazines and translated into several languages.

After his experience with his son, he is passionate about helping parents reach young reluctant readers and is active in child literacy issues. As a father of five, he leads an active life in Maryland with his wife Nicole by trying to constantly keep up with their kids. In rare moments of quiet, he can be found in the back of the City Dock Cafe in Annapolis working on his next novel or on JeffGunhus.com.

Come say hello...
www.jeffgunhus.com
jeffgunhusauthor@gmail.com

facebook.com/jeffgunhusauthor

twitter.com/jeffgunhus

instagram.com/jeffgunhus

ALSO BY JEFF GUNHUS

ADULT FICTION

Night Chill

Night Terror

Killer Within

Killer Pursuit

The Torment of Rachel Ames: a novella

MIDDLE GRADE FICTION

Jack Templar Monster Hunter

Jack Templar and the Monster Hunter Academy

Jack Templar and the Lord of the Vampires

Jack Templar and the Lord of the Werewolves

Jack Templar and the Lord of the Demons

Jack Templar and the Last Battle

www.ingramcontent.com/pod-product-compliance
Lightning Source LLC
Chambersburg PA
CBHW020959120726
47905CB00009B/2771